W9-APK-101

The Other Side of the World

of the

a novel

Jay Neugeboren

TWO DOLLAR RADIO
Books too loud to ignore

Also by Jay Neugeboren

NOVELS
Big Man
Listen Ruben Fontanez
Sam's Legacy
An Orphan's Tale
The Stolen Jew
Before My Life Began
Poli: A Mexican Boy in Early Texas
1940

STORIES
Corky's Brother
Don't Worry About the Kids
News from the New American Diaspora
You Are My Heart

NON-FICTION
Parentheses: An Autobiographical Journey
The Story of STORY Magazine (as editor)
Imagining Robert: My Brother, Madness, and Survival
Transforming Madness: New Lives for People Living with Mental Illness
Open Heart: A Patient's Story of Life-Saving Medicine and Life-Giving Friendship
The Hillside Diary and Other Writings (as editor)

for Eric and Eliza

TWO DOLLAR RADIO is a family-run outfit founded in 2005 with the mission to reaffirm the cultural and artistic spirit of the publishing industry.

We aim to do this by presenting bold works of literary merit, each book, individually and collectively, providing a sonic progression that we believe to be too loud to ignore.

Copyright © 2012 by Jay Neugeboren
All rights reserved
ISBN: 978-1-937512-02-6
LCCN: 2012950610

Author photograph: Michael B. Friedman
Cover: Credit Data courtesy Marc Imhoff of NASA GSFC and Christopher Elvidge of NOAA NGDC. Image by Craig Mayhew and Robert Simmon, NASA GSFC.

Parts of this book have appeared in somewhat different form in *Ploughshares* (2011), *You Are My Heart* (2011), *Hadassah Magazine* (2012), *Notre Dame Review* (2012), and *Jewish Fiction.net* (2012).

Typeset in Garamond, the best font ever.
Printed in the United States of America.

No portion of this book may be copied or reproduced, with the exception of quotes used in critical essays and reviews, without the written permission of the publisher.

This is a work of fiction. All names, characters, places, and incidents are products of the author's lively imagination. Any resemblance to real events or persons, living or dead, is entirely coincidental.

TWO DOLLAR RADIO
Books too loud to ignore

TwoDollarRadio.com
twodollar@TwoDollarRadio.com

"Mine is a most peaceable disposition. My wishes are: a humble dwelling with a thatched roof, but a good bed, good food, milk and butter of the freshest, flowers at my window, and a few fine tall trees before my door; and if God wants to make my happiness complete, he will grant me the joy of seeing some six or seven of my enemies hanging from those trees. Before death I shall, moved in my heart, forgive them all the wrong they did to me in their lifetimes. One must, it is true, forgive one's enemies—but not before they have been hanged."

—Heinrich Heine, *Thoughts and Ideas*

Tag Sale

*O*n the morning Seana showed up for my father's tag sale, I was in Borneo, so that I didn't get his letter giving me the news until I was back in Singapore. Before his letter came, I'd had no plans to return to the States, and my father, who—quintessential Max—had the finely-tuned habit of rarely if ever putting pressure on me and, thus, of not allowing hopes to become expectations, had never asked if or when I might be coming back.

I'd been working in Singapore the previous three years for a company that dealt in palm oil, and during the years I worked for them, palm oil had surpassed soy bean oil as the most widely produced vegetable oil in the world. My job, mostly, was to monitor various stages of development, production, and sales—to make sure the contractors we hired did what we'd contracted for, and that what we promised to deliver was delivered safely and at the agreed-upon price. It was the most lucrative job I'd ever had, and though life in Singapore was tolerable—I worked hard, played hard, and was on the receiving end of a multitude of perks—it didn't thrill me. Borneo did, however, and during some of my visits there—mini-vacations I was able to tack on to business trips—I'd thought of sending my father a round-trip plane ticket so I could show him why it was I found Borneo so enchanting, and why I sometimes fantasized living there for the rest of my life.

But it wasn't the news about Seana showing up for my father's tag sale that made me put this kind of fantasy on hold and, instead, to put in for a leave-without-pay in order to return home. What did that was Nick Falzetti's death.

It was because of Nick that I'd gone to Singapore, and he had died in a freak accident on the first Saturday night after my return to Singapore from a weekend in Borneo. Nick and I had been buddies, on and off, when we were undergraduates at the University of Massachusetts in Amherst, and for a few years after, and when, during our tenth college reunion we hung out together, he'd sold me a bill of goods on moving to Singapore so I could live the kind of good life he'd been living.

Nick's parents lived in Tenants Harbor, a small town a few miles from the Maine coast, about halfway up the state to Bar Harbor and Acadia National Park, and his ex-wife, Trish, whom I'd gone with before she met Nick, lived with their son Gabe not far from Nick's parents. I wanted to pay my respects to Nick's family—to his parents and to Trish—but after I'd made the decision to do so, what began to get me down was thinking about the kind of messy stuff Nick, Trish, and I had gotten into way back, and once I'd gone and booked my flight and wrote my father that I was coming home, I found myself imagining, far more than was good for me, what it would be like to be with her again. And I began thinking, too, that she might be far too pleased by news of Nick's death for anyone's good.

By the time I arrived home, my father's tag sale was history, and Seana, who bought the works, had moved in with him. A good deal for them both, she claimed: She got all his leftovers—and he got her.

Here's the ad my father had put in the local papers:

Tag Sale. Retired University Professor offering material from unpublished and/or abandoned novels and stories. Items include: titles, epigraphs, opening paragraphs, opening chapters, final paragraphs, plot notions and summaries, character sketches, lists, research notes, random jottings, and select journal entries. Saturday and Sunday, 9 AM to 4:30 PM. Rain or shine. 35 Harrison Avenue, Northampton. No book dealers, please.

Seana—Seana Shulamith McGee O'Sullivan—had been one of my father's graduate students in the late eighties—his best and brightest, and also, to his ongoing delight, his most successful. Although Seana's first novel, *Triangle*, was far too raunchy to have been chosen by Oprah—it was about a mother-daughter-father *ménage à trois* that had a deliciously happy ending—it wound up outselling most Oprah selections and staying on *The New York Times* best-seller list for over a hundred weeks.

I met Seana for the first time in the spring of 1988, when my father let me sit in on one of his at-home writing workshops. I'd just passed my thirteenth birthday—I know this because I'd been Bar Mitzvahed three weeks earlier—and I remember watching Seana sitting cross-legged on the floor next to the fireplace, chewing on and off at a hangnail on her left index finger while the women in the class kept giving her looks of disdain and envy she clearly relished.

My father always cooked a sumptuous dinner for his students—never boiled up spaghetti or ordered out for pizza—and he served it on our good china, on a white damask linen tablecloth, with napkins to match, and while he and I were doing the dishes afterwards, I asked about Seana and the way the women in the class had been looking at her. "Ah," my father sighed. And then: "I mean, after all, son, what young woman *wouldn't* be resentful and envious of Seana? All that talent and productivity... and beautiful too!"

For the tag sale—after education, the region's second largest industry, my father contended—what he'd done was to lay out on our front porch and lawn stuff that had not made its way into his published work, and that, in the time he estimated he had left—he was seventy-two and calculated his remaining *productive* years at sixteen—he did not expect ever to look at again.

In addition to being one upon whom nothing was lost, he wrote, he wanted to be one *from whom* nothing was lost. That, he explained, had been the modest *raison d'être* for what he'd come to call, before Seana's arrival, 'The First and Last Annual Max Eisner Literary Tag Sale.' But then, as in any good novel, the wonderful and unpredictable had occurred: First (and only) person in line on a bright, chilly New England Saturday morning in early October, there was Seana—gorgeous, voluptuous, brilliant Seana, and in her mature incarnation—eager to pluck up *everything* so that, she announced at once, she would make sure that nothing *would* be lost.

What I found myself imagining when I read about my father's tag sale was that the first sets of folders Seana came to that morning were laid out on three mahogany nesting tables that, one inside the other, had lived in a corner of our living room, by the driveway window, all through my childhood. My father had taken the tables from his mother's apartment in Brooklyn after she died—they'd sat in a corner of his living room throughout his childhood (one of his mother's famous "space-savers")— and even though my father and I lived in a three-story Victorian house, and had a large living room, along with a larger dining room, smaller music room and library, and lots of surfaces on which to set down food and drinks, my father would, as his mother had, put out the three tables whenever we had company.

When I imagined the tables on our front lawn, one beside the other, what they also brought to mind were my father's wives and girlfriends, each of whom, as he grew older, was younger than the one before, and all of whom seemed, in the way I pictured them, like a series of older, larger women within whom—as in a set of Russian *matryoshka* dolls—younger, leaner, more beautiful women lived.

My father had had five wives, starting with my mother (who was two years older than he was), and there were also a dozen or so long-term girlfriends, though none of the girlfriends had ever moved in with him. Still, my father was not, he'd state whenever I asked about a new relationship—this usually in response to his inquiries about *my* love life—a philanderer. "I've always been an unregenerate serial monogamist," he'd say, "though I really *do* love women."

In all their varieties, he might have added, and as different as we were in most ways, in this we were alike, because whenever a friend would offer to fix me up with someone and ask what my *type* was, I'd be stumped. Like my father, I had no particular preferences because, like him, I found most women, whether girlfriends or friend-friends, more interesting—and better company—than guys. And because just about always—the thing I know my father valued above all, once you'd gotten past whatever it was you found initially attractive, and maybe because, it occurs to me, it was *his* pre-eminent quality—they were usually *kinder* than guys.

Be kind, my father would say to me from as far back as I can remember, and for a long list of situations—whether it had to do with guys I played against in sports, store clerks who were incompetent, strangers who were rude, or friends and relatives who were nasty—be kind, for everyone you meet is fighting a great battle.

The quote was from Philo, he said, and I grew up imagining that the name belonged to the man who'd invented the kind of pastry dough you use to make strudel or *spanakopitas*. When I was ten or eleven, though, I found out who Philo was, and the way it happened tells you things about my father you wouldn't suspect from the quiet, somewhat shy man he was most of the time.

I was changing out of my uniform after a basketball game at our local YMCA on a Saturday afternoon when my father came into the locker room to see how I was doing, and while we were going over the game, one of the guys along our row of lockers called another guy a faggot. Without hesitating, my father walked over to the boy and told him that using such a term was vulgar and unacceptable, that he hoped the boy would never use it again, and that, to this end, he intended to speak with the boy's father. My father waited for the boy to get dressed, after which he accompanied him to the Y's lobby, where he told the boy's father—a huge guy, six-three or -four, wearing a Boston Bruins hockey shirt—what had happened.

When the man told my father to mind his own goddamned business, my father repeated what he'd said to the boy: that use of such a word was vulgar and unacceptable, and that it demeaned not only the person to whom it referred, but, more profoundly, the person who had the unexamined need to employ such a word.

The man laughed in my father's face, then jabbed him in the chest, told him that it took one to know one and that he'd better watch his own ass or he'd wind up skewered butt-first on a flagpole. Grabbing the front of my father's shirt, the man said that he bet the last time my father had seen pussy was when he shoveled out cat shit at the A.S.P.C.A.

A woman at the Y desk picked up a phone—a crowd had gathered—but my father gestured to her to put it down and, very calmly, he addressed the man who was holding his shirt, and the way he did it made me think 'Uh-oh!', because even though my father could be a polite and accommodating man most of the time, he could, at times, be seriously roused, and then—watch out!

"Sir," he said to the man. "I would have you know that I have known more fine women in my lifetime than have ever existed in your imagination."

The man warned my father not to be a professor smart-ass, made a fist, and said the only reason he'd been holding back till then was because he didn't like to hit little old men. At this point, my father, who was five-foot-six and weighed perhaps one-fifty, stepped forward and pointed to the ceiling. "Well, look at that," he said, and as soon as the man looked up, my father stomped down hard on one of the man's feet, and let loose with a swift one-two combination to the guy's mid-section. When the man doubled over, my father gave him a terrific roundhouse chop to the side of the head that dropped him straight to the floor.

"In my youth, you see," my father said, and without breathing hard, "I studied at the Flatbush Boys Club with the great champion Lew Tendler, who himself had learned the trade, in and out of the ring, from the immortal Benny Leonard."

The man opened his eyes, but stayed where he was while my father advised him never to discount the benefits of a good education in teaching us that the use of verbal insults against those we deem inferior only served to reveal our own ignorant shortcomings.

After word of the incident got around, my father became a hero to my friends, who, when they hung out at our house, would ask him for boxing tips, and it turned out that my father knew more than a little bit about the sport. He had published a novel, *Prizefighter*, when he was in his twenties, and it was based in part on the life of Barney Ross, a Jewish boxing champion who'd also been a war hero, and had, from the morphine they gave him for pain when he was wounded, become a drug addict, and then a recovered drug addict. My father had been a pretty good bantamweight himself in Police Athletic League competitions, though he never did A.A.U. or Golden Gloves, and when my friends asked, he'd offer them basic stuff about feints and jabs and being alert to an opponent's weaknesses, and, using Ross as an example, about the will to win, which derived, he asserted, from fighting for something larger than yourself.

My father told us Ross's story: how Ross's father was a Talmudic scholar who owned a grocery store in Chicago and was killed by gangsters in a hold-up, and how the family was made so poor by the father's death that two of Ross's brothers, along with his sister, were placed in an orphanage. The result was that whenever Ross was in the ring, he'd imagine he was fighting against his father's murderers, and when he won the first of his three world championships, he used the prize money to rescue his brothers and sister from the orphanage.

After he'd finish telling us about Ross—or about Tendler, or Leonard, or "Kid" Kaplan, or Abe Attell, or Daniel Mendoza, or other great Jewish fighters—and after he'd given us a few pointers, he'd stop, hold up an index finger to indicate that the most important advice was coming, and then touch his tongue with his finger and emphasize that because it could produce words that allowed you to avoid a fight, or if you had to fight, that allowed you to *distract* your opponent, the tongue remained far and away your most important weapon.

"And always, always," he would add, "be kind—fight as hard as you can, but at the same time don't forget to nurture the kindness in your heart, the way Barney Ross did"—and one time when he gave out the saying, a friend asked if it was from Ross, and my father said no, that it was from Philo, and my friend asked who Philo was, and my father explained that Philo had been a philosopher from Alexandria who lived about fifty years before Christ, was known as Philo-the-Jew, and had been instrumental in the founding of Christianity by having combined elements of Greek mystery religions with Jewish theology.

My father usually had answers to most questions my friends asked, and if he didn't, he'd say, "Now that's an interesting question—may I get back to you on it?" In truth, I grew up in awe not so much of things like his boxing expertise, but of his mind, of its sheer range and intelligence, though he would dismiss praise from me and others by acknowledging that yes, maybe he had a few smarts, but if he did they were merely a result of the lucky genetic hand he'd drawn at birth.

In this, he said, he liked to think he had something in common with James Michener, though my father's own writing—the one novel, along with a few short stories, and two books about other writers (Henry James and Willa Cather)—could not, of course, compare with Michener's work, either in output or style. Although Michener had a low reputation among academics, my father considered him 'a great humanist,' and would outrage his colleagues—something he never minded doing—by teaching a course every few semesters on Michener's essays and novels.

He owned all of Michener's more than fifty books, many of them real door-stoppers, along with copies of some of his screenplays, and to encourage students, he would point out that Michener (whom he referred to as 'the Rabbi Akiba of fiction') hadn't published his first book until he was past forty years old. He may not have been the greatest prose stylist, my father would say—something Michener himself readily conceded—but his books were richly informed, made readers of millions of people, and were—their great distinction—unlike those of any other writer, living or dead.

Like Michener, who never used researchers until he was hooked up to dialysis machines in his last years, my father was gifted with a photographic memory: if he read a page once, he had only to relax enough to locate the page somewhere in his mind and the sentences would be there for him. What helped make things easy between us was that it never seemed to bother him that I wasn't drawn to matters intellectual or literary, and clear, too, early on, that I lacked not only his intelligence, but his phenomenal memory. Nor was I a particularly good student—I worked hard to get a B average in high school, and at UMass, where I was a business major, I worked even harder to get a three-point average. Still, as long as I applied myself, did the best I could, and, what my father considered most important of all—remained curious about the world—he seemed satisfied.

"The wonderful thing about you, Charlie," he said to me on the afternoon of my college graduation—repeating what he'd said on previous such occasions: my Bar Mitzvah, my graduations from junior high and high school, and what he'd say each time I started a new job or brought home a new girlfriend—"the wonderful thing about you is that you've never disappointed me."

Sometimes I wondered why. It wasn't that I'd screwed up so terribly, but more that I'd never succeeded especially well at any one thing: I hadn't married, or bought a house or an apartment, or made a ton of money, or—the nut of the thing—ever really had any clear idea of what I wanted *to* do with my life. More to the point, and what worried *me* from time to time: I'd never had much of a desire to do anything in particular with my life.

When I'd say this to him—that I sometimes wished I was more like this person or that person—friends who'd become doctors or lawyers or teachers or businessmen, who owned homes and had kids and the rest—he would seem puzzled. Why did I compare myself to others? Think of yourself as having taken the scenic route, he'd say. Or he'd tell me that in this I was really just a quintessential man of my times—a free agent, much like those professional athletes who moved to different teams and cities every few years. And weren't we, after all, *all* free agents these days?

He was forever alert to the ways others might compare me to him, so that the testimonials to my character I'd get from him through the years, which he must have thought would alleviate my insecurities (they never did) went essentially like this: That I was a fine young man leading a life unlike the lives of most of my contemporaries—that I had not lost my capacity for joy, that my values were sound, and that I remained open to possibility.

Big deal, I'd think. Or, when I was in a better mood, "Words words words," I'd say back to him, at which response he'd smile, and say something about the apple not falling far from the pear tree, but it was this kind of perpetual cheerfulness, along with his seeming blindness to the ways in which I was a fuck-up, that often irritated me. By the time I was in my mid to late twenties, his words of praise, along with the repeated injunction to be kind to everybody, especially when it came to the shits of the world, left me pretty cold. Why be kind to people who were mean and fucked over other people? Why forgive people for unforgivable acts? For all his sophistication and shrewdness— his incredible knack, especially when it came to women and books, to discerning crap from quality—he also had a surprising willingness to suffer fools gladly.

I must have seen myself as one of those fools, since I had a fairly well-developed talent for depriving myself of those things—like sticking with interesting women who actually *liked* me, or making sure to spend more time with Max—that might have offered more focus and direction—*and* more comfort and joy. Thus my tendency to change jobs (and girlfriends) regularly, to find jobs as far from home as I could, and to stay away from home for years at a time.

There was something about the tag sale, though, and, more, about Seana moving in—she wasn't much older than several women I'd gone with—that pushed me to say things to him I'd never been able to say before: that though I was glad things were going well, and I didn't want to piss on his new parade, there seemed something *unreal* about his endless good cheer. Especially, I wrote, given how much loss he'd experienced. For starters, there was the fact that his first wife (my mom) had ditched him (and me), and that two of his other four wives had died on him, so how come, I asked, there was no acknowledgement—not even when he was raising me by himself, and there wasn't even a housekeeper around to help—of just how lousy and encumbered a lot of his life must have been?

"Well, Charlie," he wrote back, "'twas not ever thus, let me assure you…" He understood why I might be puzzled by the ways he showed himself forth in the world, but what he'd come to believe had allowed him to be so cheerful, to use my word (*healthy-minded* was the term he preferred), as he thought he'd made clear on several occasions—but perhaps I hadn't been paying attention, he wrote, or had chosen not to pay attention—had to do with a period of considerable darkness in his life, a period that began a few months before my first birthday during which he'd come as close as one could to choosing to leave this world.

Because I'd been an infant at the time, I would of course possess no conscious memory of this moment—one he'd come to think of as his missing year (an admittedly foolish way of thinking of it, he noted, since it was anything but missing)—yet once he'd survived the year, an enormous clump of feelings and fears—of debilitating vexations—that had previously bothered him were, for the most part, deprived of their power.

That was the sum of what he wrote, without giving any details (in a postscript he noted that the period he referred to lasted fourteen months and three days, but that there was a certain pleasurable tidiness for him in thinking of it as a single year), and so I found myself wondering if he'd written about this period of his life, and if Seana had found any of it in the stuff she'd taken from him.

When I woke up on my first day home—the trip took a full twenty-four hours (to avoid Hong Kong, I flew via Tokyo and landed at JFK in New York, then took limo service to Northampton)—Seana was sitting next to me on the side of the bed, looking more beautiful than ever. She had been out of the house when I'd arrived, doing research at the local library, so I had no idea how long she'd been there watching me sleep.

The last time I'd seen her had been nine or ten years before, in Chicago, where I'd been working for an insurance company as an auto accident appraiser. I'd shown up at a reading she was giving at a downtown bookstore for her second novel, *Plain Jane*, which was about an American woman in her mid-thirties who, after a divorce and an abortion, takes a job teaching art to teenagers at an international school in southern France, and becomes romantically involved with the headmaster. It was based, in part, on *Jane Eyre*—the headmaster is married, and his wife, a gifted painter who suffers from bouts of depression and mania, lives in seclusion in a cottage near the school—but, as Seana made clear in the question-and-answer period after the reading, when she reminded the audience that instead of *marrying* the headmaster, her heroine *murders* him and gets away with it—'Reader, I buried him,' was the book's opening line—her novel was intended not as homage to Charlotte Brontë, but as Seana's way of using a situation she found intrinsically intriguing—another one of O'Sullivan's triangles, she allowed—to get at the dark side of matters that, in her opinion, Brontë had turned into sentimental nonsense. 'Mawkish' was the word she used to describe Brontë's book, and afterwards—we had drinks together in her hotel's bar—she confided that although what gave her the most pleasure in life was the act of writing itself, she did love getting a rise out of audiences by being mildly *outré*.

"*Outré*?" I asked.

"Outrageous, eccentric," she said. She was aware that people thought her books weird, which didn't hurt sales, and the good sales gave her the freedom to write what she wanted to write, and to live the way she wanted to live. The truth, though, was that she never thought of her books as being weird.

"I'm essentially a realist," she said, after which, watching for my response—which was no response at all, since even if I'd been sober at the time, I don't think I would have understood what she meant about *Triangle* or *Plain Jane* being *realistic* novels—she began giggling. Then she leaned toward me and kissed me on the mouth, very gently, and I was so stunned that all I could do was sit there and grin. "You can kiss me back if you'd like," she said, and I did, and we kissed for a long time until, a finger to my forehead, she pushed me away from her. "That was very good, Charlie," she said, and she wished me sweet dreams, and left.

Now, when I looked up at her from my bed, I saw that her reddish-brown hair was still cut page-boy style, that her eyebrows, which she never plucked or trimmed, were as dark and thick as ever, and that she had not had a chipped front tooth repaired. I'd always admired her for leaving the tooth the way it was because its imperfection had the effect of making me aware of how weirdly beautiful the rest of her was.

"It's my apostrophe," she had explained once when I asked about it. While playing stickball with some guy-friends in Holy Cross schoolyard in Brooklyn, near where she grew up—which wasn't far from where Max had grown up—she'd broken off a corner of the tooth, and the resulting shape—"Why it's a giant white apostrophe!" her high school English teacher at the time, a nun named Sister Maureen, had said—seemed a good thing for a writer to hang on to, Seana had theorized, since in addition to representing something that had been omitted—and wasn't what a writer chose to leave out more important than what he or she chose to leave in?—the word derived from the Greek, and signified a turning away from a large audience in order to direct your words to one person in particular.

"Hey Charlie," she said a moment after I opened my eyes.

"Hey Seana," I said.

She caressed my forehead and said she hoped we were still friends.

"Why wouldn't we still be friends?" I asked.

"Well, for starters, I took over your room for a while, though I've since relocated to the third floor guest room."

"Then you're not…" I began, and stopped. "I mean, you and my father have separate rooms."

"Sure."

"I just…"

"You really are an innocent, aren't you?"

"That's what Max always says."

She leaned down, brushing my forehead with a kiss, and said that I'd had a long trip and probably wanted to wash up and get myself settled before dinner. She'd brought my bags up to the room, and there was a glass of ice water and a snack—cheese and crackers and assorted goodies she'd left on my desk—and later, after I got my bearings, she had something she wanted to show me.

I looked at the clock on my bureau, saw that it was nearly seven, but the shades were drawn, and I wasn't sure if it was seven in the morning or the evening.

She saw the puzzled look on my face. "It's evening," she said.

"How long was I asleep?"

"Three hours, maybe four. I'm not sure exactly when you arrived, but you were buzzing away—beautiful Z's—when I returned from the library. You're good at it."

"Good at it?"

"At sleeping. It's a talent I wish I had."

I sat up. "What's the surprise?"

"No surprise. Just something I'd like your opinion on."

"That's all you want?"

"Don't get fresh with me, young man," she said. "But yes, that's all I want—your opinion on something I'd prefer not to ask your father about, all right?"

"Sure."

"And there is one other thing." She opened the door to leave.

"Some time—*whenever*, as they say these days—I want your story. I want you to tell me *your* story."

"Sure," I said. And then: "Is this the way you usually get material for your books—do you go around collecting stories from everyone you meet?"

"Not at all."

"Then why…?"

"*Why*?" She shrugged, and when she spoke again she did so without looking at me. "*Why*? Because I guess I figure it's the quickest, best way for you and me to get to know each other now that we've both grown up."

For dinner, my father made one of our favorites—*blanquette de veau*, with a spinach and wild mushroom salad on the side—and he served it with a smooth, light-bodied Italian wine. I was still in the grogs from the long flight home, and the wine kept me there, but my father and Seana were in high spirits, especially when they went on riffs where they imagined the way various of his colleagues (some of whom had been Seana's teachers) might have reacted to the tag sale, and to the deal he and Seana had reached on the morning of the tag sale.

In general, they agreed, most English department faculty members had little use for living writers, though they didn't mind the *cachet* that came their way from knowing a writer who'd become a celebrity like Seana, or—what they got off on even more—being able to tell people they were friends with a colleague whose novel had been turned into a movie. In this, Seana said, they were like most people, thinking the highest compliment they could pay you was to say your book would make a great movie—as if novels were merely movies *manqués*.

"Is that why you made sure your first novel would be one that could not be made into a movie?" I asked.

"Not at all," Seana said. "It certainly *could* be made into a movie—anything can be made into a movie these days."

"A most depressing thought," my father said.

"They made *Lolita* into a movie," I said.

"*Lolita*?" my father said. "Compared to *Triangle*, *Lolita* is very *pale* matter, totally lacking in *fire*."

Seana groaned.

"And what about *Jules and Jim*?" I said.

"Grim and gloomy stuff," Seana declared, "and with heavy-handed thematic overlays—The Great War and all that—and without anybody ever really enjoying it."

"*It*?" I asked.

"The sex," my father said. "What's so extraordinary about *Triangle* is the sheer joy the family takes in its sexual escapades, the great and uncomplicated delight in one another, and in who they truly are."

"Shhh," Seana said. "You're embarrassing the author."

By this time, Max had opened a second bottle of wine, and was telling us about how at faculty Christmas parties he'd walk up behind a colleague, tap the man or woman on the shoulder, and before the colleague could turn around, ask—"So tell me—how's the new novel coming?"—to which the colleague would usually reply, "Almost done," or "Coming along," and then there'd be a double-take, and the inevitable question: "But how did you *know*?"

Somewhere between salad and dessert—my father's delicious bread-pudding-with-maple-syrup—I fell asleep, and when I opened my eyes, Max was pouring more wine—we were on our third bottle—and raising a glass to my health. As to his own health, he said, he was feeling terrific—stronger than ever. He glanced down at his lap, then looked at me.

"Now I can bend it," he said.

Seana rolled her eyes and declared this was the perfect example of the kind of *shtik* that had charmed his students—had made them use the word 'puckish' when they talked about him.

"A term I deplored," my father said.

Seana leaned toward me: "Your father never fooled around with us—with his female students—the way the other profs did."

"One should not shit where one eats," my father said.

"Still," Seana said, "there were those among us who thought it a shame."

"There can be great pleasures in renunciation," my father stated, after which he stood, inclined his head slightly toward Seana, and began removing dishes from the table while reminding me that, as he'd mentioned in one of his letters, he was planning a trip to his old neighborhood in Brooklyn, and that he hoped I'd join him. Perhaps Seana would come too.

Seana shrugged, said she preferred not to go home again if she could help it, thank you very much, and her face took on a look of such sudden sadness—her hazel-green eyes going to dark brown, her smile sucked inward—that I wanted to reach across the table and take her hands in mine, tell her that everything—*everything!*—was going to be all right. My father continued to clear the table while Seana remained where she was, immobile, so I stood and, on wobbly legs, began gathering plates and silverware.

"Please sit," my father said, after which he announced that it was past his bedtime but that he knew we young people had things to talk about—Seana had so informed him earlier in the day—and that we should leave the rest of the dishes, along with the pots and pans, until morning.

He kissed Seana on the forehead, then came around the table, told me again how good it was to have me home, kissed me on the cheek, and asked me to give serious thought to accompanying him to Brooklyn, perhaps the following week.

"I need to go to Maine first," I said. "To visit Nick's parents."

"Of course," my father said, and reminded Seana that Nick had been a friend of mine from college who had lived in Singapore—who was responsible for my going there to work—and that Nick had died recently.

"You didn't like him," Seana said.

"Correct," my father said. "I didn't like him, although I didn't wish him dead. I found him a somewhat hollow and manipulative young man."

"You never told me that," I said.

"He was your friend, not mine, and doubtless possessed qualities that made you favor him with your friendship."

"My father's right about that," I said to Seana.

"Right that this guy was an ass?" Seana asked.

"Right that it was because of Nick that I went to Singapore."

"So?" she said.

"So I'm just setting the record straight."

"But surely your decision was not based wholly upon your friendship with Nick," my father said.

"Not wholly," I said.

"Good," my father said, "because although Nick and your friendship with him were clearly crucial to your choice, what I've preferred to believe is that your primary reason for going to the Far East had to do with your thirst for adventure."

"That too," I said.

My father turned to Seana. "I'll tell you something about my son that, given his often *faux-naïf* demeanor when it comes to matters intellectual, you might not suspect," he said. "Charlie was a voracious reader when he was a boy, and the books he loved most were about faraway places with strange sounding names. When he was seven or eight, I started him off with a complete set of *Bomba the Jungle Boy*, and while other boys his age were reading *The Hardy Boys* or sports novels, Charlie was immersed in tales that took him on exotic journeys to the four corners of the world."

"It's true," I said and, hoping to pull Seana out of her gloom, I told her about my favorite author in high school, James Ramsey

Ullman, and the book reports I did on his novels—about climbing Everest, going across the Karakorum desert in China, and up and down the Amazon—along with books like *Kon Tiki* and *Green Mansions*, and before that—at about the time I was reading *Bomba the Jungle Boy*—the Tarzan and Doctor Dolittle books.

"When Charlie was eight years old," my father said, "he came to me at the start of summer vacation with a question he'd been pondering. 'Do you think,' he asked, and in the most serious way, 'that by the end of the summer, I'll be old enough to go out into the world to seek my fortune?'"

"Oh my," Seana said.

"And let us not forget Gerald Durrell," my father said. "Charlie adored Durrell, so that when people asked him what he wanted to be when he grew up, he would say he was going to be an animal trainer and work in a zoo. Gerald—Lawrence's brother—was a zookeeper at times, you see, as well as a naturalist and environmentalist."

"I hope he was a better writer than his brother," Seana said. "Have you ever read those Alexandria novels? Impossibly soppy. Soppy, sloppy, soggy—over-written, noxious, romantic, pretentious…"

"But what don't you like about them?" my father asked, though when he smiled to show he'd meant his question ironically, Seana didn't smile with him. "Given the impressions his early reading made on him," my father continued, "small wonder Charlie has moved around so frequently, and has become so enchanted by the world he's discovered in the Far East."

Holding tightly to the stem of her wine glass, Seana leaned across the table. "So tell me something, Charlie," she said. "Do you enjoy seeing beautiful landscapes despoiled and ravaged? Do you take pleasure in seeing men, women, and children exploited and driven to early graves in order to provide lubricants for our machines, and poisons for our food and arteries? Do you take pride in your portion of responsibility for the deadly conditions that prevail in the enchanted world you've been inhabiting?"

"Of course not," I said, and resisted the urge to start talking about just what I *did* feel about Borneo and palm oil. "It's complicated," I said. "If you'd been there you'd understand that it's very complicated..."

"What isn't?" Seana said. "Nevertheless, our conversation has served to put me in mind once again of George Sand, a woman rarely far from my thoughts, and in particular—the obvious inspiration for the accusatory grilling I've just subjected you to—of her dying words: *Ne détruisez pas la verdure.*"

"Do not destroy the greenery," my father said.

"I don't need a translator," Seana snapped. "And 'greenery' stinks—doesn't begin to capture what she meant."

"When Seana was considering continuing on for a doctorate," my father explained, "she talked of writing her dissertation on George Sand."

"On Sand *and* Eliot," Seana said, correcting him. "The two great Georges. Gorgeous Georges? Curious Georges? Our own Ms. Oates notwithstanding, George Sand, you will recall—Amandine Aurore Lucile Dupin, and for greater part of her adult life, the Baroness Dudevant—was the most prolific female author in history. Nobody reads her anymore, though I would point out that Virginia Woolf's father, Leslie Stephen, a man of exceptional erudition and discernment—like you, Professor Max—admired her enormously."

"As did many men," my father said.

"Truly and duly noted," Seana said, her voice slurred. "Pagello above all." Seana turned to me. "Pagello was an Italian doctor—a country doctor, but not out of Kafka, and he fell in love with Sand, and she transported him with her across Italy and lived with him in Paris, and then she ditched him, and he returned to Venice, where he married and fathered children. He died at the age of ninety-one, nearly sixty years later. Your father once considered writing a novel about him."

"That's true," Max said.

"Actually, I know who you're talking about," I said. "I saw a movie about him where he gets to shag Juliet Binoche. A piss-poor movie, if you ask me."

"A novel *manqué*? my father asked.

"*Mutilé* would be more like it," Seana said. "And as for you, Max—didn't I hear you say it was past your bedtime?"

Seana stood, steadied herself by leaning on the table, said that it was true that she and I had things to talk about, and that, to prepare herself, she would now proceed to brew a cup of coal-black coffee.

She swayed a bit as she made her way to the kitchen, stopping at my chair, where she touched my shoulder briefly, even as my father said again what a joy it was to have me home. He wished us both pleasant dreams, and headed upstairs.

The list Seana gave me—titles with brief one-sentence explanatory tags attached to them, like log-lines you see in tele-vision listings for movies—was in her handwriting, which was exquisitely graceful, a skill of small value, she asserted, and one shared by most girls who'd survived a childhood of Catholic schools. My father's full list—titles with and without the tags—was extensive, she said. Amazing, actually—page after page of titles and snippets in search of authors and stories—so that what she'd done was to choose a baker's dozen that on a first reading seemed the most obviously promising, and, more to the point, ones that she liked to imagine Max had had in mind for her—for novels he imagined *she* might imagine into being were she to come across them one day.

What she wanted from me was not my opinion—how could one have an *opinion* of an unwritten novel that *might* be based on a title and a squiggle of words?—but my immediate and, more important, my *unreflective* reactions.

Because what made me an ideal collaborator, she added pointedly, was that she believed me capable of a truly thought-less response.

"Thanks," I said.

She stared past me with glazed eyes, then blinked. "Okay," she said, as if she were waking up. "You're right. Okay then. I've thought about this and here's what I've come to—that I've never *collaborated* with anyone before, so I'm doubtless wary of doing so, and covering my wariness—my sadness? my fear?—with aggression. A familiar pattern because—and I'm on a slight roll now, Charlie, so don't interrupt, please—unlike Mister James, a writer more generously sociable than most, who wrote that the port *from which* he set out was the essential loneliness of life—hardly an unusual journey for an Irishman—I've always believed my compass was set in an opposite direction: that the port *to which* I've been heading was the essential loneliness of my life. Can you understand that?"

"Yes," I said.

"Yes," she repeated, and she pushed several pieces of paper across the table. "So here's the list—what I wanted to ask you about. And now that I've given it to you, do you know what that makes me?"

"List-less?"

"It is apparent that you are more your father's son than either of you understand."

"Maybe. But consider this too—that because you made your deal with him, he's become listless too."

She tapped on the list with the eraser end of a pencil. "To the task at hand, young man," she said. "Read them and then tell me, please: Which ones appeal most? Which ones seem of no interest? Which ones inspire your curiosity, and—question *numéro uno*—which one do you think I should use as the basis for my next novel—or, to make it easier on you, why don't you choose three, say—but in ranked order of preference."

I picked up the pages.

"Is that too much to ask?" she said. "Too much responsibility for an innocent young guy like you?"

"Innocent and thoughtless," I said, correcting her.

"Oh Charlie," she said. "You shouldn't take my words as seriously as I sometimes do. I was just trying to get a rise out of you. My apologies—okay?"

"Okay," I said.

This is the list she gave me:

Pagello's Surgery. Memoirs of an aging Italian country doctor who had once been George Sand's lover.

A Missing Year. A veteran of the Korean War, suffering intermittently from suicidal impulses, returns home to Kansas in order to marry a fellow soldier's widowed wife even while he struggles to come to terms with the death of that soldier, an act of murder he may or may not have imagined.

Hector on 9/11. Story of a Puerto Rican teenager who, on the day the World Trade Center towers come down, has an exceptionally successful 24 hours of romance with his social studies teacher and several frightened teenage girls, all of whom are in extreme need of tenderness and consolation.

Tag Sale. A retired professor at a New England college organizes a tag sale in which he attempts to sell material from his unpublished and/or abandoned novels, and the ways in which this act affects the destinies of people dear to him.

Sky Captain. An Irish priest, chaplain to the crew of a merchant marine training ship, dies in a Marseilles brothel and is transported back across the Atlantic in the ship's freezer among sides of beef, cartons of hamburgers, and crates of dead chickens.

Hearts and Minds. A fifty-five-year-old chemist, in line for a Nobel prize and in need of a heart transplant, receives the heart of a 19-year-old black woman who has died in an automobile crash; following the transplant, he abandons his scientific research in favor of the life of a *bon vivant*.

Her Private Train. An historical novel based on Theodore Roosevelt's 1905 wolf hunt—the tale told primarily from the p.o.v. of his daughter, Alice Roosevelt Longworth—for which hunt TR set out for the territory of Oklahoma in a private train of 22 cars, with 70 fox hounds, 67 greyhounds, 60 saddle and packhorses, 44 hunters, beaters, wranglers, journalists, and one woman.

Charlie's Story. A charming young man in his mid-thirties takes up residence in an international city in the Far East, and becomes involved with a less than charming man whose fate has (wonderful) transformative effects on our hero.

The James Brothers. In heaven, Henry and William join with Frank and Jesse to steal the pearly gates.

Max Baer and the Star of David. The tale of Max Baer's relationship with a black couple who, before and after he becomes heavyweight champion—a Star of David first adorning his trunks when he defeats Hitler's boxer, Max Schmeling, in Yankee Stadium—serve him faithfully as Man Friday and housekeeper, and in which tale we discover that the couple are not husband and wife but brother and sister, and that their child is Max Baer's son.

Make-A-Wish. A gifted young violinist, knowing she has but a year to live, shows up at her mentor's door and declares that, like those children who get to meet their favorite athlete or rock star before they die, she has chosen to live with him for the duration.

Jules and Jim Go to White's Castle. In 1947, two young Brooklyn Dodger fans make a pilgrimage to Maine to visit their favorite writer, E. B. White, in order to persuade White to write a book in which he has the boys befriend Jackie Robinson, thereby enabling Robinson to survive a signal moment in his first year in the Major Leagues.

We Gather Together. A Thanksgiving reunion wherein the children and grandchildren of a warring Irish family bring the family back together on the occasion of the silver anniversary of their parents' divorce.

The story I kept thinking about on our way across Massachusetts and up toward Tenants Harbor was *Make-A-Wish*, even though—because?—I had *not* chosen it as one of the three I thought would make the best novel for Seana to work on. The three I chose were *Charlie's Story*, *Tag Sale*, and *A Missing Year*, mainly because they contained elements I could relate to from Max's life or my own.

Which, Seana had declared while we sat at the kitchen table my first night home, had nothing to do with whether or not any of them would make a good novel. Because something had happened to you, or might happen to you, had zilch to do with what made fiction work. In fiction—this is what she said she'd learned from my father—imagination and empathy: being able to conjure up lives and times *unlike* your own—were everything.

"Does that mean that what I've been believing all these years—that *Triangle* was based on your relationship with your mother and father—had no truth to it?"

"Don't try to get funny with me, young man," she said. "My life's my life, and my stories are my stories."

She fixed us tumblers of Drambuie over ice, then came around the table and sat next to me, an arm across my shoulder as if we were old schoolyard buddies, and said that she'd been thinking about Nick's death, and had decided it was a bad idea for me to go up to Maine by myself, and that she was going to go with me.

"Even if I ask you to?" I said.

"Even if you ask me to," she said, and then, before I could try to kiss her—and oh boy did I want to!—she drained her drink, chucked me on the arm, and left me in the kitchen. I waved good-bye to her after she was gone, but instead of thinking of her sweet mouth, or trying to recall what it felt like the time we did kiss, or imagining what it would be like if I went into her room later, lay down beside her, and began kissing her—I found myself picturing the two of us arriving at Trish's house, with Trish embracing me, and the two of *us* kissing.

What I'd also begun wondering about, from the moment I read the *Make-A-Wish* synopsis, was whether the story about the violinist was really about Seana, and if, like the woman in the story, Seana had come to our house in Northampton because, knowing she was dying, she wanted to be near *her* mentor during the time she had left. The idea for the novel had been my father's, but I had to wonder if Seana had either confided her situation in him at some point, or if he somehow guessed that the only reason she would take up nesting rights in our house was because it was the one place where she felt safe—at home— and because she wanted to be close to him on her way out. I stood, felt my knees wobble, and put a hand on the back of a chair to steady myself. The room tilted to one side, and then to the other, as if it were a ship going through high, rolling waves, and I told myself that I'd done much too much wondering for one evening, and that it was time to go to sleep so that I might, if I got lucky, become lost in a wild and lovely storm-tossed sea of dreams.

After we'd made our way across the small cuff of New Hampshire that connected Massachusetts to Maine, and stopped for lunch in a shoreline diner outside Kennebunkport, I remembered what I'd been thinking the night before, and asked Seana if *Make-A-Wish* had anything to do with her.

"It was your father's idea, not mine," she said.

"Sure," I said. "But you said you thought he might have

imagined some of the stories—at least the ones you showed me—in part because it was his way of giving you notions for novels that you imagined he might have imagined would be novels you might imagine."

"Don't get meta-fictional on me," she said.

"Meta-who?"

"Actually, if you need reassurance, let it be known that Seana Shulamith McGee O'Sullivan subjects herself to regular check-ups—cervix, breasts, colon, heart, lungs—the works—and that the best medical teams have failed to discover anything to worry about. Which means I have to keep writing."

"But I thought you *love* to write. You told me that nothing gives you more pleasure than writing."

"I love to write," she said, pointing a fork at me. "But you're missing the point, Charlie." She tapped the flat side of the fork against the side of her head. "Use your noodle, fella. Whose story is it?"

"Oh," I said. And then again: "Oh."

"Oh," she said.

"But he seems *fine.*"

"So do we all, some days."

"But," I began, and leaned forward. "I mean, do you really think that's what it's about?"

"No," she said.

"But why—?"

She shrugged and lifted her coffee mug, as if in a toast to Max, then sat back. "Who knows?" she said again. "Probably because I enjoy playing you—playing *with* you?—seeing what's going on behind those moist brown eyes of yours. I used to love it when Max had to be out of town and he asked me to babysit you—he said I was there to house-sit so that you wouldn't be offended and think he thought you couldn't take care of your-self. But it was the same then: when you're especially happy or sad—or scared—your eyes have the same beguiling quality your father's eyes have, did you know that?"

"Maybe," I said. "But all that stuff about ports and loneliness—what was *that* all about? Some perverse way of… of…?"

"Stuck for words, Charlie?"

"Let's just forget it, okay?" I said. I picked up the check. "Let's just forget it and blow this joint."

"Do you have one?"

"Very funny," I said. "But you know what?"

"What?"

"You're not that funny," I said. "You're weird—I'll give you that—and—like some of the characters in your books—with a distinctive mean streak. For sure. But you're not funny."

"I'll take that as a compliment," she said.

A short while later, in the car, Seana fell asleep, her head against the window, a rolled up sweater for a pillow. She snored lightly, her mouth open, and I tried to stay angry at her for making me believe, if only for a moment, that my father was living on borrowed time, but then it occurred to me that maybe he really was, and that when she saw my reaction, she had changed course.

I wondered, though: What difference did it make if I knew for sure—if he knew for sure—if he and Seana knew for sure, or if none of us knew anything? I tried to imagine what he might do if he *did* know—if he'd make any changes in the way he lived, and decided he wouldn't, which was when I realized that the idea of getting rid of the unused parts of his writing life might have come from the knowledge—and fear—that he wouldn't be here much longer, though a second later this led to the thought that the tag sale might have only been what it was: the kind of thing Max did now and then for no other reason than that he felt like doing it.

North of Portland, I turned off the main highway—Seana

was awake now, but quiet—and took a detour west toward Naples so we could swing by the place where I'd gone to summer camp as a kid—Camp Kingswood—and where I'd been a counselor the first two summers I was at UMass. I'd been to Maine a bunch of times in the years since I'd been a camper and counselor there—Nick and Trish were married in Maine, and the year Nick and I graduated from UMass, we'd gone up there and had a wild few days with a group of friends, eight or ten of us, partying, drinking, and screwing our asses off.

Now, seeing Camp Kingswood again—leaves gone from the trees, you could see the old bunk houses, and the lake beyond, the lake calm, flat, and steel-gray in the autumn chill—I found myself telling Seana about how, starting with my first summer there, I'd fallen in love, not so much with Maine's lakes or coastline, but with its trees, the evergreens especially—pine, hemlock, juniper, and, my favorite, Norwegian spruce.

What I'd loved about Maine, I said, was what I'd come to love about Borneo, even though the two landscapes had hardly anything in common, and that was how thick and deep the forests were, along with my sense that they were still—evergreen and hardwood here, tropical forests there—the way they might have been millions of years ago.

I talked about the different kinds of mangroves in the coastal regions of Borneo and how their root systems looked like tangles of swollen spider webs, and I talked about peat swamp forests, and how they could burst into flame spontaneously, or be set on fire by people clearing them, and how the fires could rage over hundreds of acres for months at a time and were almost impossible to extinguish because so much of the burning went on below ground, in the deepest layers of the peat. And I talked about forests I'd been to on my most recent visit to Kalimantan—Dipterocarp forests—probably at the same time Seana had been moving in with Max. About every four years—I'd been lucky enough to be there when it happened two years before—the onset of dry weather conditions, combined with *El Niño*, resulted in an extraordinary explosion of color, where tens of thousands of trees in these forests, many of them a hundred and twenty or thirty feet high, and any single one of them bearing four *million* flowers, burst into bloom. It was the most amazing thing I'd ever seen.

"Four million?" Seana said. "You counted?"

"Estimated," I said.

"But these trees are dying—they're being logged away to make room for your palm oil plantations, yes?"

"Yes."

"Palm oil was used in the making of napalm, wasn't it?"

"Yes."

"So you are a shit," she said.

"Probably. Still, I was wondering if you'd like to visit the forests with me and get to see them before they're gone?"

"Sure," she said. And then: "'Death is the mother of beauty,' right?"

"Max used to say the same thing—a line from a poem, right?"

"'Sunday Morning,' by Wallace Stevens—I heard the lines from Max the first time too. But you say you don't feel guilty?"

"About what?"

"About taking pleasure from seeing the beauty of these forests because you know they're dying."

"What good would guilt do?"

"Actually," she said, "and take it from an Irish girl who knows about such matters—when it's not self-destructive, guilt can be a splendid muse."

"In some places I've been to in Borneo," I said, "there can be more than seven hundred different species of trees in a twenty-five acre plot, which is more than the total number of tree species in the United States and Canada combined."

"Impressive."

"It's one reason—being able to get to Borneo easily and often—I've stayed at the job in Singapore."

"And you'd go there—to Borneo—if you knew you were dying, yes?"

"Yes."

Seana was quiet for a while, after which she said she'd come to the conclusion it would be a good idea if I was the one who wrote *Charlie's Story*, that she liked listening to me talk—to what she called the sweet, innocent timbre of my voice—and that maybe I could make this voice work on the page.

"I'm not as smart or talented as Max," I said.

"Neither am I."

"Not so," I said.

"Well, who knows, Charlie?" she said. "But you do have the main thing most writers begin with: you loved to read when you were young. Because no matter what other reasons writers may give for why they write, most of them, in the end, will tell you that what made them want to be writers was that they loved to read when they were kids, and that they wanted to be able some day to write books that would be for others like the books they'd loved when they were growing up."

"Max used to say pretty much the same thing when people asked him why he wrote," I said.

"Oh yes," Seana said. "And your father said you had a great thirst for advenure, right? So what could be more of an adventure than making up a story—creating a world that never actually existed, and peopling it with imaginary people you come to care about more than you often care about people you know, and all the while—all the while, Charlie—never knowing what's going to happen to them next?"

"When you start writing your novels, you *really* don't know what's going to happen to the people in it?"

"No," Seana said.

"Sounds good to me," I said.

"Some writers—Nabokov most famously—claim they *always* know what's going to happen next—that a writer is like an omniscient god who controls the destinies of all his characters."

"Doesn't sound like much fun," I said.

"That's because, despite a sometimes useless habit of being more innocent and timid than is good for you, you're an essentially unique, adventurous, and playful young man," she said.

"Maybe," I said.

"Neither of us are as *playful* as your father is, though."

"Not yet anyway," I said.

"'Not yet anyway,'" she said, repeating my words, and when she did she looked away so that I couldn't see her eyes. Then: "Don't you think that's sad, Charlie?"

I wanted to say yes, but instead I answered her question by telling her that the blossoms in the Dicterocap forests were pale and dusty, and looked something like hibiscus blossoms—wide, flat, and fringed like crepe paper, and the color of blood oranges—and that their leaves were light green and fleshy.

"Every four years, did you say? Which means that in two years we can go there, you and I—book a trip together, yes?"

"Is that what you writers do—*book* trips?"

"You're not that funny either," she said. "But sure—I'm game to go."

I told her it was a deal, and explained what I'd learned on my trips there: that the massive flowering of the trees, and the fruiting that followed, had been a gift to the animals, especially to wild boar, who thrived on the seeds and spread them everywhere. I said that nobody knew how many centuries local populations had depended on those times when there was an abundance of seeds—and lots of pork to gorge on—but that anthropologists believed the relationship had lasted for as long as human beings had inhabited Borneo.

What I didn't say was that most scientists had concluded that logging had probably reduced the density of the forests below the critical level needed to maintain reproductive cycles, and that the ecosystem was, therefore, irreparably damaged.

When we got to Tenants Harbor, I telephoned Nick's parents—his mother answered, a lucky break—and I said I was in the vicinity with a friend and would like to stop by. Mrs. Falzetti said to please come, but to give her a half hour or so to tidy up. Seana was surprised I hadn't called from Northampton, and I said I'd waited until we were nearby because I didn't want to give them a chance to reject a visit out-of-hand, which I figured would have happened if Lorenzo, who could be nasty at times, had picked up the phone.

We had some time to kill, so I drove us out to Port Clyde, a few miles away, and we walked along the boat landing, where the ferry to Monhegan Island docked. The air was crisp, near freezing, but without wind, and Seana slipped her arm into mine. The ocean, like the lake at Camp Kingswood, was steel-gray and calm, but I knew how changeable the weather could be—how a pearl-gray sky could turn to slate-black within seconds, and how winds could become ferocious and waves could come roaring in and swamp small boats.

"Did you ever spend time here with Nick, just the two of you?" Seana asked.

"Yes," I said. "Once—a total disaster—when we stayed with his mother and father. And I visited him and Trish a few times after they were married. For a while—before they were married, when the three of us would come up here together—I thought I might settle in these parts—not in a town around here, but on an island off the coast, where I could be totally alone and wouldn't have to see or talk with anyone."

"There *are* people around," Seana said. "Still, it is peaceful and lovely here. Maybe Max and I can rent a house here for a few months—it would be a good place for getting work done. No distractions."

"Except for Max," I said.

"You never said how Nick died."

"You're right. I never said how Nick died."

"Do his parents know how he died?"

"I assume so. The embassy called from Singapore, and I called too."

"And what did you tell them?" Seana said. "And can you stop being such a tight-ass with me about it? Is there some deep, dark secret here?"

"No," I said. "Just stupidity. Nick could be incredibly stupid sometimes—a real stupid son of a bitch. A lucky son of a bitch too a lot of the time."

"But not this time."

"Not this time," I said, and I told her what had happened: how, on the first Saturday night after I'd returned from Borneo, he got drunk at a party he threw in his apartment.

"He was showing off," I said, "and I was out on his balcony— I was pretty plastered too, and busting his chops—and he came at me, and I managed to step aside at the last second and he couldn't stop—miscalculated—and pitched over the railing. His apartment was sixteen stories high."

"And…?"

"And I tried to catch him—to grab him—but it was too late, of course, and when I sobered up, I went to the morgue and ID'd the body—puked all over the place, and over Nick too. Projectile vomiting, like a baby…"

"Good," Seana said.

"*Good?*"

"A vegetable kind of justice."

"I thought you're not supposed to say bad things about the dead."

"Why not? Given the way you and Max talk about him, it sounds as if he got what he deserved, including your leftovers."

"Sure," I said. "The way you got Max's leftovers, right?"

"You *can* be nasty."

"Sometimes."

"Well, I *do* like that in you, Charlie," she said. "But tell me this: given your dislike of Nick's father, along with your claim about not being affected by guilt, why the compulsion to pay your respects?"

I was ready for her question, and said that Nick had been an only child, same as me, and that all through my teenage years, and occasionally since, I'd imagined what my father would feel if he had to watch my coffin being lowered into a grave, especially if it happened at a time when he was without a wife or live-in girlfriend, and when I'd told this to Nick, he said he'd had similar thoughts about him and *his* father, but that there was nothing for me to worry about, because knowing Max, he bet that if Max were single when I kicked off, he wouldn't stay single long.

"I'm with Nick on that," Seana said, "but imagining what people will feel after you're dead—that's ordinary self-serving stuff we all indulge in now and then. It doesn't account for why we're making this trip."

I said that even though Mister Falzetti was a lousy piece of work, it was still something to lose your only child, and that there was this too: that after Nick died, I kept remembering what Max said once when he'd come home from the funeral of a colleague's daughter: that the rabbis taught that although there was a word for a child who lost his parents, and for a husband or wife who lost a spouse, there was no word for someone who lost a child, so terrible was the loss.

"That's the mush side of your father's brain talking," Seana said. "Sentimental crap. When he gets into his rabbinic groove, spewing homilitic pap, I head for the exits."

"You've never had a child to lose," I said.

"So?"

"So how would you know what it's like?"

"Loss is loss."

"I don't buy it," I said. "There are losses, and there are losses. They're not all equal."

"And imagination's imagination," Seana said. "It can go anywhere and feel anything. You don't have to lose a child to feel what it would be like to lose one."

"Methinks she doth protest too much," I said.

"Give it a rest, Charlie," she said.

"What I think is that if you'd ever had a child yourself, and if…"

"*Goddamn you!*" she said, and whacked me hard across the face with the back of her hand, then walked away, fast.

I caught up to her, grabbed her by a shoulder, and turned her around. "*Hey*—!" I began, but before I could say anything else, she wrenched her shoulder free and pushed me away.

"I gave you fair warning," she said. "I gave you fair warning, and I'll do it again. Don't you *ever* talk to me like that. Don't you ever, *ever* talk to me like that, do you hear? I'd have made a good mother if I'd wanted to—a damned good mother."

"I agree."

"Prick!" she said, and she drew back her hand to whack me again, but then let it drop to her side, and walked off toward the near end of the boat landing.

Neither of us spoke again until we were back in the car and were approaching the Falzettis' house. The house was large, and set on a slight rise that overlooked a small fishing harbor that contained one of three islands owned by Andrew Wyeth and his wife. The Wyeths' island was set in the mouth of the harbor and covered about twenty acres, with a beautiful old lighthouse at one end that the Wyeths had used as their home before they'd bought two other islands in the area, and before they'd moved back to Pennsylvania. I told Seana about the Wyeths, and suggested that if we stayed a few days, we might visit their other two islands, which were much larger than this one—four to five hundred acres each—and that Wyeth's wife had turned these two islands into wildlife refuges where local fishermen could base their operations.

"Thanks for the good news on the environmental front," Seana said, and she punched me on the arm, lightly. "So okay—here's what just happened: because I'd convinced myself you were tougher-minded than your father, I became momentarily disillusioned—upset with myself—for having been blind to the squishy regions of your sensibility. You were right about Max, though. He'd be a distraction."

When Nick's mother opened the door—she was a short, compact woman with light blue eyes that, like Nick's, were almost translucent, and gray hair that had a hazy purple sheen to it—I hugged her and told her how sorry I was about Nick, and as I did I recalled that the first time Nick invited me to his parents' home we were halfway through a meal she'd set down for us before I realized she was his mother, and not the housekeeper.

Mrs. Falzetti said it was good to see me again and that I looked wonderful, then wiped at her eyes with the back of a hand. I introduced her to Seana, who had been one of my father's students, I said, and—the story we'd contrived on the way north—was on her way to a writer's retreat near Acadia National Park, and (but why was I surprised?) Seana said something sweet and appropriate about it being impossible to feel what it would be like to lose one's only child.

Mister Falzetti came to us then—"Call me Lorenzo," he said at once, and I hugged him too, which seemed to surprise him—his body stiffened—and told him how sorry I was about Nick, and that Nick had been my closest friend and had always looked out for me. Mister Falzetti was wearing a navy-blue blazer, a powder-blue mock-turtleneck, gray flannel slacks, and white deck shoes. I'd first met him at a UMass homecoming football game nearly twenty years before, and he looked the same now as he had then: lean, strong, and, in his yachting outfit, though without a captain's hat, what my father would have called 'natty.'

He looked at Seana then, and seemed taken aback that she was there, but recovered quickly and spoke to her in his usual cold, confident way: "You're Seana O'Sullivan, aren't you," he said.

"That's correct."

"I'm an admirer of your two novels," he said, and he led us into the living room, which was handsomely appointed in a soothing combination of contemporary furniture—sleek plastics and stainless steel—and antiques: an oak sideboard, a large French country table, rush-covered ladder-back chairs, electrified oil lamps, and, around the room, discretely placed, a dozen or so model ships, some of which, I knew, Mister Falzetti had made: fishing boats, sailboats, steamboats, ocean liners, and fully rigged tall ships like those you see in pirate movies.

If you'd met him in this setting, or in the home Nick had grown up in, in Longmeadow, Massachusetts, an upper middle class suburb south of Springfield—the house in Maine had been the family's country home until Mister Falzetti retired and they moved here full-time—you would have thought he'd probably gone to Harvard or Yale, and had been the CEO of an old-line WASP corporation. But it wasn't so. "What my dad does is to turn shit into gold," was the way Nick had described his father to me. Mister Falzetti had grown up in the North End of Boston, one of nine kids from a poor Italian immigrant family, and had started out, at fourteen, digging sewer lines for a company in Newton, after which, when he was sixteen, he'd moved to a small, mostly Polish farming town in Western Massachusetts where he set up his own business—mowing lawns, plowing driveways, pumping out septic tanks. Though he never finished high school, he was a fanatic about education— the one thing, he liked to say, the bastards can't take away from you. And when it came to smarts—Nick loved quoting him on stuff like this—being a Wop among Polacks was like being the proverbial one-eyed man in the kingdom of the blind. By the time he was twenty-one, he owned his own company, which pumped out shit and sludge from people's basements and septic systems, dug up their leach fields, put in their sewer lines, and plowed and repaired their driveways, and he'd also been able to corner lucrative contracts for school bus routes, waste treatment operations, and road work—salting, plowing, repairs—in a half-dozen Western Massachusetts towns.

"So let's get to it, Charlie," he said as soon as he'd poured wine for me and Seana. "Tell us about Nick, since, except perhaps for poor Trish, you knew him better than anyone. Tell us about our boy: was he happy near the end?"

"Not especially," I said.

"He drank a lot, didn't he."

"He drank a lot."

"The man from the embassy said that his alcohol level at the time of death was off the charts."

"Probably."

"Then tell us something else: Are you glad he's dead?" he asked, and before I could answer, he pointed a finger at me. "The truth now, Charlie. Don't dissemble with me. Is it a *relief*? Were you glad when it happened or, in the immediate aftermath, let's say, when the actuality—its irreversibility—hit home?"

"No."

"You're a liar, but a credible one," he said. "Nick always admired that quality in you—your ability to fool people into thinking you were just an ordinary, okay guy. 'My friend's a regular good-time Charlie,' he used to joke. You were the only person he knew whose way of being was a refutation of the truism that one cannot both be sincere and seem to be sincere at the same time."

"I miss Nick more than you can know," I said.

"I intend no criticism," Mister Falzetti said. "We're all upset, each in our own ways, but I'll tell you this: you did make a ter-rific team, you two—like Tom Sawyer and Huck Finn, I used to think—Nick ever ebullient, risk-taking, wild, and so shrewd he ultimately did himself in, but in love with life, my son was!—and you, almost as smart as Nick but with an essential—what shall we call it?—naïveté? reserve? timidity?"

"Call it sleep," Seana said, and walked by us, to a large bay window on the south side of the room.

"That's Henry Roth, of course," Mister Falzetti said. "He lived not too far from here, on a shit-ass farm plopped down between villages named Freedom and Liberty. The way I see it, he fled New York and came here to live so he could teach him-self not to write and not to be a Jew."

"He didn't succeed at either," Seana said.

"Correct," Mister Falzetti said and, moving across the room to Seana, pointed to the lighthouse. "Now take poor Wyeth," he said. "The son of a bitch timed his death all wrong—packed it in three days before they inaugurated that young black tennis player, so he didn't get anywhere near the press and publicity he craved."

"Tennis player?" I said.

"The young Ashe boy, he's in the White House now, isn't he, even though he has AIDS? I call it a miracle."

"Arthur Ashe is dead, and has been for some time," Seana said.

"Perhaps," Mister Falzetti said. "But what difference? I admire the cool athleticism and affect, the way he rope-a-dopes his opponents, plus—all-important—the fire within. The man's a worker—I refer to our president—and he's a fighter too, you just wait and see. Plenty smart—smarter than Wyeth, who chose to live under his father's thumb his whole life. That's where the rage came from, of course."

"We were hoping the two of you would stay for dinner," Mrs. Falzetti said. She sat by a stone fireplace, in a narrow wooden chair, her hands clasped on her lap. The fire was low and bright, and drew the chill from the air. In the floor-to-ceiling bookcases that surrounded the fireplace I saw what looked like the same books that had been in the living room in Longmeadow, and that Nick bragged were not just there for show: *The Encyclopedia Britannica*, *The Harvard Classics*, *The Great Books* and *Syntopicon*, and uniform sets of novels by nineteenth and early twentieth century authors: Dickens, Twain, Hardy, Trollope, Scott, Stevenson, Eliot, James, Cather, Dreiser, Howells, Forster, the Brontës…

"It would please us if you would," Mrs. Falzetti said. "We could talk about Nick, and look through old photo albums. And if you haven't yet found lodging, we have a small guest cabin out back you're welcome to use."

"Thanks but no thanks," Seana said. "Perhaps we can rain-check the invite, and join with your husband's desire to dance on graves on some other occasion."

"I understand," Mister Falzetti said. "I *can* be irritating at times—offensive, some say—but I've read and admired your books, as I said, and there's no lack of offense there for those so inclined. Your work's marked by what I'd call a grim severity, and I like severity, admire it in prose as much as I do in people."

"It really would be no trouble at all," Mrs. Falzetti said. "And we needn't talk about Nick if doing so would make you uncomfortable."

"And I've read interviews with you," Mister Falzetti said. "The few you've allowed, that is—quite shrewd to minimize them and keep the mystery going, which is something Wyeth, for one, never understood—and I've noticed that you never mention your family. So a question for the author: How come no mention of family?"

"Because I have none," Seana said.

"Oh?"

"I excommunicated them at an early age."

"But—let me guess—you did have a mother and father. Most of us, I'm told, have mothers and fathers."

"Maybe," Seana said. "Depends upon how you define your terms."

"There's something to be said for that," Mister Falzetti said. "For example: if you think of that young black man's strength of character and the fact that he only knew his father for a single month of his life, and if you then consider the lives Nick, or even Charlie here, have had—young men who've never had to dream up their fathers, it tells you something."

"Tells you what?" Seana asked.

"That's correct," Mister Falzetti said, and he refilled Seana's wine glass. "But tell me about Shulamith, if you will, since it's a middle name you've chosen to keep. Are there Jews in your lineage?"

"There are Jews everywhere," Seana said.

"True enough," Mister Falzetti said. "There may even be Jews in my family, from a time when the Moors overran Southern Europe and mingled with the Italians and Spanish. Did you know—forgive the tangent, but did you know that the Roosevelts—Franklin, Theodore, and Eleanor—were descended from Dutch Jews named Rosenfeld? Rosen-*veldt*, to be exact."

Seana sat down next to me and squeezed my arm. "Oh Charlie, let's blow this joint, okay?" she said quietly, mocking me affectionately with my own phrase.

Mister Falzetti poured himself more wine. "Now, your father's short story about *The Protocols of the Elders of Zion* coming true, is, in my opinion, his single most brilliant creation," he said. "It rivals the best in Roth—in any of them: Henry, Philip, or Joseph—and it's a damned shame he only wrote one novel, because that novel is a real knockout. I always thought he could have been another Nabokov, the mind and gift he had."

"Has," I corrected.

"Ah—your father's still alive then, which makes me happy for you both," Mister Falzetti said, "although it cannot but be hard on you at times, Charlie—to be in the presence of his unrequited ambitions. Or did he live vicariously through your books, Ms. O'Sullivan?"

"Did you live vicariously through your son, Mister Falzetti?"

"Of course not. If anything, the reverse is true—Nick admired me more than was good for him."

"A shame, for if only you'd emulated him…"

"You're quite good at repartee," Mister Falzetti said. "But then words are your métier—the unapologetic and cruel wit of your characters is often the most endearing element in your novels. Now Nick could be word-clever too, of course, even if he never—"

"Nick's *dead*, Mister Falzetti," I said, finding myself unable hold back—to keep my irritation from showing. "So why don't you just give it a rest, okay? Nothing any of us can do will bring him back."

"Oh I know *that*," Mister Falzetti said. "But I was told that you let him go, Charlie—that you held onto him for an instant before he made the plunge."

"*Hey—come on!*"

I started to stand, but Seana pushed me down, stood, and lifted her wine glass so that it was only an inch or two from Mister Falzetti's nose. "Now I bet you're the kind of guy who puts himself to sleep some nights by imagining there's a touch of evil about you that makes you truly fascinating," she said, "when the truth is that you're really just a creep."

"And you're the kind of woman Evelyn Waugh might have adored—a mean-spirited Catholic fabulist," Mister Falzetti said and, very gently, he nudged Seana's glass aside and moved past her to the fireplace. "The reason I preferred *Plain Jane* to *Triangle*," he continued, "is because it was utterly lacking in conscience, or in anything called conscience, as the poet would have it."

"Yeats," Seana said, "'The Tower.'"

"I surely won't attempt to compete with you in a literary duel," Mister Falzetti said, "but I will complete my thought, which is that it's the absence of conscience in your work that I find so endearing. Unlike Waugh, whose characters are ingeniously eccentric but whose dark humor, alas, is marred by his schoolboy Catholicism, or Patricia Highsmith, say, whose characters are often charmingly amoral—true psychopaths—your characters are quintessentially normal, and very American. It's not only that your heroine gets away with murder—it's her lack of contrition—her ease with what she's done that delights. Plain Jane indeed!"

"You know what?" Seana said, and she gave Mister Falzetti her most winning smile. "If I'd had a father like you, I'd have killed myself too."

"Oh but Nick did not kill himself," Mrs. Falzetti said, her voice assured in a way that surprised me.

"Eugenia's correct," Mister Falzetti said. "It was an accident. The embassy and the police assured us that it was an accident. Isn't that so, Charlie?"

"It was an accident," I said.

"That's what I believe," Mrs. Falzetti said, "although at times Lorenzo has other notions, and I trust I'm not talking out of school to say that ever since we received the news, Lorenzo has been living in a state of shock that has given rise to a prolonged and somewhat antic state of denial."

"And I believe we've overstayed our welcome," Seana said.

"Lorenzo worried about Nick more than he can admit," Mrs. Falzetti continued. "He loved our son inordinately, and in his heart I believe he has always felt responsible for Nick's troubles."

"Come, come, Eugenia," Mister Falzetti said. "Let's not bother these young people with our disagreements."

"What I'm saying does not excuse Lorenzo, of course," Mrs.

Falzetti said, "but it does help account for his behavior of late. That's what I believe."

"It's what you want to believe," Mister Falzetti said, and he kissed the top of his wife's head. "Eugenia is not the same woman she was before Nick left us. It may not seem so to see her on a day like this, but she can be a pistol. Can't you, dear?"

"I certainly can," she said, "although I do not possess the potential to be quite as insufferable as you. Therefore, I apologize to our guests. Manners, please, Lorenzo. Manners must get us through."

"Manners, yes, but also surprises and shrewd purchases," Mister Falzetti said. "I bought up lots of Wyeth early on—that's not under the heading of 'surprise,' which we'll get to by and by—but when we were friendly, and before fame rotted his brain, Wyeth sold me his stuff at bargain-basement prices, along with work from the father. He couldn't get rid of his father's stuff fast enough, and I knew back then what we've come to understand since: that the father's work will last far longer than the son's. Burned Andy's cheap, arrogant ass when he found out what I was getting for my stash, one by one, father and son. So don't you worry about us, no matter how far into the toilet this lousy economy goes."

"Which reminds me," Mrs. Falzetti said to us. "Do you worry about what the recession has done to our economy?"

Seana started to laugh, but covered her mouth. "I'm not laughing at you or your question, ma'am," she said. "And the answer is no—I don't worry about the economy, and neither does Charlie, though we appreciate your concern."

"I inherited Nick's accounts," I said. "I'm in good shape for a while to come."

"I'm happy for you," Mrs. Falzetti said. "Nick did have a generous streak in him—he's left everything to Trish, you know."

"We hope to visit Trish," I said.

"Trish is a fine young woman," Mrs. Falzetti said. "She's done a wonderful job with Gabe and Anna. Anna is seventeen months old and quite normal so far, I'm pleased to report."

"Ah—you've gone and said the magic word," Mister Falzetti exclaimed. "*Normal!* And speaking of normal, I believe it's time for our little surprise, so you will give me two more minutes, won't you?"

"Don't," Mrs. Falzetti said, but I couldn't tell if she was talking to us, or to Mister Falzetti.

"I can assure you it will be worth your while," Mister Falzetti said. "A rare opportunity to see how we entertain ourselves up here, where the winters, as you know, can be long and dark."

I was ready to leave, but when Seana sat where she was without moving, I stayed put. I felt distinctly numb, though, in the way I'd feel after a long walk along the coast when the cold and the damp could seep into your bones.

A minute later Mister Falzetti twirled into the room. "*Ta-da!*" he exclaimed. He still had on his blazer, but was wearing bright red lipstick, and a wig of blond curls, a hair net pulled down over it. He put his arm around Mrs. Falzetti.

"So what do you think?" he asked. "Honestly now. Wasn't this worth waiting for?"

"He usually only does this on Saturday nights," Mrs. Falzetti explained. "I feel distinctly embarrassed, and once again I do apologize."

"Nothing to be embarrassed about or apologize for," Mister Falzetti said. "We all have our quirky sides, but most of us are too shy—too *timid*—to show them forth. Think of the great pain people live with because of unexpressed desires! Think of the fabulous lives we *might* lead that we never get to experience. Think of Nick, and of how nasty, brutish, and short his life was—of all he hoped to do and never will."

I wondered if Nick had ever seen his father like this, and then realized: yes or no, what difference to who he was, or to his fate? I felt an urge to *defend* Nick—to say to Nick's father what Nick might have said: that though his life had been short, he'd done what he wanted when he wanted, but when I imagined Nick chiding me for being romantic and sentimental again, I decided to say nothing.

"Stop," Mrs. Falzetti said. "Please stop, Lorenzo."

"Nasty, brutish, and short," Seana said. "Doubtless true. Still, he wasn't poor or solitary."

"Correct again," Mister Falzetti said, and he licked a fingertip, wiped away an invisible hair from a corner of his mouth. "It's one thing, of course, to imagine new and different lives on a piece of paper, but far different—far more *tangible*, wouldn't you agree?—to let the imagination live in the *actual* world. Why not indulge ourselves, then, no matter how foolish and ridiculous our indulgences? Why not live the lives we desire, given that this is not a first draft—that this is all there is? Would you like to see me perform one of my music hall numbers? Would you like to kiss me?"

"Sure," Seana said.

"I had a feeling, from your books, that you'd prove willing," Mister Falzetti said.

"Did you?" Seana asked. "Or were you hoping you could *épater* me just a wee bit?"

"Perhaps," he said. "Did I succeed?"

"Who knows?" Seana said, and cracking her glass against the side of the fireplace so quickly that I hardly noticed the motion—my eyes were fixed on Mister Falzetti's mouth, where the lipstick had been applied the way a little girl might have applied lipstick on her first try—and with part of the glass still in her hand, and with a swift downward movement, but without splashing blood on herself, she sliced his bottom lip open.

"That should shut him up for a while," she said. "You know what they say about having too much of a good thing." Then she leaned toward Mister Falzetti, but instead of kissing him, she licked at the blood that ran along his chin as if, I thought, she were slurping ice cream that was melting down the side of a sugar cone.

"Thank you, dear," Mrs. Falzetti said.

"You're welcome," Seana said, and then: "Duct tape."

"Duct tape?"

"Duct tape," Seana said. "Duct tape should seal things until an ambulance gets here. Do you have duct tape?"

"Oh I'm certain we do," Mrs. Falzetti said, her voice animated in a way it had not been since our arrival. "Lorenzo has an excellent workshop at the other end of the house. He's quite handy, you know."

"And some gauze if you have it," Seana said, after which she took her cell phone from her purse and dialled 911 while Mister Falzetti, his hand cupped under his chin, the blood pooling in his palm, smiled at us in a way that was not unlike the way Nick had smiled when, on his balcony, he'd charged at me: as if feelings of imminent triumph were being quickly replaced by child-like bewilderment.

After we'd checked into the Ocean House Hotel in Port Clyde—an early nineteenth century rooming house for local fishermen that had been turned into a bed-and-breakfast, and that was a short walk from the boat landing where the ferry docked—Seana and I drove up Route 131 to Thomaston to visit Trish. I'd called Trish from Northampton to tell her I'd be visiting Nick's parents, and asked if it would be all right to stop by, and she had responded with a typical Trish answer: "When have I ever denied you, Charlie?" she'd said, and in a low-key monotone that had been a turn-on for me once upon a time, but which I'd come to realize had nothing to do with her trying to be seductive or mysterious, and was merely an expression of her intermittent, ongoing glooms.

I mentioned that I'd be coming with a friend, and when I told her who the friend was, she asked if I was shitting her or what.

She reminded me about how smitten she'd been with *Triangle* (she remembered that Seana had been one of my father's students), so was I just making this up in order to get past her hi-tech security system and into her pants again, or would Seana O'Sullivan *really* be coming with me?

When I said that Seana would really be with me, Trish said to come anytime we wanted, early or late, and if we felt like roughing it, we could stay over. She wouldn't ask and wouldn't tell, she said, but she congratulated me on my conquest, and said I was proving to be more like my father than anyone had imagined possible—anyone but her, of course, and she trusted she'd get credit for having seen my potential at a time when few others had.

I said that Seana was just a friend, and when she said something about knowing what the word 'friend' could mean to a guy like me, I pointed out that Seana had moved in with my father before I'd returned from Singapore.

"Well, based on her books, I figure she's into sharing," Trish said. "So congrats again—and to your old man too—and we'll see you soon, buckeroo. But one favor, okay?"

"Sure."

"Do your best not to look surprised when you see me. It's been a while, and I had another child, and I've become what some people might call plump."

"Plump is good."

"But know this: that I do look forward to seeing you, Charlie. You're essentially a good guy, no matter what you think and no matter what you did."

"Can I quote you on that?"

"No," she said, and she hung up.

"Oh my god!" Trish exclaimed as soon as we entered her house. "It's really you, isn't it?"

"Who else could I be?" Seana replied, clearly delighted by

Trish's uninhibited exuberance, and by Trish herself, who, though overweight, as promised, was as lovely as ever, her long, soft brown hair pulled back in a ponytail, her cheeks flushed, her slate-gray eyes aglow with eagerness and enthusiasm.

"Did Charlie tell you that *Triangle* is my very favorite novel of all time, and that I could recite most of it, word for word, my favorite scenes anyway."

"Thanks but no thanks," Seana said even as she knelt down slightly and smiled at Gabe and Anna, who were standing next to Trish, Anna holding on to Gabe's sleeve.

"So you're Gabe," she said. "And this is your sister Anna, right?"

"That's correct," Gabe said. "I'm ten years old, going on eleven—ten going on twenty-three is the way my mother often puts it—and my sister Anna is seventeen months old, but she can walk already, and she can talk when she chooses to."

Trish wore black carpenter's coveralls on top of a button-down light-blue shirt, but they didn't do much to hide the fact that she'd gained a considerable amount of weight since the last time I'd seen her—twenty to thirty pounds, at least—and I was glad she'd warned me so that I didn't gape. The house looked the way it always had—as if the people who worked the local flea markets were storing their stuff there: clothing, suitcases, backpacks, dishes, pots and pans, Mason jars, wicker baskets, hat boxes, lamps, catalogs, magazines, and books piled everywhere.

What I wasn't prepared for, though, and I saw that it pleased Trish to see my surprise, was Gabe. He looked more like Nick than ever and, the shocker, seemed very sturdy. The constant restlessness that had brought on various diagnoses—ADD, ADHD, autism, Asperger's—seemed gone. His blue eyes were nearly as black as his hair, which fell to his shoulders—a shock of it lay at a diagonal across his forehead like a crow's wing—and he stared at me without blinking. I couldn't shake the feeling—I recalled that this had been so even before he was a year old—that there was a fierce and determined old man inside him that was staring out from a little boy's head.

"Hey Gabe," I said, and put out my hand. "It's good to see you again."

"You're Charlie," he said.

"I'm Charlie," I said.

"I don't remember you, but my mother showed me your photograph."

"I'm Charlie," I said again, "and I remember you from when you were a little boy."

"My father's dead," he said.

"Sad to say, yes—your father's dead."

"You saw him die," he said.

"I saw him *fall*," I said.

"That's accurate," Gabe said, "and I accept the correction. But it's not useful information."

"Your father was my closest friend," I said.

"I know that already," Gabe said. "Would you be interested in seeing his ashes?"

Trish leaned toward Gabe, but without touching him. "Not yet, sweetheart," she said. "Be patient, all right?" She turned to us. "Lorenzo—Mister Falzetti—gave the ashes to me—brought them here in a box one day, said he'd decided they'd mean more to me than to him, and I didn't have the heart—or strength—to argue. With Lorenzo, it's always easiest to let him have his way."

"Like father, like son?" I asked.

"Who knows?" Trish said. "Who *cares* really?"

"Did you bring us any presents?" Gabe asked.

"Oh Gabe!" Trish scolded, but softly. "I've asked you not to…"

"It's okay," Seana said. "Yes, we brought gifts for you and for your sister."

"Perhaps we can accept the gifts now and you can see the ashes later," Gabe said.

"Sounds like a plan," Seana said.

"But before we get too far into gift-giving," Trish said, "how about a loving hug for the grieving ex-wife?"

"Of course," I said. "Sorry I didn't…"

I moved toward Trish, but Seana was there first, and when she embraced Trish, Trish collapsed as if a strut inside her had snapped.

"I'm sorry too," Trish said, and she started crying, her body convulsing in small spasms. "In fact, I'm *very* sorry. I'm *damned* sorry. I'm one sorry, sorry girl. Sorry… sorry…"

Seana pulled Trish closer to her, even while Anna, thumb in mouth, was pillowed between them.

After a while, Trish caught her breath and stepped away. "Now it's your turn, Charlie," she said, and she came to me and rested her head against my chest.

"You *are* plump," I said. "Plump and warm."

"You used to say you preferred women who were ample."

"Still true."

"I do well on amplitude tests," she said.

"No one better," I said, and a moment later: "And hey—I *am* sorry about Nick."

"He never saw fatherhood as a vocation, I suppose," she said. "I mean, he was a real bastard—mean as shit when he was wasted—and a lousy father even when he tried in his half-assed way. Still, he was all the father Gabe had."

"And Anna? I mean, what about Anna's father, if I can ask?"

"Several of the usual small-town suspects," Trish answered. She wiped at her nose. "I cooked supper for us. You're in for a treat."

"That's correct," Gabe said. "My mother and I made several of our best recipes—baked stuffed haddock, string beans with mushrooms and onions, candied yams, and another potato dish, I forget its name."

"*Dauphinoise*," Trish said.

"That's correct," Gabe said. "And for dessert, we're having a blueberry crumble, which you can have with or without ice cream."

"I fussed," Trish said proudly. "I *like* to fuss. I was *happy* fussing—getting ready for your visit—and Gabe was a big help."

"That's correct," Gabe said. "My mother calls me her *sous-chef.*"

"And sometimes he's my Sioux *chief,*" Trish said.

"Ha ha," Gabe said, his voice flat. "That's very funny. So *now* can we have our gifts?"

"Probably," Seana said.

"*Probably?*" Gabe cocked his head to the side. "You're teasing me, right?"

"I'm teasing you," Seana said.

Gabe smiled for the first time. "I like it when people tease me," he said, "although they're not always successful at it the way you just were."

Seana took a stuffed animal from the canvas bag she was carrying—a brightly colored parrot into which you could slide your hand to make it into a puppet—and handed it to Anna, and then she gave Gabe the model airplane kit we'd bought for him: a Glenn Martin Bomber.

"Thank you," he said. "My grandfather makes excellent model ships, but I prefer airplanes, especially those from World War One. How did you know?"

"Lucky guess," Seana said. "And I consulted with Charlie here. He's an expert at gift-giving."

Gabe eyed me. "I know!" he exclaimed. "My *mother* told you about my hobby, and she told you I'd been hoping to get a Glenn Martin."

"Maybe," I said.

"After supper, I can show you the models I've already made. I have Fokkers, Aircos, SPADs, Junkers, Vickers, Halberstadts, and a Sopwith that's a triplane with three wings, which is quite rare. My grandfather helps me build the planes sometimes, and he's quite patient with me. Even though I'm the smartest student in my class, I also have a large temper for a boy my age. I can be difficult at times."

"Self-knowledge is a wonderful thing," Seana said.

"At school, I'm required to have my own teacher with me all day, in addition to the regular teacher for the other students," he explained to Seana. "It's called special education."

"Figures," Seana said.

"Figures?"

"Special education for a special guy, and you're pretty special, aren't you?"

"I certainly hope so," Gabe said.

After we helped Trish put the children to bed—Gabe showed us his model airplane collection and then read a story to Seana while I read one to Anna—Trish took down a small metal box from a cabinet over the sink, and asked if we wanted to smoke some funny stuff with her.

She pushed away a bunch of clothes and laundry so we could sit side by side, and stuffed what looked like pencil shavings into a small clay pipe. She lit the pipe, inhaled, held the smoke down in her lungs, exhaled, and passed the pipe to Seana.

"Sweet," Seana said after she'd taken a long drag.

"Lovely, lovely," I said after I'd let the smoke permeate my lungs and float up toward my brain. "This is quality stuff."

"That's because some of it's Nick," Trish said.

"*Nick?!*" I said.

"Did you *really*?" Seana asked.

"Uh-huh. Just a small sprinkling, though."

"How wonderful," Seana said.

I felt nauseated, dizzy. "You actually put some of Nick's ashes in here?" I asked.

"Uh-huh," Trish said. "I thought of doing this—what we're

doing now—I mean I had it in mind ever since your phone call—as being a kind of private memorial ceremony Nick would appreciate, wherever he is. He's part of us now..."

This was when Seana's cell phone rang. "It's Max," she said, looking at the phone's display screen and grinning. "His timing has always been impeccable."

While Trish and I passed the pipe back and forth, Seana talked with Max, and told him we'd visited with Nick's parents, were now visiting with Trish and her children, and that she'd found another home away from home—a quiet place where the two of them could be happy campers while working on their books. She told him we'd already paid for a room at an inn we weren't going to use, and suggested he drive up and be our guest there.

"That would be so *cool*," Trish said. "Even though I only met your dad a couple of times, I fell in love with him, Charlie, and used to wish he'd been *my* father. Is that okay?"

"Sure," I said.

"I mean, it's like I miss him *because* I wanted to know him and never did, and maybe now my chance has come. Is that okay?"

"Sure," I said again.

"We all miss you, Max," Seana was saying. "We do. And that includes me because I become very sad when I'm away from you."

"Me too," I said, and I asked Seana to ask my father if he wanted to say hello to his beloved son.

"He says he only called because he misses us and that I should say 'Goodbye and good luck' to you," she said a moment later.

"That's the title of my favorite Grace Paley story," Trish said. She rested her head against Seana's shoulder. "But you're still my favorite author, so there's no need to be jealous."

Seana was asking Max to repeat something, and she held the phone near us so we could hear him.

"Good night, my dear children," was what he said then. "And don't forget to be kind to one another."

I heard a clicking sound, and then a dial tone.

"Is that all?" I asked.

"That's it," Seana said.

"Well, that's *his* hang-up, I suppose," I said.

Trish laughed. "You always had a way with words, Charlie. Even Nick used to say so, and he could really put out the word-play stuff when he got rolling."

"Do tell," Seana said.

"All grass is flesh," I said while I massaged the back of Trish's neck. "That was one of Nick's lines. All grass is flesh."

"Okay then," Trish said. "And now I have an important question. Does what you said before about the room at Ocean House mean you're going to crash here tonight?"

"Of course," Seana said.

"Oh I do love you," Trish said, and she kissed Seana on the cheek.

Seana placed the pipe on my lap, took Trish's face between her hands, and kissed her on the mouth.

"*Wow!*" Trish said when they separated. She took the pipe from me, closed her eyes and inhaled. Then she and Seana flicked tongues with each other for a while, after which, while they kissed and hummed, I filled the pipe again, and tamped the good stuff down without spilling any.

"Essence of Nick," I proclaimed some time later. "A new fragrance for a new generation!"

I thought my inventive sloganeering might inspire words of praise from Seana, but she was too deep into Trish—without my having noticed, Trish had unbuckled her coveralls and let the shoulder straps hang down—to be aware of me. And I was too stoned to be surprised or shocked by what was going on, or to wonder much about why it had never, until this moment, occurred to me that the relationship between the mother and daughter in *Triangle* might have been based on experiences Seana had been having through the years with *women*.

"What about me?" I asked quietly.

"Your time will come, sweetheart," Seana said, but without turning away from Trish. "Be patient."

"Patience is one of the cardinal virtues," Trish said. "She's also one of my friends—Patience Roncka. She grew up in the Portuguese community, and she's my best friend here. She met Nick early on, but she never really knew him—not in the biblical sense, I mean."

"Neither did I," Seana said. "Did I miss anything?"

"No," I said.

"Oh Charlie, you're wonderful too," Trish said, and she turned to me, her eyes on fire with happiness.

In the morning, Trish was first to wake up, and she whispered that she could hear Anna talking to herself in her crib, and would have to leave us for a while.

"This is like a dream come true," Trish said. "Correct that. It's not like a dream come true because it *is* a dream come true since I imagined the whole thing—well, some of it, anyway—before you ever got here."

"So which was better," Seana asked, "the dream or the reality?"

Trish laughed. "I'm not telling," she said.

"Smart girl," Seana said.

"I feel like I'm living in a book you wrote just for me."

"For us," I corrected.

"For *us*," Trish said. "Even better."

"My pleasure," said Seana, who was spooned against my back, her breasts warm against my skin.

"God, I hope so!" Trish said.

I took Seana's hands in mine, at my chest, and pulled her closer while I tried to take in what was going on—what was actually *happening*. My head was clear, and my senses alert— I'd rarely if ever had hangovers from smoking pot; rather the opposite—I'd usually woken up especially clear-headed after a night of smoking the stuff. I knew, of course, that I'd been drawn to Seana from the first time I'd met her, and had often *fantasized* moments like this, but now, even though the moment I was living in seemed a dream come true for me the way Trish said it was for her, there was a difference, I wanted to say: because of the fact that I'd *known* Seana for more than twenty years—for most of my life!—what had happened and what was happening seemed very *natural* somehow—as least as inevitable and familiar as it was wonderful...

"And oh—wait a minute," Trish said. She was propped up on an elbow, facing me. "Before I go, I have to tell you something—a secret I've been saving. Is that okay?"

"Sure," Seana said.

"Okay. Here it is: Before you came, I took a chance and went off my meds—my anti-depressants."

"Me too," Seana said.

"*You* went off your meds?" Trish said.

"Yes, and a good thing too, to judge from the results."

"I mean, are you *really* on meds?" Trish said.

"Many of our finest writers are on meds," Seana said. "Mine's Celexa—twenty milligrams, once or twice a day, depending. RPN, as they say. And you?"

"Cymbalta—sixty milligrams a day, and it's a killer—wreaks havoc with my sexuality *and* my digestive system."

"Sixty is too much," Seana said. "Try going down to forty."

"I'm not on *any* anti-depressants," I said.

"Poor Charlie," Trish said, kissing me on the nose. "So forlorn. But we love him anyway, don't we?"

Seana nuzzled the nape of my neck. "Mmmmm," she said.

Trish got out of bed, dropped an orange muu-muu over her head, then kissed each of us, me on the forehead, Seana on the back of her neck, and, stepping over toys and around baskets of laundry, called out to Anna that she was on her way.

"Did Max ever tell you about his Uncle Ben?" I asked when Trish was gone.

"No," Seana said. "Max never told me about his Uncle Ben."

"Ben was his favorite—his father's younger brother, who died at sea while in with the merchant marines—but that's another story—and he was cremated. The ashes wound up with Max, who kept them in a small covered Japanese bowl on our fireplace mantle. This was when I was a little boy, and whenever I pointed to the bowl, he'd say, 'The way I look at it, a Benny saved is a Benny urned.'"

Seana groaned and, both arms around my waist, pulled me tight against her. "I like you a lot, you know," she said, "even though you're a much younger man, and more like Max than is good for me."

When we woke the next time, I said I'd been thinking about Max—worrying about leaving him alone in our big house. I was feeling nostalgic about him—lonesome really, though perhaps not for him so much as for things we'd done together we wouldn't ever do again.

"Lonesome's okay," Seana said. "But nostalgia's a bitch, a veil for rage most of the time."

"'A veil for rage,'" I said. "I like that—Wallace Stevens?"

"No."

"Seana Shulamith McGee O'Sullivan?"

"No."

"A veil for rage because remembering stuff that way, especially childhood, masks how miserable it really was?"

"You're smarter than you look," she said.

"But I am definitely feeling lonesome for the guy," I said, "and I'm wondering why I'm feeling this way *now* and if you're feeling the same…"

"You know it," she said.

Earlier, I'd been remembering something that happened on

one of our first trips to New York. Max had given me a tour of his old neighborhood—shown me the famous places: the Brooklyn Museum, the Botanic Gardens, Prospect Park, where Ebbets Field used to be—but what I'd been remembering about the trip wasn't anything we did or saw, I told Seana, but what happened on the subway.

"Going into Brooklyn we'd stayed in the front car so I could watch the train rocketing through tunnels and switching tracks, and I remember being excited—and frightened—by the possibility we might crash into an oncoming train, or that I might see somebody fall from the platform onto the tracks as our train entered a station," I said. "Then, on the way back to Manhattan, our subway car was crowded, lots of people standing. It must have been rush hour, and there was one huge black man taking up three seats and, with a glowering expression, daring anyone to question his right to do so. He wore a red bandana on his head, pirate-style, and a sleeveless T-shirt—the kind my father said Italians called wife-beater shirts—that showed off how buff he was.

"Without warning me about what he was going to do, Max bent over and spoke to the man. 'Excuse me, sir,' Max said, 'but I was wondering if you would be kind enough to make a bit of room so that my son and I might sit.' The man did a double-take, frowned, then said 'Sorry,' shifted to the side, and made room for us, after which, at station stops, and when we were stuck between stations a few times, my father engaged him in conversation, starting off by admiring a tattoo of a large-breasted mermaid that adorned the man's shoulder—it turned out that the man, who gave his name as Willy Williams, had, like Max, served time at sea—and inquiring about Willy's line of work. Willy said that after a stint in the Navy he'd been a millwright—a kind of jack-of-all-trades—in an Indianapolis auto factory, but had come into hard times, and my father offered the fact that he was in the education business, and that he might be able to provide useful contacts and information. Had Willy been to the local VA facility? he inquired—careful, I noticed, not to call it a hospital—and Willy said he'd been meaning to go, but hadn't gotten around to it.

"My father took out an index card on which he wrote his name, address, and phone numbers—office and home—and when we got out at Penn Station, Willy shook my father's hand. 'You're the man,' he said, and then he shook my hand and said that one day I'd be the man too."

"Did your father ever hear from him?" Seana asked.

"I don't know," I said. "I never asked, he never told."

"Maybe he'll show up when we're in Brooklyn together," Seana said. "You never know. Weird things happen if you make room for them."

For breakfast Trish made blueberry pancakes, along with link sausage, fried scrapple, and hash browns. Anna, sitting in a high-chair and using her fingers, ate everything, and when I remarked on how unusual this seemed to me for a child her age—how un-American!—Trish beamed with pride and said she believed the best thing for children was to feed them what you fed yourself and not to give in to their whims because if you did you put limitations on what their taste buds would accept when they became grown-ups.

"And speaking of the future," she said, "I forgot to tell you about something I was thinking last night about the past—about another one of my dreams. Do you want to hear?"

Gabe was sniffing at the air and talking about how good the house smelled. Not breakfast, but the other smell, like the smell in the kitchen whenever his mother spilled spices on a hot stove. His favorite smell of all, though, was burning wool or burning *hair*. Sometimes, after his mother gave him a haircut, he said that she let him take hair she'd cut off and he'd pinch the strands with metal tongs and hold them over one of the burners until they sparked and sizzled.

"I never play with fire otherwise," Gabe said. "Cross my heart and hope to die."

"What I remembered last night was about who I wanted to be," Trish said.

"Who?" I asked.

"Who who," Gabe said. "I'm an owl too."

Anna giggled. "Hoo-hoo," she said. "Hoo-hoo."

"Who I wanted to be was the young woman who puts a daisy in the barrel of a soldier's rifle at an anti-war rally," Trish said. "Do you remember her? I had a poster of her up on my wall at UMass."

"My mother says she used to be a flower child," Gabe said.

"Hoo-hoo," Anna said again. "Hoo-hoo."

"*Flo-wer pow-wer,*" Trish whispered in Anna's ear while she nuzzled her. "*Flo-wer pow-wer.* Do you have *flo-wer pow-wer,* sweetheart?"

Anna laughed, and repeated the words, which came out clearly, though without the 'l': "*Fow-wer pow-wer… Fow-wer pow-wer…*"

Under the table, Seana took my hand in hers. "I like it here," she said to Trish, "and I was wondering: Have you considered selling time-shares?"

"No," Trish said. "But it sounds like an idea whose time may have come, even though with the money Nick left me I probably won't have to take in boarders for a while."

"Can you tell me about my father?" Gabe asked.

"Sure," I said. "What do you want to know?"

"Everything," Gabe said.

"As it happens, I may have a good deal for you this morning," I said. "But you have to be patient. Can you be patient?"

"Sometimes," Gabe said.

"Okay," I said, and I took a deep breath, one eye on Seana while I spoke to Gabe. "So here's the scoop: My father and Seana have been encouraging me to write a book about *your* father, and I've been thinking I might just do it."

"*Really?*" Gabe said.

"A book about *Nick*?" Trish said.

"Not just about Nick. The book would be about Nick and me—about our lives in the Far East."

"In Singapore," Gabe corrected.

"In Singapore," I said. "Yes. And if I write the book, I'm thinking I could also write about our lives before Singapore, when we were in college together."

"Will you write about how my father *died*?" Gabe asked.

"Probably," I said.

"Not good enough," Seana said, and she went to the stove, where Trish was whipping up batter for another round of pancakes and spoke to Trish. "Will *you* tell us stories about Nick even if they're not for publication?"

"Maybe," Trish said. "Who knows?"

"Stories that took place in the olden days?" Gabe said.

"Olden and golden," Trish said. "When families were happy the way we are this morning."

"In my family—O'Sullivans and McGees, and on my mother's side, Kearneys and Mahoneys—we found happiness and inner peace by humiliating one another on a regular basis," Seana said.

"Though we're not Irish here in Thomaston, we still drink our fair share," Trish said. "And rumor has it that Ozzie and Harriet retired to rural Maine and are living among us."

"Ha ha," Gabe said. "My mother tells a lot of jokes about Ozzie and Harriet, but I don't know who Ozzie and Harriet are."

"They're illusions," Seana said.

"My favorite family is Abbott and Costello," Gabe said. "We have a collection of their movies on DVD. Do you like Abbott and Costello?"

"I *love* Abbott and Costello," Seana said. "If Costello were still alive, I'd marry him."

Gabe started to laugh, a high-pitched laugh that got louder and louder until, his face bright red, he gagged and had to spit out what was in his mouth.

"Can you tell us what was so funny?" Trish asked when Gabe had stopped coughing.

"What's so funny is Costello," Gabe said. "But he'd make a silly husband because he'd do everything wrong all the time."

"He'd keep me laughing, though," Seana said, "and I believe he'd be wonderfully affectionate."

"But he'd be—" Gabe paused, then did the best imitation he could of Costello—"a *baaaaad* boy…"

"Well, we like bad boys," Seana said. "Don't we?"

"Story of my life," Trish said.

"Because if you marry a bad boy," Seana said, "you get a father, husband, and child all rolled up into one, and who could pass that up?"

"Would you marry me some day when I grow up if I'm still a *baaaaad* boy?" Gabe asked.

"Of course," Seana said. She brought another stack of pancakes to the table, along with a fresh pitcher of warm maple syrup, and told me she was glad I was going to write *Charlie's Story*, because that was what she believed Max had intended in the first place.

"What the hell is wrong with you?" I whispered.

"Wrong?"

"Why'd you say you'd marry Gabe when he grew up?"

"Because I wanted to," she said.

"But don't you know he's going to take your promise seriously?"

"The way he took *your* promise to write about his father?"

"But I didn't *make* a promise—I said I *might* try to write a book about me and Nick. But you *promised* to marry him some day…"

"So?"

"So be careful, that's all. He's not like other kids. He's not…"

"He's not what?" Seana asked, loud enough for Gabe to hear.

"Forget it," I said. "Jesus, but you're a case sometimes. You should be more careful, that's all."

"If I were careful all the time, I wouldn't be Seana," she said.

"That's true, Charlie, and you shouldn't forget it," Trish said. "And also, didn't we agree last night that it's important to believe in a *future*—to believe there'll actually be one?"

"I recall that we did," Seana said.

"In my opinion, that's what last night was about," Trish said. "Otherwise, why are we here?"

"We're here because Nick's dead," I said.

"That's merely the proximate cause of our visit," Seana said, and she walked to the stove, where, while glaring at me with eyes devoid of anything resembling affection, she kissed the back of Trish's neck in a way that made Trish shiver.

Gabe leaned toward me from across the table. "In less than eight years I'll be eighteen," he said.

I felt a pale whooshing and clicking inside my head then, as if the fumes from what we'd smoked the night before were drifting away into dark rooms, the doors to these rooms closing one behind the other, after which a voice rose up from the floor of my brain and called to me: *Hey Charlie—don't you think you're getting in just a little bit over your head this time?*

"*All* done!" Anna said. Trish wiped Anna's face with a washcloth, lifted her from the high-chair, and told Gabe that in fifteen minutes he had to be ready for school. Gabe got down on the floor next to Anna, and the two of them began playing a game that involved moving clothespins in and out of empty yogurt cups. "I'll be ready on time," he said. "I always am."

"After Gabe leaves, I can tell you about Nick if you want," Trish said.

"Whenever," Seana said, and she turned to me. "Will you take notes?"

"For somebody so smart you can be pretty stupid sometimes," I said.

"Oh yeah?" she said, her voice pure Brooklyn.

"Yeah," I said.

"Well then, chuck you, Farley."

"Hey you two—we're all friends here, remember?" Trish said. "None of this nasty stuff allowed, especially in the morning. You'll send me straight back to my caves of gloom, and I'm hell to be around when that happens. Charlie can vouch."

"I can vouch," I said.

It was past ten in the morning, and we were still sitting around the kitchen table, drinking coffee, Anna on the floor playing with her clothespins and yogurt cups—Gabe had been picked up by the school bus more than an hour before—and Trish was telling Seana about her and Nick: how they met on our infamous double-date, me with her, and Nick with a hot, young Israeli student named Shoshana. What happened, Trish explained, was that she and Nick couldn't keep their eyes off each other all night—we'd gone bowling, and then to a late night drinking spot in Hadley called The Rusty Nail, where they had punk-rock bands and access to a smorgasbrod of drugs—and how, afterwards—the next morning, in fact—Nick had asked my permission to call her.

"He acted honorably toward you in doing that—in not just going after me," Trish said, "and I was thrilled."

"That he acted honorably?" I asked.

"That he acted honorably toward you and that he wanted to go out with me."

"You had it wrong," I corrected. "He wanted to get *into* you."

"Well that was okay with me," Trish said. "And with you too, Charlie, so don't deny it."

I shrugged, and Trish began telling Seana about the first time the three of us got it on together, which happened a week later in a hotel Nick took us to on the coast of Maine, near Ogunquit. It was off-season, and we stayed in a large room in a place straight out of a Hopper painting, with an in-room fireplace and a spectacular view of the ocean, and waves crashing in on rocks all night long. Nick brought along a stash of Golden Montana— 'the champagne of Mary Jane,' he called it—and before long we were sky-high happy and doing things you only fantasize doing most of your life, or read about other people doing.

"Nowadays, it's all on *You Tube*," Trish said. "Everything you can imagine, and in all possible combinations and permutations. It makes me sad."

"Because it leaves so little to the imagination?" Seana said.

"Maybe," Trish said. "But for a more personal reason. I mean, a lot of our friends were doing what we did, but it makes me sad because it turns what we did, which I thought was special, into something common."

"Oh yes," Seana said, and was about to say something else— about things she'd done in *her* earlier years?—when the doorbell rang—a buzzing instead of a ringing—followed by a loud, insistent rapping. Trish went to the door and let in a state trooper, and for an instant, my bourgeois conscience back on the job, I thought he might have come to tell us we'd violated some state law. *We don't allow things like that up here, mister*, I imagined him saying.

The trooper, built like a tight end—about six-five and two-forty—had taken off his hat and had his arm around Trish. From the soft, polite way he was talking with her, and from the way she rested her head against his chest, and then from the way her eyes filled up when she turned to us, I was suddenly afraid something had happened to Gabe.

Trish walked toward us slowly, tears streaming down her cheeks, and I opened my arms wide, for a hug, but she stopped when she was a few feet away. "Officer Guardi—Richard—needs to talk with you, Charlie," she said. "I'm sorry. Really sorry. Really, really, Charlie…"

"Shit," I said.

"Fuck," Seana said. "Fuck and double-fuck."

"It's my father, isn't it," I said to the trooper.

He nodded. "I'm awfully sorry, Mister Eisner," he said.

"I knew it," I said. "I just knew it. "We shouldn't have left him alone."

"Nonsense," Seana said.

"We *shouldn't*," I insisted. "We shouldn't have—even if he wanted us to."

"And we're being punished for having done so, right?" Seana said. "Punished for our pleasures."

"I didn't say that. I just said we shouldn't have left him alone."

"Can it, Charlie," she said. "He's gone. End-of-story, as young people say these days."

Then she turned to Trish, who opened her arms wide for her. Seana held to Trish, let her head rest on Trish's shoulder, and I was suddenly confused. Why was she embracing Trish when it was *my* father who had died? Why was she shutting me out? And if I went to her, and tried to pry her from Trish's embrace…

"I'm awfully sorry, Mister Eisner," the trooper said again. "We received a request from the Northampton police to try to locate you. I checked hotels and motels in the area—we had the license plate number of your father's car—and at the Ocean House, in Port Clyde, they said you'd mentioned visiting some one in Thomaston."

"Did he—did he do it himself?" I asked.

"I don't have details, sir. For that you'll have to call Northampton. I have a number for you—two numbers, in fact." He tore off a piece of paper from the kind of pad you use for giving out speeding tickets, and handed it to me. "Officer Burke. Michael Burke. He said he'd be there all morning, and that you can call him on his cell phone anytime—the number's there. He said he went to high school with you."

I turned and saw that Trish was sitting in a chair now, sobbing away, Seana next to her, stroking Trish's hair while Anna clung to Trish's leg and told her not to cry. "Don't cry, Mommy," she kept saying. "Please don't cry, Mommy. Don't cry, Mommy Mommy Mommy…"

The floor, tilted up at a forty-five degree angle, was rapidly approaching my nose, squiggles of black dots swirling in its path. I sat down, bent over so that my head was lower than my heart, and after about thirty seconds I sat up straight again.

None of us spoke for a while, which made the room much too quiet—the trooper was gone, though I hadn't noticed him leaving—so I picked up the telephone and called Michael Burke, and when I identified myself, he said he was sorry for my loss, and assured me he would take care of everything until I was back in Northampton. My father had died peacefully in his sleep, of heart failure, he said—that was the initial finding by the doctor, and he didn't expect it to change. When the lights in much of the house had stayed on for more than twenty-four hours, a neighbor became concerned, and rang the doorbell and banged on the door and, receiving no response, had called the police. I thanked Michael and told him we should arrive back in town by early evening.

I told Trish and Seana what Michael had told me—that it seemed Max had died peacefully in his sleep—and I added that he would have turned seventy-three on his next birthday, but that, as I'd often heard him say, he believed that everything past the proverbial three score and ten was considered extra—a gift—so that seventy-two wasn't a bad run.

"Still," Seana said, "when you're seventy-two, seventy-three doesn't look so good."

We were quiet again, and after a minute or two I decided to fill the silence with words by telling a story about my father, though it was a shame, it occurred to me, that I'd already told Seana the one about him and the man in the subway. Still, with Max, I knew, if you used up one story, another usually arrived pretty quickly to take its place.

"You know who my father's hero was?" I asked.

"Barney Ross?" Seana said.

"No," I said.

"Jackie Robinson?"

"Not that kind of hero."

"Primo Levi?"

I shook my head again.

"Henry James?

"Only until he found out what an anti-Semite James was."

"I forgot about that," Seana said. "So I give up. Who was your father's hero?"

"My father's hero," I said, "was a baggage guy at Bradley Airport. He met him when he and a colleague were going to a convention together. The colleague—his name was Friedman, Wolf Friedman, or maybe it was Freeman without the 'd'—was a guy who got off on being snide to everybody. He'd published a few books of poems, and wrote about Frank O'Hara and that crowd, and was the kind of New York guy—I think of him as being from New York, though it turned out he came from Omaha, Nebraska, where his father was a kosher butcher—but he was the kind of guy who has to make a joke out of everything. And he used to brag about the critiques he laid on grad students—on their writing—and how under his *tutelage*—that's the word I remember Max said he used—he could get them to break down in class and cry."

"That was Freeman—without the 'd'—all right," Seana said. "A schmuck-with-earlaps, first class. I got him good, though, at least twice. Remember, in *Plain Jane*, the butcher who gets castrated by a group of Algerian men for raping one of their daughters? I named him Freeman Woolf. But that was just an old-fashioned novelist's revenge."

"And in real life?" I asked.

"Freeman was famous among grad students for being a stinker," Seana said, "and he was after me all semester to meet him for this or for that, so once grades were in—ever the practical young woman, *moi*—I agreed to meet him in a bar in Holyoke, and we were in a booth, and it was dark, and he was breathing hard. He put a hand on my lap and leaned close, and I blew on his ear and kept my eyes on his crotch. As soon as he was ripe, I reached over and grabbed his teeny-weeny and squeezed until he begged me to stop or to unzip him, and when I let go, I said I was curious about something—that I'd been wondering what his pecker got like when he had a hard-on."

"Though I doubt my father used a similar tactic," I said, "he probably said clever things to Freeman too. But Max never bragged to me about ways he put people down."

"Your father was a man of elegance and discretion," Seana said. "A *mensch* of *mensches*, as we say in Gaelic. He could be playful in unpredictably inventive ways. But he was rarely mean."

"*Rarely?*" I asked.

"Nick could be mean," Trish said. "Like his father. But Eugenia and I get along well—she comes here when I have my down times, and she's great with the children. And a lot tougher than she seems. But even so, I want you to know about a decision I made this morning."

"Go for it," Seana said.

"As Charlie knows, my parents are both dead," Trish began, "and I don't talk to my brothers and sisters anymore."

"I have no brothers," Seana said. "But same story here."

"That's sad, isn't it?" Trish said.

"Not if you knew my sisters," Seana said.

"I'm like Nick," I said. "Neither of us had brothers or sisters to not talk to. Friends like you two were always my family."

"Lucky guy," Seana said. "In my book, the idealization of family does as much harm as believing that falling-in-love with a one-and-only being the be-all and end-all of life. Friendship—having good friends you can count on, like you two—like Max—always trumps family."

"Can we drink to that—and to Max?" Trish asked.

"A splendid idea," Seana said, and then: "Okay by you, Charlie?"

"Yes," I said, and would have said more, but was afraid that if I did, I would break down completely.

Trish poured three glasses of Jamison's for us, and, silently, we raised our glasses, clinked them, drank.

Seana spoke, with a brogue: "'For what could be worse than drink?' the young Irishman asked, and his father answered, 'Thirst.'"

"So after Nick left us," Trish said, "I made Lorenzo and Eugenia legal guardians for Gabe, and later on I added that they be guardians for Anna too, because at least if something happened to me, Lorenzo and Eugenia would have the wherewithal to raise them, or to see that they were taken care of, which I knew I couldn't count on Nick for. But now that Nick's gone, I've changed my mind, and I've decided to call my lawyer and ask him to draw up new papers making you two the guardians."

"But you haven't asked us if we agree to *be* guardians," Seana said.

"*Do* you?"

"Maybe yes, maybe no," Seana said. "But a question first: Your departure from this world isn't in the works, is it?"

"No."

"Promise?"

"Yes."

"Cross your heart?"

"Yes."

"Then, as judges are wont to say, we'll take it under advisement, okay?" Seana said.

"And you, Charlie?" Trish asked.

"I agree with Seana," I said. "I'm flattered, Trish—honored, really—but I think we should give it some time. I know what you're like when you get high, and I'm not sure, with the news about my dad, that *I'm* capable of thinking clearly right now, even if I seem to be rational…"

"And you've been off your meds," Seana said.

"Okay, okay," Trish said. "Sure. And thank you both very much. Thank you. I feel better now—a *lot* better. I mean, not better that your father's gone, Charlie, but…"

"It's okay," I said.

"…but even when I go back on my meds—lower dose, right?—and you're gone and I try to get back to what passes for normal life, I know I'm going to stay firm about my decision. I just know it because it feels so *right*—it just does," she said, and then to me: "Do you still want to have your own kids some day?"

"Yes," I said.

"If you didn't have any, would that be a loss—something that would diminish your life?"

"Yes," I said.

"I remember how enthusiastic you were when we talked about maybe having kids together, you and me—but you were calm too—like it was something you'd always known about yourself. It made me care for you a lot."

"When you and Nick had Gabe," I said, "I was happy for you and sad for me—that I wasn't the father."

Trish put her hand on mine. "You weren't, Charlie. I know you worried about that, but you can trust me on this. You're not Gabe's father, okay?"

"Max was just like a mother to me," Seana said.

"*What?*" Trish said.

"Max was just like a mother to me," Seana said again.

"Oh," Trish said, and nodded several times. "Sure. I think I understand."

"Do you *really*?" Seana said.

"As I was saying," I said, "my father and Freeman were on their way to a convention somewhere—Baltimore, I think—yes, it was definitely Baltimore because when Max came home he promised to take me to the aquarium there—and Freeman was ragging on one of the guys who check in your stuff curbside at the airport. I don't know if the man was white or black—I don't think my father would have made such a distinction..."

"But if he memorialized the event in prose, he would have," Seana said. "He would have been specific, so that you would have *seen* the man. You would have believed you *knew* him."

"I've always pictured the man as being black and toothless—the men who did that work at Bradley were mostly old and black—" I said "—and after Freeman checked his bags and left, my father apologized for the way Freeman had treated him—rude, and no tip to boot—and the baggage guy gave my dad a big grin, and said, 'Oh that's all right, sir—I've sent his bags on to Los Angeles.'"

"Your father would have done the same had he been in that position," Seana said. "Max had great empathy—a large capacity for negative capability."

"I don't see what's negative about what he did," Trish said.

Seana kissed Trish, and said she'd explain what she meant later. Then, so I wouldn't feel left out, she kissed me too.

"Simple Simon met a pieman going to the fare," Seana said. "Said the pieman to Simple Simon, let me taste your wares."

"So?" I said.

"So I met your father and moved in with him on a day in which he'd set out his wares. Nor was he wary. Nor was I. Though he can at times be wearing. Are you aware of that, Charlie, you only begotten son? Max the pieman, not Simple Simon...?"

"Did you taste them—his wares, I mean?" Trish asked.

Seana started laughing at Trish's question, but, as if seizing her laugh in an invisible fist, stopped abruptly and, slowly and in a low voice, began reciting Max's name, *"Morris Herman Eisner... Morris Herman Eisner... Morris Herman Eisner..."* and then started punching me, first with one fist and then with the other—left, right, left, right—while continuing to repeat his name: *"Morris Herman Eisner... Morris Herman Eisner... Morris Herman Eisner...."*

I didn't try to block her blows, and when she saw I was just going to sit there and take it, she hit me a serious one-two combination, chest and shoulder, after which she got in my face and asked me if I was a wimp or what, and when was I going to hit back.

"Maybe later," I said.

"Is that a threat or a promise?" she asked and, stepping away, tried to repeat her question—to show she was making a joke—but she couldn't get the words out, and she collapsed on me. "Oh Jesus, Mary, and Joseph," she said. "Oh Jesus, oh Jesus, Charlie—what will we do without him? Tell me, please. *Tell* me..."

"What I can do is to write the story you believe he wanted me to write," I said.

Seana sucked in an enormous batch of air then, and gradually got herself under control. She didn't say anything, but she put an arm around me, which I took as her way of showing approval for my decision. The floor had been descending slowly and steadily, like the near half of a drawbridge falling back to where it was supposed to be, and now that Seana had stopped crying, I figured it was okay for me to let go, and so with her to one side of me, Trish to the other, and Anna holding tight to my right ankle with two hands, I let myself heave in and out for a while and, my throat good and raw even before I began, I roared out all the curses I knew, and then made up a few new ones.

Charlie's Story

*I*n order to understand Singapore, the most important thing to know, Nick had told me at our UMass reunion, was that you weren't allowed to chew gum there. For natives, chewing gum—or even possession of gum—was a crime punishable by heavy fines, and for foreigners like me and Nick—or for tourists, or for anyone doing business there—cause for immediate deportation. The same went for using a toilet and not flushing when you were done.

There was more: You could be fined for spitting, jaywalking, littering, chewing tobacco, or for owning obscene material, play money, or toy guns. For more serious crimes, there was prison and caning—they were big on caning—and for trafficking in drugs (500 grams of marijuana would do the job), the death penalty. Per capita, Singapore had the highest number of death penalties in the world.

It also had the densest population of any country in the world except for Monaco, and the highest standard of living, along with the most desirable quality of life, especially for business and professional people, of any city or nation in Asia. An island of less than two hundred fifty square miles (not counting about twenty square miles of small islands that were largely uninhabited), it had all been rainforest once upon a time, the way some of Borneo still was.

From a miserably poor third world country (its population was about the same as that of countries like Norway and Denmark—just over five million), it had, in less than half a century, transformed itself into the most efficient place in the world to do business—a completely air-conditioned, high-tech preserve that offered exceptional levels of service, comfort, and safety.

Its harbor was the most gorgeous in the world, Nick claimed, more beautiful even than Hong Kong's. Unusually wide and deep, it could accommodate more than seven hundred vessels at a time, large or small (Singapore became a major east-west port after the opening of the Suez Canal in the late nineteenth century, when it was part of the British empire), and at night, lights sparkling on the water as if they were stars in the darkest of skies, it was especially beautiful. But what, in addition to its physical beauty and technological efficiencies, made Singapore more deliciously inviting than Hong Kong, according to Nick, was that, whereas Hong Kong was vibrant and exciting—Shanghai, Rome, and New York City wrapped up in an exquisite Asian paradise—Singapore was blissfully bland.

To live in Singapore, Nick explained—despite its ethnic mix (Chinese, Maylay, Indian), and despite the food, customs, and traditions that came with these cultures, along with the cultural residue from the British, and from the World War Two Japanese occupation—was to live nowhere. And given what the world was like, Nick had concluded, living nowhere was the place to be.

His theories about living nowhere were hardly new—he'd been pushing the same line at UMass (and not long after he'd quit the football team, early in his junior year—he'd been All Conference at halfback the previous season, with pro scouts showing interest), when he'd carry on about the homogenization and Americanization of the world: how instead of living somewhere, people were now living anywhere.

If you were transported blindfolded to a shopping mall in Houston or Seattle, Atlanta or New Orleans or Boston, he'd point out, and you took off your blindfold, how would you know where you were? All across America, small towns were dying, and the people who lived in them were praying for Wal-Marts and contracts for new prison construction to save them. Large cities, ravaged by crime and drugs, were rotting away, and if and when they renewed themselves, they did so in ways that made them look like every other city trying to renew itself. Whereas until recently most people had grown up *somewhere*—in towns, cities, and neighborhoods whose identities were marked by particular cultures, ethnicities, and traditions—most of us now lived *anywhere*. So that the secret, Nick said, was not to want to drown in yearnings for what things used to be like, or might be like again, but to see that living anywhere was merely a way-station on the road to something infinitely better: to be living nowhere, and that, he said, was what would set you free.

The thing to do, therefore, he argued, was not to get trapped by the past or the future, but—how Zen could you get? he'd laugh—to accept the world and yourself for what they were, to live in the moment, and—not quite as Zen—to rejoice in earthly pleasures. And there was no better place in the world to do this than in Singapore.

After my father had met Nick a few times, he talked about him—this when I'd come home mid-week (I lived on campus at UMass, about a dozen miles away in Amherst) in order to pick up hiking gear for a trip Nick, Trish, and I were planning to Mount Washington—in a way he rarely talked about any of my friends, telling me he found him remarkably intelligent, but cautioning me to be wary of him.

My father was married to his fourth wife at the time, Geraldine Strober, a professor of chemistry at Hampshire College. About seven months later, Geraldine, thirty-six at the time (two decades younger than Max), would die of ovarian cancer, and my father, honoring her wish not to die in a hospice or hospital, would care for her at home through her final months. On this night, however, she was as delightful and warm—as seemingly healthy—as she'd ever been, telling stories about growing up as an army brat at Jefferson Barracks in Missouri, where her father had served, and where her grandfather, a major with the Sixth Infantry, had become friends with Major Tadeo Terriagaki, an officer of the Imperial Japanese Army who spent six months attached to the Sixth Infantry, and who, a few years after his stay at Jefferson Barracks, would figure prominently in the attack on Pearl Harbor.

A year or so earlier, my father had heard Geraldine give a lecture on Primo Levi's career as a chemist, and his ingenuity in solving problems relating to paints and solvents. Enchanted, he discovered that she required all her students, whether in basic chemistry courses or graduate seminars, to read Primo Levi, especially *The Periodic Table* and *Survival in Auschwitz*. In assigned papers and end-term exams, she proposed problems of a kind Levi might have faced in his laboratories in Turin or Auschwitz, and would ask students to explain how they would go about solving them, and, for extra credit, to speculate on the relation of Levi's scientific vocation to his literary sensibility.

Max composed an answer to the extra credit question and, under a pseudonym, left it in her Hampshire College mailbox. When she responded with a note saying his was the most brilliant essay she'd received on the subject that semester, but that she didn't recognize the name—Morris Herman—as belonging to one of her students, he revealed his true identity. They were married six weeks later.

After supper on this visit, my father suggested we take a walk, just the two of us, the way we'd often done after supper during my junior high and high school years. And when, during our walk, I told him how lucky I thought he was to have married Geraldine, and that I hoped I might meet a woman like her some day, he said I'd surely meet women like Geraldine and that they'd doubtless fall in love with me. In fact, he confided, Geraldine had said that were I a few years older, and not his son, she wouldn't have hesitated to throw him over for me.

The Smith College campus was only a block away from our house and I loved our walks there. Sometimes we talked, and sometimes we didn't, and it made no difference either way. The campus was lovely, with handsome nineteenth century red-brick buildings, well-tended lawns, lush perennial gardens, a gorgeous pond (on which we ice-skated in winter), and a remarkable variety of trees. The campus was registered as an arboretum, its trees labeled with their Latin and common names, and my father, having taken walks there nearly every day for most of three decades, often said the trees there had become to him like old friends: he watched them grow and change; he watched them become ill and recover from illness—from harsh winters, broiling summers, and occasional maladies; and sometimes he watched them die. And when they died, he said, they usually died the way we did, from the top down.

What I also loved about our walks were the chances they gave me to meet Smith College students. Then as now, Smith was an all-women's school, and many of the women—'Smithies'— would cross the Connecticut River to take advanced writing and literature courses from my father at UMass. During our walks, we'd meet some of them and he'd introduce me, so that when I walked around campus on my own, or around downtown Northampton, and ran into one of them, I'd say hello, we'd get into a conversation, and sometimes I'd get invited to see their rooms, or to parties in their dorms.

Although the women were not much older than I was, and hardly sophisticated pros at things we did together sexually, because we assumed from the start that what we were doing couldn't lead to a serious relationship, we were free with one another in ways they probably weren't with guys their own age (or older), and I surely wasn't with girls my age.

What was intriguing about Nick, my father said during our walk, was that he seemed uniquely free because he was that rare species of being for whom the distinctions between right and wrong, and good and evil seemed to have little relevance. Nick struck him as a man who was, to use a psychological term my father didn't especially care for, *well-resolved*—a fascinating if unlikely example of the kind of person a successful psychoanalysis might produce. Max went on to talk about writers he'd known or knew about—Bellow, Mailer, Arendt, Sontag—and how one result of their years on the couch had been to endow them, especially in the risks they were willing to take in and for their work, with a profound sense of entitlement.

So it was with Nick, Max said, though in a non-literary way. He had not often, if ever, met an intelligent man of Nick's age who radiated the kind of self-assurance Nick did. Since he doubted Nick had spent any time in therapy, much less analysis, my father concluded that Nick's sense of entitlement was simply part of his nature: he did what he wanted to do when he wanted to do it not because he'd trained himself to feel the right to do so, but because he saw no conflict between means and ends— between his desires and his actions.

That evening and a few times later on, most memorably during a talk we had the day before I left for Singapore, my father qualified his earlier impressions: he could certainly understand why I was drawn to Nick and had become good friends with him. He even invoked *The Odyssey* to demonstrate his trust in me and my decision. *The Odyssey*—and he was here, he said, merely paraphrasing a mini-lecture he gave in a humanities course he'd taught for years—was essentially about the education of a hero, and of a hero who was being educated not, as in *The Iliad*, to become a great warrior, but to become a peaceful prince whose wisdom would derive from what he experienced during his travels.

A man made his mark, the Greeks believed, by undertaking long voyages during which he associated with exceptional individuals, and by arriving home with valuable possessions, chief among which would be wisdom. What young man—and one not yet burdened with familial obligations—would not be driven by what the Greeks called a demonic urge, and not welcome an opportunity of the kind Nick was offering me?

There were also the usual things that allowed for friendship—physical attraction, along with common interests, tastes, and experiences (sports, women, UMass)—but what had played the largest part in his revised opinion of Nick was something obvious that he'd previously overlooked: the excellent judgment Nick had shown in choosing me for a friend.

Still, his warnings about Nick made their home in one of the unfurnished rooms of my mind, and, given how things would turn out in Singapore, did more than that, and in ways, I liked to think, my father would have approved.

When I'd met Nick at our reunion (he and Trish had split up five years earlier), he pitched Singapore to me by saying that working there would be like being a cop or a fireman, but without the physical dangers, and with infinitely better perks. Cops and firemen put in their time—twenty years of risk, swag, bullshit, and boredom—and were rewarded with pensions that allowed them to retire on comfortable incomes for the rest of their lives, and to take up second careers while they were still young men.

In Singapore, it was the same, only better—you could work hard and play hard, and get rewarded out the wazoo with buckets of money and all the pleasures money could buy. You could pull in a small fortune—get laid, get paid, get high, have people squat, shit, and bend over whenever you wanted them to—and leave it all behind not in twenty years but in less than a dozen, and never have to work again. Unless I was into some sappy version of the American Dream—into having a devoted wife, two-point-three kids, membership in a swish country club, and a home featured in *Architectural Digest*—what could keep me away?

In addition to which—we were hanging out at Chequers, a bar we'd gone to after basketball games during the UMass glory years (when the team had risen in national polls from number three-hundred-something to number one), and we were both fairly well lit—the real dirt on what gave life in Singapore its own bland thrum of glory, he said, was that living there on one's own—living nowhere, unconnected to somewhere or anywhere—you were *free of responsibility*. Which meant being free from things that shackled most guys our age: wives, kids, jobs, mortgages, debt, alimony, child support.

That was when he talked about my relationship to Max. He knew he might offend, he said, but he'd rather risk my anger than watch me continue to stumble around, and he urged me to hear him out.

"Do I have a choice?" I asked.

He jabbed me in the arm, hard, and said that we always had choices. For example: He could punch me if he wanted, and I could punch him back if I wanted, and we could keep going and break up the bar (something he'd been known to do during his football days), and we could wind up with one or both of us in the emergency ward or the slammer. To prove his point, he punched me again, harder this time, so that the drink I was holding splashed onto my shirt, and when, after a moment's hesitation, I pulled back my fist to return the blow, he seized it in *his* fist (he had huge hands for his size), and warned me not to be foolish—"I love you, Charlie, don't you know that?" he said, something I remembered him saying before, when he'd whispered the words in my ear at a time when I'd been so looped out of my mind, with him, me, and Trish rolling around in bed together, that afterwards I wasn't sure if he'd said it or if I'd dreamt he'd said it.

This time, he had my hand in a kind of death-lock and, his face close to mine, he kept smiling and repeating his we-always-have-choices line while I kept trying not to show how scared I was that if I didn't call him off, he'd break some of my fingers. But then, without my having to give in, he just let go and talked about me and Max again.

He had no quarrel with Max, he began. In fact, he said, laughing, he admired him to-the-max, and gave him a ton of credit for being as hands-off and non-judgmental a father as he'd ever met. This was impressive not only because Nick's father was the opposite, but because it was totally anomalous, in his experience, for a first generation Jewish-American man to be laid back toward an only son the way Max was. What worried him weren't any dreams or wishes Max might have had for me, he said, but dreams and delusions I had about Max, and how attached I was to him.

He'd asked himself why a guy like me, oozing with brains and talent, had wound up shuttling from one half-assed job to another. Where was the guy he used to know—a guy who kept his priorities in order, whose persistence matched his grit, especially when it came to playing ball or shagging women, and who had, he suspected, if only I'd give in to it, a real fire in the belly for taking risks that could make the most outrageous dreams come true? So that when, the day before, he'd started making the case for my coming to Singapore and I'd rebuffed him, the answer had been there: My problem, he realized, was that I couldn't commit to anything that allowed me to put myself in first position. And I couldn't do this because I couldn't bear the idea of leaving Max back home by his lonesome.

The real reason I hadn't been able to commit to anything was my concern that Max might suddenly need me: that he might become ill, disabled, or senile. What I'd done, according to Nick, was to make a contract with myself to *always be available*—to always be free, and on a moment's notice, to move back home and care for *him*.

Being an only child to an only parent, my fear had been: *What happens to me if Max is gone?* And hey—what guy in my position wouldn't have such a fear? But what I'd also gone and done, Nick said, was to have inverted this, projected it, reversed it—he didn't know what the current psychobabble term was—and put my feelings into Max so I could worry about what would happen to him if I were gone.

But this made no sense, Nick said, because Max was the last guy in the world who'd want to tie a son down by obligation or guilt, and he pointed to the obvious—Max's five wives—as proof. Hadn't it occurred to me that Max had married so many times and, in between, rarely left himself without a live-in lady-friend, because he was working overtime to let me off the hook—because he wanted me to see that there'd always be someone else who could, when occasion arose, take care of him?

In truth, I argued back, it seemed to me Max had had so many wives and girlfriends because he liked women. It never occurred to me that he liked them and married them in order to set *me* free, and I wagered that if I were to present Max with Nick's theory, he would have laughed it away.

"Exactly my point," Nick said. "Neither of you can see what's happening because it's been the secret, unspoken deal you've had going all along. Sure he likes the ladies, and he understands them, which is why they take to him so often: he knows that no matter how independent and accomplished they are, the great aphrodisiac for them is the famous *need-to-be-needed*."

I told Nick he was full of shit—not about women maybe, because I'd seen enough grade-A women become suckers for sad sacks to know the truth of what he was saying—but about Max. My hesitation about jumping in with Nick didn't come from his cock-and-bull about me and Max, but from the fact that everything he'd told me about Singapore, and about what turned him on about being there, persuaded me it would be exactly what he said it would be: bland and boring.

"Oh you won't be bored," Nick said. "I promise you."

"Because—?"

"Because you'll be with me, and because we both know it's time to up the ante—to take pleasure from things we haven't even dreamt of yet. Take my word for it, Charlie. Have I ever steered you wrong before?"

"Rarely," I said.

"*Rarely?*" he laughed. "I'll put it another way then. Since you said your life's going nowhere fast, why not take up my offer on a trial basis—a six week or six month lease, round-trip expenses paid for? Plus—and here's the last, best reason to say yes—if you won't do it for yourself, how about doing it for me?"

"That way I won't be putting myself in first position, is that it?"

"You got it."

A few drinks later, I shrugged, put my arm around him, said, "What the hell," shook his hand, and told him we had a deal, and to tell me what to do.

"Get your vaccinations," he said.

Nick didn't talk much about Borneo in all the hours we talked about my going to Singapore, but it was Borneo that made the difference—made me sign up to renew the six week lease, and the six month lease, and any other lease anyone would have put in front of me.

But Borneo didn't happen until the beginning of my seventh week in Singapore, when Nick and I visited three of our palm oil plantations there, by which time I'd settled into my job and apartment, and during which time I learned just how accurate Nick's descriptions of Singapore had been.

Bland was an understatement. Singapore was the very model

of a benevolent dictatorship, with trade-offs everyone seemed to accept without even noticing that they had: a few human rights and civil liberties lost—a life of comfort, efficiency, and safety gained. Singapore made the most tranquil American suburb seem like a cauldron of chaos and danger. All public services—trains, busses, traffic, street cleaning, garbage collection, electrical service—functioned smoothly. The government controlled the number of cars on the road (I never saw a car more than a decade old), and free, eerily quiet shuttles, along with an ultra-modern rail system, connected all major points in the city. Things rarely seemed to go awry (or if they did, they were fixed almost before you knew the repair crew had been there), and people were endlessly, maddeningly *pleasant*.

The health care system (offering both Western and traditional Chinese medicine) was world-class, with easy access to doctors, clinics, and hospitals. There were banks on virtually every street corner, fitness centers, swimming pools, tennis courts, health clinics, and mini-markets attached to most condominiums, and a wealth of country clubs offering long menus of amenities. Singapore turned out to be, that is, nothing less than what Nick and the government claimed it was: a model of Western innovation and efficiency with, in its values, traditions, and people, an Eastern face.

I arrived the third week in July, when the monsoons were blowing through, and though this was a time of year with the least amount of rainfall, the monsoons brought with them intermittent, heavy thunderstorms and the year's most unrelentingly unbearable heat and humidity. When I had to be outdoors, I perspired so profusely that even my ears sweated, and I'd go through three or four shirts on some days (I kept spares in my briefcase). The heat and humidity turned out to be year-round companions, and despite Nick's warnings, I never stopped being undone by the toll they took on me, and came to live as much of my life indoors as I could: in air-conditioned offices, apartments, stores, restaurants, and bars that were comfortable, clean, and cool.

Our college reunion had taken place in early June, at a time when I was living in New York and working on an interim basis as an English and social studies teacher at a private high school on Manhattan's Upper East Side, where I also helped coach the tennis and baseball teams. I'd been enjoying the teaching and coaching, and, even more, the city's infinite offerings—concerts, museums, parks, restaurants, pubs, ballgames, women—along with the sheer insane diversity of the place.

I loved walking the streets—would set out ritually every Saturday morning and, using an old 1939 *WPA Guide to New York City* Max had given me (a guide written and edited, he pointed out, by, among others, John Cheever and Richard Wright when they'd been young, unpublished authors), explore a part of the city I'd never been to before, mostly in Manhattan, but some-times in the other boroughs. To understand New York, Max often said, you had to understand that despite its being a global center of commerce, entertainment, and ideas, it was also, in its essence, a set of villages, and seeing the city this way—through his eyes—made me feel, each week, as if I were setting off into the unknown—for neighborhoods that were discrete, exotic nations entire unto themselves.

I loved hearing the multitude of languages you'd hear on any given day—Spanish most of all, but also Russian, Italian, Hebrew, French, German, Japanese, Albanian, Indian, Portuguese, Yiddish, along with those (Hungarian? Roumanian? Farsi? Arabic? Finnish? Chinese? Korean?) whose music and cadences I had to guess at. I loved the contrasts: homeless people sleeping in doorways a few feet from apartment houses with multi-million-dollar penthouses; rundown, abandoned buildings side by side with bright new avant-garde, upscale res-taurants (this was especially common on the Lower East Side, where Max's parents—my grandparents—had lived when they came to America); blocks of high-rise apartment buildings that housed hundreds of thousands of people in an acre or two of concrete, while overlooking enormous expanses of lawns, ball fields, woodlands, and gardens in city parks.

New Yorkers were not overtly friendly—women, especially, would rarely return a glance or smile—but if you stopped and asked for directions, or for the time (I never wore a watch, so I could initiate conversations this way), New Yorkers were the most helpful people I'd ever known. I loved shmoozing with store owners, bargaining with sidewalk vendors, eating by myself in restaurants, overhearing conversations and lovers' quarrels, and, mostly, meandering along streets—Broadway especially, on Manhattan's Upper West Side (where I rented a one-bedroom apartment)—that overflowed with thousands of people I didn't know.

What I loved most, though, as I had when I was a boy, was riding the subways. And this time it wasn't so much the physical stuff that enchanted—the tracks and tunnels, rats and dirt and noise—but the mix of people. In any one subway car on any day of the week I'd get to see individuals of more varied and wondrous colors, shapes, dress, sizes, and ethnicities than most people in the rest of the world saw in a lifetime: Asian, Hispanic, Russian, Slavic, Scandinavian, black, white, old, young, tall, short, fat, skinny, disabled, disheveled, and decrepit. Sometimes I'd close my eyes as soon as I sat down in a subway car and make a mind-bet with myself as to how many different nationalities— how many different species of human being—I'd see sitting on the stretch of seats directly across from me. And if there was no doubling—no more, say, than one black man or one Asian woman—I'd tell myself I'd won double.

Living in New York for the first time in my life, what I also loved—how not?—was the feeling it gave me of being close to Max by imagining I was experiencing some of what he'd known when he was a young man growing up in New York before he'd married, before he'd published, before he'd settled in Northampton, and before I'd been born.

Despite the fact that Singapore was, in its harbor, financial centers, and skyscrapers, a thriving center of global commerce, and that people who worked there worked at least as hard as people did in New York (until I worked with the Chinese in Singapore, I'd thought nobody worked as hard as New Yorkers), and despite the fact that it was amazingly diverse, both in its native population and in its expatriates and itinerant merchants, it seemed as different from New York as Amherst was from Bangladesh, and it seemed to exist merely and provisionally as a place, to use Nick's phrase, 'for processing product.'

By the time I arrived, Nick had taken care of pretty much all my essential needs—apartment, car, work pass, health care, health club, insurance, domestic help—and all I had to do, and most of what I did do that first week, after I'd slept off jetlag, was to let him shepherd me from one bank, bureau, and agency to another.

Our company's offices were on the twenty-eighth and twenty-ninth floors of a building in what was known as the CBD (Central Business District), with spectacular, unobstructed views of the marina area, the harbor islands (Coral Island, Paradise Island, Treasure Island, Pearl Island), and the Straits of Singapore beyond. Our company—Singapore Palm Oil Technologies Limited—produced and sold palm oil, and to do this, we bought, leased, developed, and managed palm oil plantations for which my responsibilities were pretty much the same as Nick's: to make sure that what we promised to deliver was delivered safely, and at the agreed-upon price. Our job was to monitor every stage of the enterprise—from contract negotiations to locating plantations and/or creating new ones, and from the deforesting of land to the planting and cultivation of trees, the hiring of workers, the harvesting of fruit, the transformation of fruit into oil, the shipping of either the fruit or the oil (crude and/or processed), and the delivery and acceptance of product. What this meant, whether the oil was produced by small companies or large (in old-fashioned village ways or on modern industrial plantations), was that we were involved in what happened, and in the most literal way, on and in the ground.

My flight, via Hong Kong, arrived in Singapore early on a Sunday morning. Nick met me at the airport and drove me straight to his pad, where I slept for fourteen straight hours, after which, on and off for the rest of the week, starting early Monday morning, we made rounds of insurance and real estate offices, government agencies, law offices, and banks, and, still in a stupor—enhanced at breakfast that first morning by two Bloody Marys (heavy on horseradish and vodka)—I filled out forms, signed papers, nodded comprehension, had my photo taken some half-dozen times, and wrote checks. Nick showed me the apartment and car he'd picked out for me, got me settled in my office, and introduced me to people at work (two secretaries and three clerks, all Chinese, were assigned to me).

Whenever he had to excuse himself to take care of stuff that needed immediate attention, I sat in my office, gazed out at the harbor and horizon, and read through stacks of brochures, reports, and papers he'd assembled for me—mostly about the wonders of palm oil, which, I learned, had already passed bananas as the number one fruit crop in the world, and which could be used not only in the production of food, soaps, detergents, and cosmetics, but also as an inexpensive biofuel. Palm oil was *the future of the world*, brochures and company literature proclaimed, and who were we, Nick advised, to argue against such sublime prophecy? Others, however, I soon discovered when I went online to inform myself about palm oil—especially about what the creation of palm oil plantations were doing to Borneo and the environment—didn't see palm oil as anything like the pure blessing Singapore Palm Oil Technologies Limited claimed it was.

At exactly five-forty in the afternoon of my second Monday in Singapore, Nick announced that, our work done, it was time to play, at which point we headed for his favorite watering hole, The Sling Shot, located on the ground floor of one of the city's major waterfront hotels, with views both of the western end of the Tanjong Pagar wharves (they extended for more than three miles), and of one of the most extraordinary Hindu temples in the world, built, Nick informed me, in the middle of the nineteenth century by Indian convicts.

The amazing thing about The Sling Shot, and what delighted Nick about it, were not the views it offered through a huge plate glass window that was its southern wall, though the views were exceptional, but its interior, which had been modeled, and with impeccable fidelity to detail—including the long bar, panelled walls, potted plants, and (even) cigar smoke scent—after The Oak Room of the Plaza Hotel in New York City.

"Go figure, right?" Nick said. We ordered drinks, toasted our reunion, and then Nick talked about work, moving directly to what, he asserted, I would discover was at the heart of it all: contracts. Corruption was everywhere and assumed, bribes a legitimate and time-honored form of negotiation, and what might have been considered illegal or unethical somewhere else was here openly talked about in language that emphasized friendship and respect. But alongside this traditionally sanctioned trading of favors there was an obsessive formality and exactitude, a legacy of English rule, where *everything* you did—when you blew your nose, or pulled up anchor, or arranged to arrange for an arrangement that would lead to an arrangement—had to be authorized by a contract that was impeccably detailed, and, once signed, was honored in each and every particular and—the good news—could be trusted.

We had a second round of drinks, Nick talked about the chain of command in our company—who we reported to, who reported to us, who was and wasn't trustworthy—and then, as we started on our third round—we were mildly pie-eyed, and Nick kept slapping me on the shoulder and exclaiming: *"You're really here, buddy! You did it! You're really here!"*—he signalled to the maître d', who brought a leather-bound book that he set down in front of me, a book handsomely tooled with gold and green curlicues, and one that seemed too thick to be a menu or wine list. I started to open it, but Nick stopped me, his hand on top of mine.

"Guess," he said.

"A wedding album."

"Close," Nick said.

"A Chinese translation of *Triangle*."

"Closer," Nick said.

"A smorgasbord of Asian delicacies."

"Bingo!" Nick said, and took his hand away.

I opened the book, began turning the pages, and found myself looking not at wedding pictures or elegant entrées, but at glossy photographs of beautiful young Asian women who might have been posing for Chanel or Oscar de la Renta ads in places such as *Vogue, W,* or *Harper's Bazaar,* except that the majority of them wore no clothes, and were doing things to themselves and other women you would never see in these magazines. In several pictures, there were two women, in some three or more (there were no men in any of them), and in some—I looked at Nick with alarm when I came to the first of these—there were girls who could not have been more than eight or nine years old.

Below each picture was a number.

"Welcome to Singapore," Nick said, "where false advertising is frowned upon."

"What you see is what you get?"

"And you *do* get it," he said, and when he did, as if on cue, the maître d' returned, and placed a cordless telephone between us.

I had left the book open to a picture of a pretty Asian woman, perhaps nineteen or twenty, dressed in the familiar, somewhat

shapeless uniform of a Singapore Airlines flight attendant—
a sweet, unrevealing batik print in blues, reds, and golds. She
looked less voluptuous than most of the others, and—the word
that came to mind even as I nodded to the maître d'—incongru-
ously wholesome.

I lifted the receiver, tapped in the number below the photo,
then placed the phone back in its cradle. A few minutes later, the
maître d' handed me a small ivory-colored envelope. Inside the
envelope was a card with a number on it: 747.

"The room, I assume," I said. "And it's here in this hotel,
right?"

Nick nodded.

"Here's the deal," Nick said. "Much as I love hanging out
with you, Charlie, I decided to be practical, and staying with me
would clip wings, yours more than mine. This way, the journey
can be as varied as you choose, and without me standing behind
you directing traffic. And there's also this: since everything's a
perk—we've got relocation allowances and expense accounts
to make a teamster official envious—without you having to
worry you're running up a tab on my turf. You can stay here, all
expenses paid—and I mean *all*—until your apartment's ready."

"What about my toothbrush?" I asked.

In the middle of the night—two-twenty-one on the bedside
clock—the door opened and two women entered the room,
one of them carrying a small satchel. The woman I was with—
her name was Bao-zhu, which she'd told me meant treasure-
jewel—put a finger against my lips to indicate that I shouldn't
be alarmed.

The two women, dressed as Bao-zhu had been in the uniforms of Singapore Airlines, seemed to glide toward me on
cushions of air. The woman carrying the satchel set it on the
floor, and spoke in a surprisingly clear and silky voice, and with
an accent more American than English.

"We are here compliments of your good friend and ours," she said. She pointed to the satchel. "I have brought your toothbrush, of course, plus several pieces of clothing and some personal items I thought you might need before you leave for work in the morning."

"Hey thanks—but am I now expected to reciprocate—to send two women to his room?" I asked.

"If you wish," she said, and smiled in a way that made me think she understood my attempt at irony. The second woman, who had moved to the other side of the bed, stepped out of her shoes and dress, and lay down behind Bao-zhu.

"You speak excellent English," I said to the woman who faced me.

"My name is Jin-gen," she said, "which means golden root, but you may call me Ginny if you prefer. I will be your translator tonight."

The woman behind Bao-zhu, her arms around Bao-zhu's waist, tapped me on the shoulder and spoke in what I assumed was Chinese.

"She wishes to explain that although her name, Jin-*feng*, is similar to mine in its first part," Jin-gen said, "yet due to its second part, it becomes quite different from mine. It means golden phoenix."

"So that I'll rise again—is that the message?" I forced a laugh. "I mean, come on—what's going on here? Is this for real?"

"Oh yes—quite real, as you will see presently. And seeing is believing—is that not a common expression where you come from?"

"Seeing is believing," I said. "Sure. But I've never done a foursome before—a quartet, right?—never even seen one."

"Then we will have the honor of being your first." She knelt beside the bed so that her face—an almost perfect oval that was heartstoppingly beautiful, and without any least sign of care or tension—was level with mine. "You are very sweet, Mister Charles," she said, "but there is no need to be nervous."

"You can call me Charlie if you like," I said.

Again, she smiled ever so slightly and, with her index finger, she pressed on my chest at the center of my breast bone.

"As I said, I will be your translator tonight. I am here, that is, to translate your wishes into reality. In this room, with us, whatever you desire or imagine is possible."

"I wonder, though," I said—a line I thought my father—or Seana!—might have found admirable—"if that's either desirable or possible."

She answered my question by running her finger down my chest, the nail scraping my skin but not breaking it, and letting her finger come to rest just above my navel.

"Okay," I said. "I think I see what you're getting at, but when you came in a few minutes ago, I was asleep, and at first..."

I hesitated.

"Yes?"

"What about my dreams?" I asked. "When you entered the room, I was dreaming wonderful dreams, and in the last one I was reading a book—I was a character in the book, actually—and I fell in love with a beautiful woman who confessed to having loved me forever, and we began to make love as if it were the first time for each of us."

"And then—?"

"The famous what-happened-next—?"

"Yes. Tell me, please. What happens next?"

"Okay," I said. "But first, I have to tell you that I'm feeling very sad. I mean, I know it's strange, given that the three of you are here, but I'm feeling sad, and I think it's because just as the woman and I were about to make love, my dream was interrupted by two women entering my room."

"So you are upset with me for stealing your dream from you, is that it?"

Bao-zhu was licking the back of my neck while Jin-feng, who'd moved to the foot of the bed, had begun massaging my feet.

"Maybe," I said.

"You will have more dreams," Jin-gen said. "You have my assurances."

In the morning, when the others were gone, I asked Jin-gen if she could return and spend the evening with me, and she said she could, and I also asked if I could call her JG rather than Ginny—that Ginny seemed like a name for a high school cheerleader, and I didn't want to think of her that way.

"You may call me Jin-gen," she said.

"Why not JG?"

"Because."

"Because why—?"

"Because it is not my name," she said.

Before she left—I was to have an hour or so to myself until it was time to leave for work and for my appointments, she explained, so the transition from night to day would not be unnecessarily abrupt, and so the moment could be noted in a way I felt appropriate—she said she would pick me up by car in front of my office building at five-forty, and she hoped I would allow her to make reservations for dinner.

"Sure," I said, and added: "Many things may be possible, though I get the feeling that disagreeing with you will not be one of them."

"You are at least as clever as you are kind," she said, inclining her head toward me in a slight bow, and leaving the room before I could ask what had made her use the word 'kind.'

A few minutes later, there was a knock on the door, and I thought—hoped—she might be returning, but it was a waiter bringing breakfast. After Jin-gen's arrival, I'd slept well when I'd slept—a deep post-coital sleep that was, as far as I could remember, and despite the assurances Jin-gen had given me, dreamless. This was something that rarely happened to me, and I'd mentioned this, told Jin-gen I loved to dream—that I often wanted to go to sleep in order to dream—and that my father had sometimes reminded me of something I'd said when I was a boy: that for me going to sleep and dreaming was like going to the movies, but even better because in all the stories I got to be the hero.

And there was this too, I realized while, from the terrace, I watched small boats (called bumboats, or cigar boats, I'd learn) darting and skittering around the larger boats as they made their morning pick-ups and deliveries—that despite the bodily pleasures and intimacies I'd just experienced, I was feeling at ease in a way I'd sometimes felt, not after a night of love, but after an evening spent hanging out with good friends.

Jin-gen stayed with me for the next seven nights, and I counted none but happy hours during our time together, and not only because of the physical pleasures, which were exquisite beyond anything I'd ever known, but because of the way, at dinner that first night, and at breakfast the next morning— and before we made love, and after we made love, and when we'd wake in the middle of the night or toward morning—we traded stories. It felt wonderful to lie beside her and feel as if I'd been given permission to tell her *everything*, and to do so not to impress her, or to get her to please me in sublime and/or (previously) forbidden ways, or to settle scores, or to let old injuries and demons loose—or for any *reason*, really—but for the sheer joy of telling stories.

I loved listening to her, and here's some of what I learned: she'd grown up, the youngest of seven children, in the province of Hunan, about forty miles from its capital city of Changsha, where, along with her parents, brothers, and sisters, she lived and worked on a collective rice farm. Her father, Yu-lin Liu, had himself been born in the city of Changsha, where *his* father, Yuan-sou Liu, had been a teacher and an acting school principal. Yu-lin Liu had been raised in a large house with many brothers, sisters, aunts, uncles, and cousins. A gifted student, he'd attended the university in Changsha for three years before being informed upon by a fellow student for a casual remark he'd made about Chairman Mao when he and the student were spending an afternoon together in a teahouse. Yu-lin Liu was convicted of 'impure thoughts,' and sent to a stone quarry on an island in Taihu Lake, in Jiangsu province, where he served for seven years as part of a labor-reform brigade.

At the time of his sentencing, he was twenty-four years old and had been married to Jin-gen's mother, Yuan-ling, for six years. Like Yu-lin Liu, Yuan-ling came from an educated family, and she and Yu-lin Liu had had six children, two boys and four girls. By the time Yu-lin returned from the labor camp in 1984, the one-child-per-family law was in effect, and when Jin-gen was born a year later, they claimed she was the daughter of Si-hui, a childless aunt who lived with Yu-lin Liu and Yuan-ling in the commune.

As soon as Jin-gen could walk and talk, her father and mother began teaching her to read and to write. Because she was a girl, along with the risk that the truth of her birth would be uncovered (and with it, her father and grandfather's criminal records), they were certain Jin-gen would never be admitted to a university, and so, when she was fifteen, the family sent her and an older sister, Wei-li, to Guangzhou—the former Canton—in the province of Guangdong, where hundreds of clothing manufacturers had been setting up factories. The plan, one that had worked for Jin-gen's oldest sister, Yu-mei, was for her to find work there and, by the force of her beauty, intelligence, and industriousness, to attract a sponsor, either Chinese or foreign (and preferably American or Dutch), who might bring her to one of the great international cities—Shanghai, Tokyo, Hong

Kong, Jakarta, or Singapore—where she could earn more than she would on the rice farm or in a factory, and where she might eventually come to a better life.

Like her sisters before her, Jin-gen lied about her age, and arrived in Guangzhou with documents, secured from a neighbor on the commune, that validated the lies. On her third day in Guangzhou, she found work in an American factory that made children's dresses, and though the work was demanding, it was somewhat less exhausting than work in the rice fields had been. From conversations with other women she learned she'd been lucky in this first job—that they preferred working in American factories because conditions there were usually cleaner, and more humane, than they were in factories run by companies from other nations. What American firms such as Nike and Gap had discovered—this confirmed what Nick told me at our reunion—was that the better the working conditions and the happier the workers, the more efficient and productive the factories, and the more reliable its products.

Every American company, from the smallest to the largest (as was true in Singapore), had to have a local partner in order to be able to do business, and the American companies did what they could, bribes included, to keep Chinese officials from shutting them down for violations of laws regarding working conditions. Still, the local Chinese officials and inspectors were, to Jin-gen's surprise, less feared by the American businessmen than their own American inspectors, who didn't hesitate to give pink slips to anyone found violating even the most minor technicalities.

In the factory, Jin-gen and her sister started out trimming and cutting threads from hems, linings, and buttonholes. Wei-li, more adept at these tasks than Jin-gen, was soon working at a sewing machine, stitching in labels. A short while later, Jin-gen, favored by one of the local Chinese foremen, became a tea-and-water girl, walking the factory floor all day and dispensing tea and water to workers from a large two-barreled aluminum canteen on her back. She lived with the Chinese foreman, whose status allowed him his own small room so that—a welcome perk—Jin-gen didn't have to spend her nights in the factory itself, where hundreds of families, many with infants and children, slept on the floor.

What surprised me were not Jin-gen's descriptions of how relentlessly hard, boring, and dis-spiriting the work was—how little life for workers existed beyond work itself (in Amherst, Nick had given me graphic, first-hand reports on this)—but the pride she took in the factories and their productivity. "We are machines, you see," she kept saying (based on my experience, I'd respond, she was anything but a machine). "But we *are* machines, Charlie," she'd insist. "We are machines and that is why we are great—China, not India!—and why the world will have to reckon with us before all others. We—the workers!—are cogs in wheels, wires in motors, fuel for electricity, chips for computers, do you see? We *are* machines! That is what we are— and that is why we are the future..."

The children's dress factory, which employed fewer than five hundred women, could, she boasted, turn out more than twelve thousand dresses in a day. And a jewelry factory where she worked after this (transferred there, the foreman took her with him), could produce ten thousand pairs of earrings by noon, and could do this from a new design given to them at the start of the workday.

There seemed no disgrace, despite her age, to being the companion of the Chinese foreman. Rather the opposite, for she had privileges that made her the envy of other women, not the least of which was her ability to send money to her family with a reasonable assurance it would get there.

Her father, I learned, was not the only member of her family to have been imprisoned. Her grandfather had spent six years in a labor camp, and on our fourth night together, while we ate in a makeshift tent on the outskirts of the city where a Chinese man and his wife cooked for us (they lived behind a curtain that separated the kitchen and small eating area from their sleeping quarters), Jin-gen told me her grandfather's story.

Before his imprisonment, her grandfather had been the acting principal at a school in Changsha, and he had hoped some day to be made principal of the school, a school he himself had attended. The local Communist Party chief, however, was also determined to become principal of the school, and Jin-gen's grandfather and the party chief became fierce rivals. In 1968, two years after Mao declared a Cultural Revolution for China, her grandfather was declared a Rightist, and sentenced to six years in a coal mine being used as a forced labor camp. Early in his fourth year in the camp—during the first three he'd been forbidden to write or receive letters—he was, for having protested his treatment by a guard, placed in solitary confinement, at which time, the guard took pleasure in reminding him of what Chairman Mao had said: that a revolution was not a dinner party.

In despair, he decided to take his own life by tearing apart his shirt and trousers and braiding them into a rope he attached to an overhead beam, and he was about to hang himself when he heard a deep sigh come from an adjoining cell. He put his ear to the wall, and heard the wailing of another prisoner. He thought he recognized the voice, listened more intently and soon realized that the man in the adjoining cell was his rival, the local party chief, who was proclaiming that he too was going to kill himself.

In that moment, Jin-gen's grandfather decided to postpone his own suicide, reasoning, as he later explained to Jin-gen's father, that if the party chief killed himself, and if he survived his imprisonment, and if the political winds shifted direction, he would have lost his major rival for the position of principal.

The party chief, however, informed by a guard that they were expecting Jin-gen's grandfather to commit suicide, also decided not to kill himself so that, upon his release from the camp, he might have a clear path to becoming principal. The result was that both men survived their incarcerations. Three years after Jin-gen was born, in 1989, her grandfather died of throat cancer. Neither he nor the party chief ever became principal of the school.

Jin-gen's father had told her the story, but had never spoken in any detail of the torture either he or her grandfather suffered. What she did tell me, however—because, she said, she wanted me to have some small sense of what these years were like for Chinese families such as hers—was that while her father was working in the stone quarry, he several times watched men place their legs on railroad tracks used to carry carloads of stone down from the high quarry to a stone-breaking area below. In this way, they hoped to lose one or both legs and, if they survived, to have the possibility of spending the rest of their lives in a home for invalids. Caution, however, was required, for if a guard saw a prisoner preparing to amputate a leg in this manner, the man would be taken away and summarily executed.

What Jin-gen found as remarkable as the events by which her grandfather and the party chief survived was that either of them had survived at all. Her own survival was less mysterious.

While she was working in the jewelry factory, the foreman introduced her to an American supervisor, Marty Garfunkel, a married man with a wife and three children in Dedham, North Carolina, who took her with him to Dongguan, a city of more than six million people that was situated a short distance from Guangzhou, and had become a center of toy manufacturing. There, Jin-gen lived with Marty and worked in a factory painting cast-iron airplanes, tanks, and soldiers. They stayed in Dongguan for nine months, until her factory was shut down because inspectors discovered it was using lead paint, at which point Marty brought her with him to Hong Kong, where he got her a job as hostess in an exclusive men's club.

Two months after they arrived in Hong Kong, Marty announced that he'd be returning to the States. Before his departure, he introduced her to a heavy-set man in his sixties who liked to call himself Charles Atlas (his real name, she discovered by looking at his passport while he was asleep one night, was Joe Wanczyk), and who, when drunk and physically abusive, would keep repeating, "I was once a ninety-eight-pound weakling, sweetheart... I was once a ninety-eight-pound weakling, can you believe it?... I was once a ninety-eight-pound weakling..." the meaning of which Jin-gen didn't understand until one of her American clients explained it to her.

Joe Wancyzk traded in currencies, and spent most of his days in his hotel suite, smoking and following exchange rates on his computer. He made large profits by taking advantage of small discrepancies in the rise and fall of currencies. He also traded in women, providing companions for businessmen (primarily Japanese, American, and Indonesian) who were in Hong Kong for limited periods of time.

Jin-gen learned that several women who worked at the club had been able to persuade their American clients to arrange jobs for them in the United States as *au pairs* (American families that had adopted Chinese children were eager and willing, they'd learned, to pay a premium to obtain Chinese *au pairs*), and when she'd been with Joe for nearly a year and he informed her he'd be returning to New York sometime soon, she asked if he would get her a job with a family in America. To her surprise, he liked the idea, and said he'd see what he could do, provided that if he succeeded, she would find ways on her days off and vacations to service clients he sent her way.

At this point, she explained, her bad luck became her good luck. As Joe's departure grew near—he'd been living in Hong Kong for eight years and, overweight and often short of breath, had become increasingly anxious about his health—he also became increasingly abusive, which made her job difficult, since men—this was particularly true of the Japanese—did not like their women to have any bruises or blemishes. Make-up, she said, only went so far, and the more Joe beat her, the less desirable she became to his clients.

This—we were lying in bed before dawn on Sunday morning when she gave me the news—was when she met Nick.

"You knew Nick in Hong Kong?!"

"Yes."

"Then the two of you were…?"

She put a hand over my mouth.

"Shh," she said, and pulled my head down to her chest. Though the news that she'd known Nick in Hong Kong surprised me, what she said next astonished me. "We were good friends only," Jin-gen stated, "and not in ways I was with other men, but that does not matter, Charlie, because what you must know first and last and always is that Nick is one of the kindest human beings who has ever lived."

"*Nick*?!" I exclaimed, and started to sit up. "Look. Nick's many things, and he's been a good friend to me, but…"

"Shh," she said again. "Listen to me. I am not the only woman to whom Nick has been kind. I can introduce you to others whose lives have been saved by him. *Saved*, Charlie! Can you understand? If not for him, we…"

Then she began to weep, and the next thing I knew I was holding her to my chest, and telling her it was okay, that I was listening, that I wanted to hear more, that I'd try to believe her.

But *Nick*? I thought to myself. *Nick Falzetti?*

When Nick and I hung out at the reunion, we'd exchanged stories of what we'd been doing since he and Trish had split, and he'd told me about working in the garment business in New York for a while—sales and marketing—and that he'd spent most of his time after that in the Far East, wheeling and dealing with clothing manufacturers, local businessmen, and with customs and tax officials. He'd started out with small firms that made their bundles in one place and then, when labor costs rose, took their businesses to the next place—India or Vietnam,

Indonesia or Malaysia or the Philippines—wherever the cost of labor was cheaper.

Creative accounting was their specialty—how to hide profits, how not to pay bills or taxes, how to pay off people who had to be paid off, and how to stiff people less shrewd than they were. But for Nick, their most venal sin was that they were vulgar—true garmentos, he said, like guys he'd worked with in New York but without the blunt, no-nonsense New York style he loved—and once he figured out how things worked, he sought out people from companies that had contracts with bigger players—firms such as Macy's, Wal-Mart, and T.J. Maxx—and hooked up with them.

The money, perks, and hours were about the same with the large firms as they'd been with the *shlock* companies, but working with the *shlock* companies had taken its toll, and for a guy who'd always prided himself on being fit, he found he was feeling sluggish too much of the time, especially during working hours, when he couldn't stop daydreaming about being somewhere else. He was also drinking and whoring more, and the more he did, the more obsessed he became about getaways and about carving out a different life, so that when, at a resort in Borneo—in Sarawak, where he'd gone for a weekend of scuba-diving—he met a South African who owned several palm oil plantations and they hit it off, he'd asked the man to make him an offer he wouldn't want to refuse.

"I've never been famous for what's in here," I remember Nick saying—tapping on his chest with his knuckles—"but it was the children who got to me. Seeing little kids—this was in the factories where I started out, not the more legit places—but seeing kids of two, three, and four years old sleeping in filth, and kids not much older working all day in mud up to their ankles, and then the way the mothers would stare at me with all their fucking pain—and with calculation equal to the pain: 'Hey, if I look miserable enough, maybe you'll give me some money, or a chit for an extra meal, or some medicine'—this got to me, and it got to me not when I was there, hip-deep in it, but when I was already gone and working for companies that didn't allow the worst of these conditions."

I remember Nick saying I probably wouldn't believe him— that if he heard what he was saying he probably wouldn't believe himself either, but that it was as if, after the fact—when he thought he was free of the glooms—some huge wave had risen up, knocked him down, and rolled over him.

He'd grabbed my wrist then and squeezed so hard I had to pry up one of his thumbs. "Sorry," he said. "But you can't know what it's like to see people living in their own puke and diarrhea, with women and older kids cleaning up the younger ones every morning so a foreman won't kick them out. To see kids going around begging, some with no hands, or only two or three fingers, or one eye, or none, and having to wonder if they were born that way, or if that was just some ordinary part of getting with the program…"

I pressed my eyes closed, to get shut of Nick's voice.

"Tell me what happened," I said to Jin-gen.

"You will believe me then—about Nick?"

"I hope so," I said, but even as I said the words, I was remembering that the whole time he was telling me about how much he felt for Asian kids on the other side of the world, he never said a word about his own son—about Gabe—and how he was doing. And in Singapore, when we'd been working together, our offices adjoining, though he talked about Trish once in a while—telling me he sent her money regularly, and reminding me about crazy stuff the three of us used to do together—he never mentioned Gabe.

"What I think," Jin-gen said, "is that your friend Nick—*our* friend Nick—has more heart than appears on his sleeve. That is one of your expressions, yes?"

"Not quite, but I like it better the way it comes from your mouth."

"Better? Better than what—better than the way your Shakespeare said it?"

"How'd you know it's from Shakespeare?"

"Nick told me when I recited the words one time—he said I was quoting your Shakespeare."

"As far as I know, Shakespeare hasn't become an American yet."

"I know *that*!" she said. "I am not a stupid, passive Chinese woman!"

"Hey, it was a joke," I said, and added that I'd meant what I said as a *compliment*—that I preferred her way of phrasing it, and I went on to ask if she knew that the line was from *Othello*, and that it was spoken not by Othello but by Iago, and I added that my father told me that people found it surprising that a character famous for being devious and evil could have uttered a line most people thought of as revealing generous impulses.

"So tell me something, Charlie, are you finished talking yet?"

"Probably."

"Then tell me something else: Would you like to hear first about Nick's heart... or about his sleeve?"

I laughed. "Both," I said and, as if to apologize for the way I'd reacted to what she'd said about Nick, I told her that Nick had talked to me, and with feeling, about factories in China where he'd worked, and about how seeing the way children lived had gotten to him.

"That is not what I am talking about," Jin-gen said. "You should listen more carefully. Nick did not save children. He saved women, but if you are too jealous to want to know about this, and of his kindness to me, I will say nothing else."

"Talk to me," I said.

"Yes," she said. "But we should eat while I talk," and saying this, she got out of bed and ordered me to stay put. When I protested, she told me again to stay where I was, and gave me her assurances that *all* her services had been well paid for in advance."

I did what she said—in the moment, I felt too defeated somehow to do anything else—and about twenty minutes later, when we were eating breakfast on the terrace, she began telling me about Nick, and about how, when he was in Hong Kong and not long before he began working for the palm oil company we both worked for now, he'd had many girlfriends.

They were often college-age women, generally Chinese but not only Chinese, she said, who were in Hong Kong to work or to study. Sometimes he went out with older women who were in the city on business. He met them in bars of fancy hotels—married woman usually, because, he said, they came with the fewest complications, and were always grateful. Mostly, though, he preferred the daughters of wealthy Chinese or Japanese entrepreneurs and businessmen. But occasionally, when he didn't want to become involved with a woman—or with her family, as one had to when it came to going out with the daughters of wealthy Chinese and Japanese—he'd pay elite escort services that employed women like Jin-gen.

The night she met Nick, he was with one of these women—a friend of hers, Cai-yu—at the men's club where she worked. This happened about two weeks before Joe Wancyzk was scheduled to leave for the States. It was past eleven in the evening, the bar was empty, and Joe was ragging on Jin-gen about complaints he'd been getting from clients, and warning her that she'd better not disappoint him with the guy she'd be meeting later in the evening.

While Joe was going at her—they were sitting at a table near the bar—she glanced at Cai-yu, who smiled brightly and pointed to Nick, making Jin-gen understand that this was the man she'd been telling Jin-gen about—the man who was going to help Cai-yu get to America. The man was watching her and Joe, but without expression, and when Joe went at her again—calling her a two-bit, bad-weather cunt, and shaking a finger in her face—and when, lowering her head, she glanced toward Cai-yu, she saw, to her amazement, that Nick was smiling at her and nodding slightly—looking at her in a way that encouraged her to go ahead and do what she wanted to do.

So she did. She pushed Joe's finger aside, told him she expected him to talk to her with respect, and that if he didn't, she would leave.

Joe stared at his finger as if he couldn't believe she'd touched it, and then he reached across the table to slap her. Fortunately, he was drunk, and she was quick. Joe missed, then stared at his open palm as if trying to understand why it had not done what he'd told it to do.

Jin-gen giggled, and said she had giggled that night too, and that when she looked up, there was Nick, who put out his hand to her, and gave her his name—Domenic Falzetti—and said that he understood she was a friend of Cai-yu and was looking for a sponsor so she could become an *au pair* in the United States.

Nick did not look at Joe, or offer to shake Joe's hand, and Joe told him to leave—to get the fuck out of there and mind his own business.

"And who are you?" Nick asked.

"I'm your worst nightmare," Joe said, and grabbed Jin-gen's arm. "She works for me," he announced. "Got it? So get lost, mister."

"Do you own this club too?" Nick asked.

"I said to do yourself a favor and get lost," Joe said.

"That was when Nick sat down next to me," Jin-gen said. "Joe stood and again ordered Nick to leave, but Nick kept smiling at him, which made Joe even crazier. He grabbed me and tried to pull me from my seat, but Nick put his hand on Joe's and told him to be polite to ladies, and I will never ever forget what he said to Joe next: 'Be kind,' he said, 'for everyone you meet is fighting a great battle.'

"'What are you—some kind of nut?' Joe said, and he pulled on me even harder, and this was when—but so quickly I hardly saw his hand move—Nick did something to Joe's chest—like a Karate chop where you attempt to break a board with a single blow, but with the flat of his hand instead of the side—and Joe's head snapped back, and he fell face first onto the table.

"His nose started to bleed, and he gurgled and choked for a while. Nick took my arm and helped me up, and I stood between him and Cai-yu, and my legs were shaking terribly. The owner of the club stood next to us, and he had two security men with him, but it was clear they were not going to keep Nick from doing whatever he wanted. When Joe got his breath back, and put an ice pack over his nose that a security man gave him, Nick leaned down and whispered to Joe that he hoped there was no next time, because if there was, they would have to crack Joe's chest open in order to fix the damage. Then Nick put a business card on the table and told Joe to have my things sent to the address on the card, along with what he owed me, and a bonus to cover my air fare to the States.

"This was when the owner of the club offered to call an ambulance. Joe, one hand on his chest as if to make sure his heart was still beating, shook his head sideways, but he didn't speak. 'We will have somebody escort you home,' the owner said, 'and since you are a good customer, I would also give to you a friendly suggestion, which is that, in order to avoid unfortunate accidents and stay healthy for leaving to America, you do as Mister Falzetti wishes.'

"I stayed with Nick and Cai-yu for three weeks while Nick arranged things," Jin-gen said, "and then I left for America, with all my papers in order, and I arrived in Boston, where the Gottlieb family—Anne and David and their two young children, both Chinese—met me at the airport. They had an enormous house in Newton—a mansion—and I lived there with them on a work visa for thirteen months."

"Then we were probably both living in Massachusetts at the same time," I said. "Less than a hundred miles apart."

"Yes," Jin-gen said. "I have realized that this was a possibility."

"And you didn't call me?"

"An oversight," she said, and then: "You are quite wonderful, you know."

"And you are too," I said. And then, a moment later: "But did Nick really say that—about being kind?"

"Yes," Jin-gen said. "It was something he said several times, and not just to me, because I have heard it from other women he helped."

"My father used to say the same thing," I said.

"Did he learn it from Nick?"

I laughed. "I think it was the other way around—or, more probably, that Nick heard me say it."

"Then we have, as you might put it, come full circle, have we not?"

Jin-gen stayed with me again on Sunday night, and at the office the next morning I said nothing to Nick about what she'd been telling me. At The Sling Shot after work, the first thing I did, even before ordering a drink, was to ask the maître d' for the book—*The Good Book*, Nick called it—and to begin looking through it.

"You won't find Jin-gen there, if that's who you're looking for," Nick said.

"Does she work for you?"

"For *me*? Not at all. Why would you think so?"

"She said she was busy tonight," I said, "but that she hoped she'd see me again sometime soon."

"That's true," Nick said.

"But if she's not in the book, and if she doesn't work for you…"

Nick shrugged. "Hey, enjoy what you can while you can, Charlie. Isn't that what it's all about?"

"Maybe," I said.

"You like it here?"

"I like it here," I said. "And oh, I meant to tell you—I got a call—I can move into my apartment tomorrow."

"Furniture?"

"They said it will be there, all set up."

"That means you have one more night of palm oil perks, you lucky bastard."

"But Jin-gen?"

"Play the field, buddy—sample the wares while you can. I know you well, Charlie, and my advice—forgive the figure of speech—is not to get stuck in old ruts."

"Jin-gen says you've helped a lot of women."

"Did she?"

"Come on, Nick—don't fuck with me—she said you saved their lives—other women—the way you saved hers. True?"

"Can't say yet," Nick said. "Who knows? What was the saying you liked to quote—from your dad…?"

"'Be kind, for everyone—'"

"Not that sentimental crap, but the other one—from a movie: 'Live fast, die young, and have a good-looking corpse.'"

"'Have a *beautiful* corpse,'" I corrected.

"James Dean, right?"

"Maybe—according to my father, it was John Derek."

Nick pointed to the book. "So come on—who interests you for tonight?"

"I was hoping Jin-gen…"

"Look. The lady sends regrets. She told you, and now I told you, or don't you get it? She really is busy tonight, and she asked me to tell you she thinks you're a good guy and that she had a great time with you."

"She's really busy?" I said.

"That's right. So come on," Nick said, pushing the book my way. "It's still on the tab. And tomorrow night we'll celebrate you being in your own digs."

"But if I want to see her, how do I get in touch—through you?"

"Never me," Nick said. "But why would you want to see her again when…"

He touched the book, leaned back, looked toward the bar. I pushed the book away, saw that he was looking at two young women—Americans, by their voices—who were laughing and smoking cigarillos. As if she could sense his gaze, one of them turned his way—she was a drop-dead gorgeous blonde bomb-shell, and the coolness of her expression said that she knew it. She met Nick's eyes for several seconds before turning back to her friend.

"She was a gift, wasn't she?" I said. "Jin-gen, I mean. She was a kind of Welcome Wagon thing, Singapore-style, you arranged because she owed you big."

"You're talking a language I don't understand, buddy. So let's each pick a winner, and compare notes in the morning. How's that sound?"

I ordered another drink, and another, and then another, and the room tilting this way and that, I opened the book and chose a woman who wasn't wearing a Singapore Airlines uniform, and who wasn't smiling. Nick chose a woman who was in a Fred Astaire pose—or maybe it was more like Marlene Dietrich. She was dressed, where she was dressed, in a partial tux—tails, with top hat and cane, and she was leaning against a pillar, and I got worried for a second they might send both women to my room, but Nick opened his envelope and showed me the number on his card, which was different from the number on mine.

"Not to worry," he said, as if he'd been reading my mind. "We're going solo tonight, one on one, the way you like it."

"The way I *like* it?" I said. "I don't follow."

I blinked, looked past Nick to the bar, and saw that the other woman—she had wavy auburn hair and a wide, bright smile—was picking something from between her front teeth with what looked like a fishbone.

"You always liked it well enough with me and Trish," Nick said, "but let's face it, it took a lot of booze, or pot, or white magic for you to get into it."

"What are you talking about?"

"You're basically straight, Charlie. We know that."

"Sure. I mean, I…"

He slapped me on the shoulder. "Hey, like I said—not to worry, buddy. Your secret's safe with me."

I finished my drink and ordered another. The woman with the auburn hair smiled at me again, and I saw that the fishbone was a toothpick.

"Or we could invite those two young lovelies to join us."

"Sure," I said. "Whatever. But I don't know what you're getting at. We had lots of fun, the three of us. But—"

"But be open to possibility, right?" Nick said. "Isn't that what you said your father taught you? Your old man had lots of good sayings, I remember. Be a Jew at home and a man on the street! Be one upon whom nothing is lost…!"

"Sure," I said. "I mean, who knows?" I smiled, and sat up straight. "*But I am a barrel!*" I declared brightly, quoting a Chinese phrase I'd learned a few days before—the equivalent of our 'I've-got-a-hollow-leg.' "*I am a barrel!*" I said again, after which I rested my head on the table. Nick lifted my head, put *The Good Book* under it for a pillow, and then his mouth was at my ear, his breath damp. "What I think, with you, me, and Trish," he whispered, "is that you always liked the idea more than the reality."

"Whatever you say," I said. "Because if I'm not a barrel, then what am I?"

"And if I'm not for myself, who will be for me? Wasn't that another one of your father's gems?"

"But if I'm only for myself, what am I?"

"Right on!" Nick said.

"Like you and all those ladies you saved, right?"

Nick helped me out of my chair. "If not now, when?" he said, and he walked me to the elevator, and then to my room. The woman I'd chosen was already there, and she wasn't wearing a tuxedo. The room was spinning fast, and the instant I lay down on the bed it spun faster. The woman put an ice-cold washcloth on my forehead, lay down next to me, massaged my neck, and whispered to me in Chinese.

Shit-faced though I was, I was aware that I was royally pissed too, and not only because I wasn't with Jin-gen, or because of the crap Nick had been throwing at me about him, me, and Trish, but because I had the distinct feeling—along with a phenomenally sick feeling in my head and stomach—that he was getting his rocks off seeing me get stuck on a woman the way I was. That the woman was a friend of his, that she believed he'd saved her life, and that he'd given her to me—chosen her for me—no matter how much he denied it, I was sure he had—made me even more pissed.

The woman with me—I never got her name—was kindness incarnate, but even while I was lost in the swirlings in my head and bowels, and, later on, in her, I couldn't get shut of the feeling that Nick was messing with me in ways that were light years ahead of my ability to figure them out.

And I couldn't help wondering about something else—something I vowed that night I'd never ever ask Nick about—whether Jin-gen had been telling me the truth about the two of them.

I went back to work in the morning—sober, but with small green men banging away inside my skull with large hammers—and I compared notes with Nick, and he teased me about how deep in the tank I'd been, and suggested I leave my car in the garage after work, that he'd drive me to my apartment so we could continue to celebrate. "You should never miss a chance to celebrate," he said, "because you never know when they'll be taking the set down, and the whole goddamn stage and building with it."

So he'd think nothing had changed between us—that I was the same guy I was before my week with Jin-gen—I gave him something else from Max.

"And as my father would put it," I said, "and this was usually when I'd be heading out on a date, or to meet some friends— 'Don't forget to have a good time, son.'"

My apartment looked wonderful—hotel-like, for sure, but with brighter, warmer colors in the carpets, furniture, and framed prints than I remembered Nick or me choosing—and there was a bottle of champagne in a bucket of ice, a red bow around its neck, waiting on the coffee table, along with a half-dozen plates of small delights. We drank and ate and drank some more, and Nick got mildly loaded and kept reciting my father's line—"'*Don't forget to have a good time, son!*' I love it! '*Don't forget to have a good time, son! Don't forget to have a good time…*'"

A few minutes after he left, there was a knock on the door and when I opened it—hardly a surprise—a beautiful young woman was standing there. She was wearing a Boston Red Sox cap, which she doffed in greeting. She walked past me, turned, and asked if I'd found everything in the apartment to my satis-faction. As with Jin-gen, her English was impeccable. Was she another of the women Nick had saved?

"All is well," I said.

"Well, your happiness is my responsibility," she said, and added that she would be grateful if I would allow her to fulfill her responsibilities.

I did, and when I woke in the morning she was gone and the dishes were washed and put away. I never saw her again.

I never saw Jin-gen again either.

Six and a half weeks after I moved into my apartment, Nick and I landed in Borneo. We flew in a two-engine company plane—what Nick called a swamp-jumper—that offered exquisite views of the South China Sea, a sea that, in the early morning sun, was all silver-blue and rippling gold—and it didn't take long before I was in love again. This time, though, I fell in love with a place, not a woman.

The first week at the hotel with Jin-gen, I began to see—along with my being able to leave the office every day before six—had, like Jin-gen, been a gift from Nick. After that week, I rarely left the office before nine or ten at night, using the hours when the rest of the staff was gone to catch up on paperwork, and to put in calls to people in Japan, Hawaii, Europe, and New York so I could catch them during *their* workdays. I spent a good part of my own regular workday, eight to six, talking to people in Borneo and Hong Kong, Shanghai, Tokyo, and China, and supervising the men and women who worked under me.

"Being able to delegate authority the way you do has never been my strong suit," Nick said when we were having a late-night drink early in my fourth week on the job. "It was one of the reasons I quit football. I did my part, but could I count on the other ten guys to do theirs?"

"Sometimes," I said.

"*Sometimes?*" he said. "Not good enough—*never* good enough. But I'm getting at something else, Charlie—something I've been thinking about since you got here: that this is probably the main difference between us."

"There are differences?" I said.

"I'm being serious," he snapped, and glared at me as if daring me to say more. "What I figured out," he continued, "is that you trust people, and I don't mean only in the office—trusting people to do what you tell them to—but you really *trust* others, and you always have."

"Probably," I said.

"I don't."

Although I was tempted to talk about why this might be so—the differences between my father and his, for starters—I remained silent. Still, he was right about my feeling easy about relying on others when I needed to know things: how much oil we shipped, or how much we promised to ship, and in what condition; which parts of a contract were already agreed to, and which parts needed to be amended; which billing charges from shipping firms were accurate, and which were padded; which reports on productivity were reliable, and which ones were full of shit; which government officials were trolling for gifts, and which budget lines to use for the gifts, and which lines for new equipment, parts, or repairs, and who to rely on to make sure the stuff was really needed; and if we ordered equipment, parts, or repairs, who were the best people to make things happen in the most cost-effective way. And—shades of Joe Wancyzk—I had an assistant I depended on to follow exchange rates so that, when the dollar fell, we could take advantage and get more bang for our buck by ordering stuff from the States.

Then Nick started in on how everybody at the office *liked* me—and how this was a difference between us too: that I was the original *nice guy* the way I'd always been. People may have respected him, and been grateful to him, but they didn't *like* him the way they liked me. We were both good with people, he said, especially with the Chinese, who made up most of our firm, high and low, the same way they made up most of Singapore. The Chinese had enormous respect for people who worked hard—there was nothing, other than being old, they admired more—but what he'd realized was that he and I were successful with them for opposite reasons.

"You're good because, same as me, you work hard, learn fast, and are good at what you do," he said, "but also because, as I was saying before, you trust people. Me—I'm good with them because I don't."

"Do you really still think of me as being the original nice guy?" I asked.

"You bet."

"But nice guys finish last," I said.

"Nice guys finish last," he repeated. "I like that—one of your old man's sayings?"

"It's from Leo Durocher—the Brooklyn Dodgers' manager when Max was growing up."

"'Lippy' Durocher, right? And wasn't he married to an actress?"

"Laraine Day," I said, but didn't offer any more information, though I was remembering that I used to like hearing my father quote Durocher because it seemed out of character for him to admire a guy who hung out with gangsters. Despite what a nice guy my father always *seemed* to be, he could be tough-minded too, I wanted to tell Nick, and the instant I thought of doing so, I felt a distinct tumbling in my stomach and realized that what I really was hoping for by quoting Durocher was to gain Nick's approval—to show him that, like my father, I wasn't quite the pushover he took me for.

"Well, when it comes to that stuff, you already know what I think, right?" he said, a hand on my shoulder.

"If you want to win in this world you have to be ruthless," I said, quoting one of his own lines back to him.

"You got it," Nick said. "Ruthless for sure. And mean—mean like the real you, Charlie boy, right?"

"You never know," I said.

On weekends, we usually partied in Nick's apartment, and either used *The Good Book*, or hooked up with Nick's friends—American, Dutch, and Japanese mostly—who brought a rich variety of women, food, booze, and drugs with them. But late on a Friday afternoon two weeks before our trip to Borneo, Nick told me I was on my own for the weekend because he had 'family obligations' to attend to.

What this meant, I assumed—he actually seemed to be bragging about it, as if he wanted to impress me—had to do with what Jin-gen alluded to: that he was involved with the daughter of a wealthy Chinese family, and in order to keep the relationship going he had to play the respectful suitor to the young woman's family, especially to the father and grandfather.

That first time he told me I'd be on my own for the weekend, I went down to The Sling Shot and looked through *The Good Book*. But women in the book, like women in my bed, were already starting to seem as bland as the rest of the city. Not because they weren't charming and beautiful, but because I began to see few differences between them other than variations in the obvious—height, weight, sexual tricks—and because I knew that no matter what they did with me and for me, it wouldn't be that different from what I'd experienced before, or would experience the next time, or the time after that—and because I also knew they'd never be able to give me what I'd had with Jin-gen. Or perhaps, it occurred to me, my sex life and love life after Jin-gen—*because* of Jin-gen?—had gone into early retirement.

So I stayed in my apartment the first weekend Nick and I didn't hang out together, leaving only to bring in food and to get in a workout at the club, and once I got through a few hours of mild restlessness, I found that it was okay being alone, and more than okay. Being by myself also reminded me of what life had been like in Northampton when Max was between wives or girlfriends—when it was just the two of us, and he'd be gone teaching, or out for dinner, and I'd have the entire house to myself, and of how I'd fix myself a snack, camp out in his office, and plop down in his wide-armed easy chair with a book. These were also times I'd have friends over, and we'd put on music, smoke pot, sample Max's liquor supply, and mess around. As good as times with my friends were, though, I found that I preferred being by myself even if—no small thing—it was only to put on one of the porno videos we were passing around, and whack off to it.

In one of Max's jokes that would sometimes come to mind while I played with myself, a rebbe asks the boys in his Bar Mitzvah class how they like their girls best—in the flesh or in their dreams—and coaxes them all, except for little Moishe, into raising their hands and admitting they prefer their girls in the flesh. 'And you, Moishe?' the rebbe asks. 'Oh rebbe,' Moishe says, 'you meet a much better class of girls in your dreams.'

This proved as true for me in Singapore as it had in Northampton, since what turned out to be most pleasurable that first weekend I was on my own was, simply, being on my own: fixing myself a favorite sandwich—roast-beef, mustard, and horseradish—and tall drinks—ice-cold sparkling water with half-limes during the day, and another sandwich and vodka tonics with half-limes in the evening—and sitting in the living room, the air-conditioning turned on full blast, and reading. And before sleep, I'd dream about women I'd known, and women I wished I'd known, and, for sure, about women—Jin-gen first in line—I'd lost. And during these hours it would occasionally occur to me that maybe I was my father's son, after all.

Kalimantan, the Indonesian part of Borneo, made up three-quarters of an island that was itself the third largest island in the world (after Greenland and New Guinea, and not counting Australia and Antarctica), and once we'd left the South China Sea behind, our plane headed inland for a makeshift landing field near a new plantation we were developing. Although Borneo had several mountainous regions, most of the island was made up of peat forests and lowland rain forests, and from the sky these forests were astonishing—so many shades and textures of green that I found myself wondering if native peoples there had as many names for the color green as Eskimos did for snow.

Then, as we approached the plantation—"Here it comes, buddy, your first sight of our brave new world," Nick said—the forests ended, and a vast treeless landscape came into view, and the instant it did, I felt as if someone had whacked me across the chest the way Jin-gen said Nick had whacked Joe Wanczyk. In the moment—I was trying to stand, but Nick pressed down hard on my arm to keep me where I was—all I could think of was getting my breath back, and of how a dozen years before—the memory, bouncing off the plane's wing, came in a flash of white sunlight—I'd felt the same thing when I'd first entered a giant redwood forest in Northern California, except that instead of standing on the ground and being surrounded by two-thousand-year-old, three-hundred-foot-high trees, I was in the sky looking down at something equally awe-inspiring.

It was as if the far rim of the rainforest over which we'd passed had been the edge of a cliff from which we were now dropping down into a world that, as far as I could see, was an endless expanse of mud that was spotted here and there with small fires and dismembered parts of trees. Batallions of orange, red, silver, and yellow earth movers, tractors, wood shredders, and dump trucks moved steadily along the ground, tearing the remaining trees and bushes from their roots while hundreds of men, like infantry, followed, but instead of rifles and machine guns, they carried chainsaws, and were slicing up and dragging trees that had been uprooted or chopped down. Our plane banked to the left, leveled out, and we headed for a landing strip edged with orange cones. At the end of the strip, a group of men stood waiting next to a pale red fire truck.

Other than foliage on shrub-like trees that lay on the ground, there was no green anywhere. "They've done a good job," Nick said. "Clear-cut the whole fucking thing in eleven days. Amazing, don't you think? We've got seven square miles of trees coming in next week from which we'll start getting oil in three years. The fuckers grow like weeds with thyroid conditions."

Small fires were burning everywhere—the cut-up trees laying on the ground looked like chunks of amputated limbs and torsos—and the roar of our engines close to the ground drowning out the sounds of their machines, the men, most wearing wide-brimmed sombrero-like hats, stopped work to watch our plane, and waved as if truly happy to see us.

"We got all the big stuff out a few weeks ago," Nick said. "Tens of thousands of board feet of good lumber. What you're looking at now is just mop-up. Amazing resources here, Charlie—half the world's tropical timber comes from this one fucking island, did you know that? Every time somebody somewhere puts a toothpick between his teeth, it's better than two-to-one the toothpick comes from Borneo, and when—"

"Stop," I said.

"Why—you going to turn bleeding heart environmentalist on me? Do me a favor and stop being Mister Nice Guy for a change—and remember what we taught you: that palm oil has more uses than petroleum, that it's a renewable biofuel that can be with us forever, and after we—"

"Give me a break," I said. "I mean, you're used to it, but I've never been here before—never seen anything like this place. It's a shock to the system, so back off."

"Okay, okay," he said. "It's just that I get *excited* whenever I see one of our places—the amazing fucking speed with which we can change things! But hey—shocked the hell out of me too once upon a time. Like I was looking at an ocean of mud that was going to become the biggest fucking set of football fields in creation."

"Enough," I said. "I asked you to cool it."

"In a minute," he said, grabbing me by the shoulders and pulling me to him as if he were going to whack my forehead with his. "Only first you give your shit-eating conscience a rest and listen up."

"Whatever you say, boss."

"And I don't need your smart-ass condescension either, because when it comes to what's happening here, you don't know shit. Because, in case the news didn't reach you, what goes on here is going on all over the planet, buddy—in the Amazon, in China, in Malaysia, in Kansas, in Alaska—you name it—and when haven't we been raping the world? Answer me that. But we come first is what I believe, even if you don't and probably never will, and what I've come to realize is that the really good news, see, is just that—that we get to see the changes up close and personal."

"Lucky us."

"Lucky us is right," he said, letting me go and opening the cabin door. He waved to the people who were waiting for us, then turned back to me, and when he spoke this time his voice shifted, and he talked easily, as if nothing in the world was bothering him.

"So look," he said, "I know what you're thinking—sure—because believe it or not, I felt the same when I first got here, but then one day I got to remembering those time-lapse films we used to watch in college, where plants came out of the ground, grew, blossomed, and died in three or four seconds—or where the sun rose and set and a whole day had come and gone before you could blink, and it dawned on me that what was happening here was pretty much the same thing."

"I don't understand a word you're saying."

"Remember when you, me, and Trish got trashed doing mushrooms," he went on as if I hadn't said a word, "and I got hold of this grad assistant to give us a private show of a bunch of those films?"

"I remember," I said.

"So lucky us is right," he said again, "because think about it for a minute, Charlie—really think about it: what happens invisibly most of the time in most of the world, or what takes years and years, we—you and me, babe—we have the good fortune— the privilege—of seeing it happen right in front of our eyes in real time."

"And if we didn't do it, somebody else would, is that it?" I asked.

"Not at all—oh not at all!—and you can bet your sweet life on that," he said, and he did so in such a condescending way— laughing at me as if I were some kind of fool—that, and not for the first time, I felt ready to kill the guy.

Then he was walking down the steps, shaking hands, and pointing to me, and as soon as he did, four of the five men, all Asian, bowed their heads in greeting. The other man—a Dutchman named Hans Martens I'd learn a few minutes later— gave me a broad grin and a thumbs up.

During the day we tramped around the property, Nick and the Asians (three Chinese, one Japanese) explaining what would be required once the land was cleared and new trees delivered: water, fertilizer, herbicides, drainage canals—how many workers, what equipment, and so on. After lunch, sitting inside a large tent, cool-water air-conditioners plugged into generators and roaring away—the heat and humidity were at least as bad as in Singapore, but with the additional perk of angry squadrons of hungry, flying insects—we went over figures and schedules, made lists of what we needed, and talked about vendors and costs. Nick handled financial negotiations, and he was good at it the way he'd been good at poker (he once claimed he'd earned his entire tuition, the year after he quit football and lost his scholarship, from poker). For the first hour and a half, palm oil was never even mentioned. The talk was about family, food, women, weather, travel, mutual acquaintances—and just when I was about to remind Nick why we were there, *he* acted as if he'd just remembered. He reached into his briefcase, took out four envelopes, one of which he handed to each of the Asians (Hans worked for us) as if presenting them with honorary degrees. After this, we got down to business and were able to sign off on agreements—mostly arranged beforehand in Singapore—in less than two hours.

My primary responsibility was to see that the palm oil seedlings arrived on time and in good shape, and I passed out copies of agreements and contracts I'd prepared, along with scheduling and contact information, all of which, to my surprise, evoked enormous gratitude, along with gifts, about which Nick had warned me, and which I'd been told I couldn't refuse: a Montblanc fountain pen, a monogrammed silver money clip, jade cuff links, and a black and white flowered kimono whose silk was as soft as a baby's skin.

In the evening our hosts prepared a feast for us—wild boar roasted slowly in a deep pit—along with bottle after bottle of splendid French and Spanish wine. Nick and I slept in separate tents that night, three men armed with machine guns standing guard until morning (Nick was carrying the bulk of the month's payroll, in cash, in the larger of his two suitcases), and after breakfast in the morning—savagely bitter coffee, and mushy rolls with sticky-sweet jam—we said our good-byes, flew off over a small mountain range, and set down a half hour later on a runway covered with a glossy olive-drab substance, located adjacent to the site of one of our larger industrial plantations.

Nick and the foreman who welcomed us—an articulate dark-skinned man I gauged to be in his forties, though his skin was so smooth he might have been ten to fifteen years older—from one of the indigenous tribes ("I am your original wild man of Borneo," he announced when Nick introduced us)—gave me a tour of the facility. The foreman's name was Saul—his mother had named him for an Englishman she said was Saul's father—and he was about my height, close to six feet, but weighed a good twenty pounds more, most of it solid muscle. The heat was unbearable here too—I felt as if I were living inside an open-air furnace—and several young women accompanied us wherever we went, fanning us with large fans that looked as if they were made of starched banana-yellow burlap, and regularly handing us wet washcloths and canteens of sweet, tea-flavored water.

Saul took us into a forest where men in trees, mostly barefoot and without harnesses, were batting down clusters of fruit from branches, some of the clusters, he told us, weighing close to a hundred pounds. Under the trees, teams of young boys and girls held onto large pieces of stiff canvas—like fireman's rescue nets—into which the clusters fell, and Hans explained that they'd begun doing this fifteen or sixteen months before— had learned it from one of our engineers, a Turkish man who'd observed the technique when he'd worked in olive groves in southern France. This was giving us an edge on our competitors, he explained, because it minimized the bruising of the nuts and fruit, which, when the clusters fell directly to the ground, had been an ongoing problem during harvest time.

I'd arrived near the end of the harvesting, and the haul this year, Hans said, had exceeded expectations. Although palm oil trees could produce their nuts and fruit within three years, they didn't peak until they were about twenty years old. The grove of trees we were looking at was eighteen years old, and according to Hans was now producing nearly nine thousand metric tons of oil per hectare.

Within a little more than two hours, when we stopped to rest and get out of the sun—Saul, sensing that the heat was wearing me down, had begun shortening his explanations—I'd gained a tangible sense of what, until then, I'd only read about: how the process worked from start to finish—from the harvesting, fermentation, sorting, boiling, mash pressing, purification, digestion (releasing the oil from the nuts), to the purification and drying of the product for storage and shipping.

The machines, large and small, including boilers that were one to two stories high, ran mostly on diesel generators, the generators housed in old, windowless, yellow school busses. Some of the processing was still done by hand, and Nick was at pains to point out that though there were mechanized, steam-driven hydraulic systems that could and did perform most basic tasks for us, the company also paid teams of young men (boys, really, no more than ten or eleven years old) to do the manual threshing: to cut the spikelets from the bunch stems with axes and machetes, and pass the fruits of their labor on to elderly women and small children who sat at long tables and separated the fruit from the spikelets by hand.

The company used battery-driven golf-cart-size cars to transport most of the nuts from the forest to the village, but there was also a steady line of men and women coming in with large baskets of nuts balanced on their heads—another way, Nick pointed out, we were taking initiatives to employ as many local people as possible.

"And with full equality for women, children, and senior citizens," I said.

"Of course," Nick said. "We help the local economy while building a strong sense of community."

"You, me, and J. P. Morgan, right?"

"I think the sun's begun to fry your brain," Nick said. "All that air-conditioning in Singapore must be turning you soft."

While we rested in the shade, Saul switched on the kind of moveable cold-water air-conditioners they'd had in the tent at our first stop. On two ping-pong size tables—in order to educate the workers, he claimed, and boost morale—he'd prepared a small exhibit of the uses to which palm oil could be put: for cooking oil, engine oil, medicines, biofuel, industrial lubricants, food additives, soaps, detergents, and cosmetics, and I acted as if this was all news to me, and refrained from asking why he didn't have a container of napalm next to the other goods.

When it was my turn, I took out charts and papers, at which point Saul beckoned to a young man of about twenty, to whom he showed the papers, which they discussed in whispers, and I became aware that for all his articulateness—his charming British accent, his impeccable courtesy and impressive vocabulary—he could not read.

When I asked where the workers lived and slept, Saul assured me they were well cared for, but Nick laughed and said Saul was being discreet when there was no need for discretion. "Most of them sleep in the fields," Nick said. "Much cooler, and that way we don't have to deduct housing fees from their pay the way other companies do." In his ongoing campaign to persuade me our company was environmentally enlightened, Nick also pointed out that the massive amounts of sludge collected from the bottoms of our boilers and purifiers were used to kill weeds, and he had Saul show me ways we recovered fiber and shells from the early stages of the process and used the residue as fuel for the boilers.

By the third day, when we'd flown forty minutes further inland to one of our smallest operations, a facility that, Nick said, had predated Singapore Palm Oil Technologies Limited's existence, I was feeling achy, dizzy, and nauseated. The constant heat and humidity, and the absence of anything resembling air-conditioning in a village of fewer than three dozen families (an elderly woman would occasionally wipe my face, neck, arms, and shoulders with a damp cloth), made me woozy and faint by midday, and seeing me stagger, Nick put an arm around me, led me back to our plane, laid me down across two seats, had the pilot turn on our air-conditioning, and told me the same thing had happened to him—that he hadn't even lasted a full day his first time here.

"You're stronger than you look," he said.

"Smarter too," I said.

"Of course," he said. "It's why you said yes to coming here to work with me."

By the time I woke, the sun had slipped below the level of the highest trees and there was a slight breeze. Back in the village, Nick had a group of men and women put on a show for me, demonstrating the traditional method of extracting palm oil—washing the fruit mash in warm water, then squeezing the mash by hand to separate the fiber and nuts from the water-and-oil mixture. Next, they passed the mixture through wooden colanders to filter out dirt and debris, after which they placed the mixture in a large iron pot, along with firewood, and set the whole thing boiling.

A few hours later—they'd arranged things as if they were putting on an exhibit at a county fair, so I could see all stages of the process one after the other and not have to wait until each stage was completed before going on to the next—they would take out the firewood, add herbs, and when the mixture cooled to just under a hundred degrees—to the body's temperature—they'd skim off the palm oil with a bowl. The oil, which had a reddish hue from the large amounts of beta-carotene in it, was easy to store and transport because, high in saturated fats, it became semi-solid at moderate temperatures.

The villagers also showed me what they saw as a more modern way of extracting palm oil—using a large screw-press to break down the nuts, then filtering the crushed nuts and shells through a screen. After boiling the mixture, they let gravity do its job, allowing the brew to cool in a large tank so that the palm oil, lighter than water, would separate on its own and rise to the top. In the final stage, the oil was decanted into a metal tank, then re-heated in ordinary cooking pots to remove any remaining impurities.

I slept like a dead man that night, and when I woke in the morning—I was in a small tent made of fine, sepia-colored mosquito netting—Nick was sitting on a stool on the other side of the tent, drinking coffee, and talking with three elderly village men.

I joined them and they immediately began telling me what a good friend to them, and to their families, Nick had been. He'd brought them work, books, medicines, and cell phones. He'd arranged for sons and grandsons to be enrolled in secondary schools in Banjarmasin, and for daughters and granddaughters to be employed as workers and guides in resort areas.

They showed me photos of children and grandchildren, the photos taken at schools and resorts where the young people, in uniform and smiling happily, lived and worked. At the same time that they praised Nick, they also lamented the fact that young people were leaving villages like theirs, and that when their generation died these villages would disappear.

Given enterprises like ours, your villages may be gone sooner than that, I thought of saying, and Nick talked about facilities our company was developing where workers could vacation, and where they could, if they'd worked for us long-term, live out their lives.

"Just like Florida or Arizona," I said.

Nick ignored me, but one of the men touched my hand and said that although Nick refused to take credit, what he said was true, and that these programs had been Nick's idea and no one else's.

I looked at Nick. "I sent in a few proposals, and the company's interested," he said. "We've taken over some old hotels and hospitals and are renovating them to create what I guess could pass for low-end vacation condos. It's a modest start, but it's a start."

"This is true," one of the men said. "Thanks to Mister Nick, my mother and aunt are already living in a home near Turtle Island."

"It's not all altruism," Nick said. "There are ways to do this that will make these places profitable."

"How so?"

"Setting up charitable foundations and using them to process liquid assets we prefer not to have to account for in more visible ways." He stopped. "But look—when we get back to the office I can fill you in on our CFO's plans."

One of the men handed me a photo of his granddaughter, a girl whose face, nearly obliterated, looked like those I remembered seeing in pictures of Vietnamese children who'd been burned by napalm. The girl had been looking into a pot to see if the palm oil had risen to the top when something in the boiling oil—most likely metal shards that had flaked off the inside of the pot—exploded. On the day of the accident, Nick had arranged for the girl to be flown to a hospital in Singapore.

The girl was eight years old, and would never regain sight in her left eye, but everything else about her, the man stated, as if to reassure me—he showed me photos of her face in various stages of reconstruction—would one day return to normal.

"Saint Nick to the rescue once again," I said.

"Just good business practice," Nick said. "Good will breeds good workers. It's what I learned in China—the factories that treated their workers like garbage got garbage for results. The factories that treated their workers like human beings made out okay."

"Speaking of which," he added, handing me a manila envelope, "we've decided to treat our executives well too."

I opened the envelope and found plane tickets, brochures, and an itinerary for 'Crowell's Great Jungle Adventures.'

As soon as Nick explained that the company was paying for four days of R-and-R for me—they'd done the same for him after his first two months—the three men began raving about the wonders I'd be seeing, wonders they themselves had seen rarely if at all, but about which their children and grandchildren had told them.

Nick, his arms around the shoulders of two of the men, was grinning happily, and I had to wonder: Who was this guy I'd been hanging out with on and off for nearly two decades? And I thought, too, about something Max often said: how little we ever really knew other people.

I looked at the cover of one of the brochures—a photo of two orangutans, mother and infant, and of a bird identified as a Scarlet-rumped Trogon, the smallest of its species, along with, in bold-faced print, a promise: that I would see endangered species and vanishing cultures while relaxing in a luxury hotel.

I showed the brochure to Nick.

"True?"

"You bet," he said.

Once I'd seen some of what the men had told me I'd see—orangutans (astonishingly graceful), a monitor lizard (more than seven feet long), a clouded leopard (beautiful beyond beautiful)—and then rivers, jungles, rainforests, underground caves, and not only dozens of endangered species, but a fair number of species (trees, flowers, birds, animals) whose existence had been discovered only within the last decade—I was hooked, changed, transformed—whatever: you name it—and I knew my life would never be the same. And I could admit, even then, that what made the difference—what made the experience so extraordinary—had to do with what Nick talked about: the fact that this world of astonishing natural beauty would soon be gone.

There were eight of us on the tour—an elderly English couple, three middle-aged German businessmen, and two young American women (Alicia, a lawyer, and Amanda, a pediatrician)—and we sat in straightback chairs like schoolchildren, trying to take in what our guide, Tamika, was telling us: that the island of Borneo was home to more than fifteen thousand species of flowering plants, more than three thousand species of trees, and to more than six hundred species of birds. In the past dozen years alone well over five hundred new species of animal, bird, and plant had been discovered on the island. Borneo was the only natural habitat in the world for several endangered species, the Borneo orangutan most famous among them, and Tamika passed around glossy photos of some of the others: the sun bear (the world's tiniest bear), the Sumatran rhino, the pygmy elephant, the proboscis monkey.

Our tour group was staying at a five-star Hilton Hotel in Kuching (which called itself 'the cleanest city in Malaysia'), and my executive suite, on the fifteenth floor, had a magnificent view through floor-to-ceiling windows of the Sarawak River. The high-tech work station was as well-appointed as my office in Singapore, and the bathroom, done in cool shades of gold-flecked marble, had a bidet, a whirlpool, a stereo system, a large flat-screen TV, and a computer-fax console. The hotel itself was an easy hour away by mini-van and boat from Bako National Park.

Tamika, a breathtakingly beautiful woman who appeared to be in her early thirties, and who was several inches taller than I was—at least six-one or six-two—wore crisp, freshly starched khakis like those American forest rangers wore. Her skin was light tan, her eyes green, her hair a deep brown and braided down her back, and her smile, enhanced by dimples in each cheek, enchanting.

"This woman is surely one of the island's natural wonders," I whispered to Alicia, "though I'm curious: do you think she's an endangered species too?"

"She's one of a kind, for sure," Alicia replied, "but not endangered."

"I've never seen anyone quite like her," I said.

"It's why we're here," Alicia said.

On the boat ride across the Sarawak River, Tamika had been warm and friendly, asking us about ourselves, where we were from, why we were there, and what we'd done before coming to the Far East. And of course it turned out she knew Nick, and thought the world of him.

"You know Nick," I said.

"Oh yes."

"Well, who doesn't know Nick," I said.

"He told me you would be coming," she said, "and he warned me about you—about how charming, intelligent, and curious you were—curious about the world, not *curieux* in the way the French use the word. He said you were anything but odd or strange."

"Thanks."

"Nick is a good man, you know."

"So I've been told."

She laughed. "You are on good terms with him, yes?"

"He's not only my best friend," I answered, "but he seems to be my only friend."

"Then you are a most lucky young man. Nick has performed more good deeds for people than I could ever count."

"A veritable Robin Hood of the Far East."

"Robin Hood?"

"Robbing from the rich and giving to the poor."

"Oh not at all." She laughed again, her hand resting on mine. "Nick takes care of *numéro uno* first, last, and always. You may count on that."

"Did you know him in Singapore?"

"Yes. And in Hong Kong before that. And I visited his family in Maine."

"You visited Lorenzo and Eugenia?!" I said, taken aback not only by the fact that she had visited them, but by the news, yet again, of how seemingly generous Nick had been to yet another Asian woman.

"Yes, and Nick's wife Trish—his former wife—and their child, Gabe, who certainly is a curious young man. It was through Nick that I found work in Maine—in Brooklin, not far from Trish and from Nick's parents. I had one of your twelve month work visas, which also came with an additional month for travel."

The Englishman was holding forth about the number of times he'd been in Borneo, the hikes he'd been on, the head-hunters he'd known, the animals he'd killed, and the sights he'd seen. Tamika turned away from him and listened to the Germans talk about the shipping company they worked for—one based in Jakarta, registered in Liberia—and asked if they knew Nick, and if they'd ever transported palm oil for our company.

"It is possible," one of them said, and inquired of the other two, but neither of them recognized Nick's name or the name of our company.

"Perhaps," I suggested, "Nick hasn't helped them the way he's helped you and your friends—women in need, yes?"

"Give it a rest," Tamika said.

"It's why I'm here," I said. "To give it a rest."

"Exactly," Tamika said. "And what I think is that you should try to be a bit less cynical, for I am beginning to fear that what Nick said about you—how exhausted—how *disillusioned* you have become—is true. So: if I can be of service in *your* time of need, you will let me know, of course, yes?"

Even though her breath was on my cheek, and I could smell the sweetness of her skin—a light, lemon-thyme fragrance—there seemed nothing flirtatious about her. Her directness, in fact, seemed as strange—as *curious*—as it was genuine, and this quality—the ability to be friendly without inviting more than friendship—unsettled me, since it was a quality I'd rarely encountered in women, especially beautiful women.

Bako was the oldest national park in Borneo, Tamika informed us, and with an area of about forty square miles, it was also one of the smallest. It possessed the widest range of climate zones of any of Borneo's parks—seven discrete and complete ecosystems—and thus was home to virtually every type of vegetation found on the island. But before we started on our visit—we were sitting on benches just outside the park's entrance—Tamika said that since she had, the day before, learned something about each of us, she thought it only fair that we should know a little about her.

Here's what she told us: Though born and raised in a nearby Bidayuh village, she'd travelled extensively. She'd been a scholarship student at Saint Anne's Catholic Girls School in Kuala Lumpur before going on to study in both Paris and New York City. In New York she'd interned at the Central Park Zoo for six months, and in Paris had studied animal behaviorism at *Université Pierre et Marie Curie*. She'd also worked and studied in Hong Kong, Singapore, and more recently, in Maine, where she'd spent fifteen months as a carpenter's apprentice in a boatyard that built racing boats.

She talked about endangered species less famous than orangutans, bearded pigs, or clouded leopards (plants, trees, flowers, and birds I'd never heard of), passed around more photos, then asked if any of us knew why species such as these were more in danger now than they'd been for Borneo's entire known history.

I raised my hand.

"Yes?"

"Two words," I said: "Palm oil."

"Mister Eisner is correct," Tamika said, and thanked me, adding that because I worked for a palm oil manufacturing company, I was a person who knew what he was talking about. Then: "Can you tell us more, Mister Eisner?"

"Please call me Charlie," I said.

"Well then, Charlie," she said. "Can you tell us more?"

"Sure," I said, and I found myself regurgitating a lot of stuff I'd learned when, during my first weeks in Singapore, I'd spent dozens of hours Googling 'palm oil' while waiting for Nick to take me to my next appointment, or tell me what my responsibilities were. I talked about how the cutting of timber and the burning of rainforests and of land that lay above peat bogs was releasing large and dangerous quantities of carbon into the atmosphere, and how the resulting fires and deforestation were more damaging to the climate than any benefits that might be gained by switching to biofuels made from palm oil. I talked about how the deforestation was depriving significant numbers of birds and animals of their natural habitats, was encroaching on the last remnants of primary rain forest, and I said that when these rainforests were gone, they'd be gone forever.

I paused, and Tamika cocked her head to the side in a way that said, 'Keep going, please.'

The clearing of forests also reduced biodiversity, increased vulnerability to fires, and had nasty effects on indigenous communities that depended on forest ecosystems for survival, I said, in addition to which, the large amounts of petroleum-based pesticides, herbicides, and fertilizers used in the cultivation of palm oil polluted local areas while at the same time contributing to greenhouse gas emissions. According to some studies, the clearing, draining, and burning of Borneo's peatland was by itself responsible for more than eight percent of the entire planet's fossil fuel emissions.

"Anything else?" Tamika asked.

"Before I left Singapore," I said, "I saw a report from the World Health Organization claiming that palm oil consumption increases the risk of heart disease."

I exhaled. "Enough?"

"For now," Tamika said, "though I am wondering if you might answer one additional question."

"Probably."

"*Probably?!*" she laughed. "Well, let me take a chance, given how forthright you have been so far. But tell us, Charlie: When it comes to palm oil and its production here in Borneo, are you for or against?"

"Got you there, lad," the Englishman said.

"Look," I said. "I was just answering your question. Whether I'm for or against palm oil production hardly matters given the push—the money—behind what's been going on here, and—"

"I did not mean to put you on the defensive," Tamika said. "We thank you for sharing so much information with us, especially given who your employer is. We really do. Our lips are sealed, of course—yes, everybody?"

The others nodded their agreement, and a few minutes later, we entered the park.

On our first day in Bako, we walked along paths bordered by freshwater mangrove forests, explored a cave where remains of human communities that existed perhaps twenty thousand years ago had been discovered, and climbed through a small rainforest to the top of a mountain that gave a spectacular view of long, empty, golden beaches, and of the South China Sea. We saw orangutans, silver-leaf monkeys, and an astonishing variety of birds: a red-crowned barbet, a cuckoo dove, a black-backed swamphen, a crested goshawk, and kingfishers, flycatchers, and snipes, and while we walked, Tamika named what we saw, and told us which birds and animals were endangered, and which were flourishing. She talked about the great Deer Cave, among the two or three biggest underground caves, which was not far from Kuching, and which she urged us to visit—it had the capacity to hold five cathedrals the size of London's St Paul's, and was home to at least three million bats who produced piles of guano that could rise to more than three hundred feet high.

After lunch we hiked along trails bordered by sumptuous

beds of wild orchids, along with flowers called pitcher plants that to my eyes were often indistinguishable from the orchids— carnivorous plants that fed on insects, and had seductive vulva-shaped, satin-skinned flowers.

What amazed—and pleased—was not only how lush and plentiful everything was—how variegated the brush, trees, and streams, how vivid and various in shape and color the birds, how well-kept the trails, rest stops, and beaches, but also how, on that day and the three that followed, we didn't encounter a single other human being. I felt at times as if we were the last people on earth, and when I said this to Tamika, she said she'd sometimes felt the same way, but the good news was that it wasn't so. Because we were here, she said, the chances that endangered species would survive were greatly increased.

I could understand why she might *hope* we could make a difference in saving a world so dear to her, I said, but in terms of cause and effect, what she said made no sense. That we were here—tourists—had nothing to do with whether or not beasts, birds, flowers, and trees survived.

"Ah, Charlie," she replied, "are you not being *merely* rational when you think that way?"

"I suppose," I said, and our discussion ended there. When we were in the boat on our way back to the hotel, however, she sat next to me and told me again that I was mistaken. It was because of visitors like me that she was encouraged to believe that much of her native land would still be saved.

I shrugged, and instead of arguing, recited a line that had been with me on and off for much of the day. "'Death is the mother of beauty,'" I said.

"Oh yes!" she exclaimed. "'Death is the mother of beauty'— of course!—that is a *wonderful* way to understand what's happening here, and it reinforces everything I believe."

"You don't understand," I said.

"But I do," she said. "Nick once said the same words when he was here."

"What I said isn't from Nick," I shot back. "It's from a poem—a line from a poem he heard from *me* that I heard from my father and that my father took from a poet named Wallace Stevens."

"Well, there is a trail there too, then, is there not?" she said.

"A *trail*?"

"In the way we make our associations and, thus, are connected to one another."

"You don't get it," I said.

"No," she said. "*You* do not get it." Then she squeezed the back of my neck between thumb and forefinger, hard.

When we were back at the hotel, she shook hands with each of us, and said she would meet us in the same place at seven-fifteen the next morning. I felt dizzy, light-headed—confused, really—and eager to get away because the last thing I wanted was to talk about what I'd seen, thought, felt, or was feeling. In a world of strange, new experiences and sudden, startling contrasts—from the utterly sublime (the beauty of the place was so exquisitely otherworldly as to be almost unbearable), to the predictably banal (the English couple, the German businessmen), and irritating (but why did the hotel's lavish perks, or Tamika's naïve optimism get under my skin?)—the only thing I wanted was to be in a place without others and without sound—a place where I wouldn't have to be with, talk with, or listen to anyone ever again.

But Tamika held onto my hand until the others were gone. I was afraid for a second she was going to offer me some kind of private tour where she'd try to prove she was right and I was wrong about saving Borneo (or the planet!), or where I'd feel obligated to try to seduce her (so that she'd have the pleasure of rejecting me?), or where she'd want to talk about Nick's good deeds, but she'd kept me from leaving only to tell me she was getting together with Alicia and Amanda after dinner—she hadn't wanted the others to feel left out—and if I wanted to stop by their suite, I'd be welcome. She let go of me then, and when she did, and when I watched her step into the mini-van and pull the door closed behind her, I realized she was considerably older than I'd thought at first—and also, a more unsettling realization: that this woman I'd found so enchanting might not be what she seemed: that she might not be a woman at all.

"You may watch," Tamika said.

I sat in an easy chair while, like performers setting up for an old-fashioned *tableau vivant*, they assumed their poses. Tamika wore a royal blue silk strapless full-length gown, and Alicia and Amanda wore white blouses and pleated gray skirts of the kind worn by girls at prep schools. Without holding hands, the three of them moved in a circle, counterclockwise, their heads tilted backward. Debussy's *La Mer* was playing softly.

"So, Mister Eisner," Amanda asked. "Who are we?"

"The three graces," I answered.

"Correct," Amanda said. "And representing—?"

"Beauty, charm, and creativity."

"Correct again," Amanda said. "But that still doesn't mean you've been granted permission to touch us."

When I'd entered the suite, they were drinking champagne and feeding appetizers to one another—raw shrimp, samosas, curry puffs, mushrooms, olives. They sat across from me, side by side on a plush russet-colored couch, told me about themselves, asked me about myself. Alicia had grown up and gone to school in Boston (Boston Latin, Radcliffe, Harvard Law School), where she now worked as a litigator. Amanda, who'd grown up in Bradford, a small Rhode Island town near Watch Hill, had gone to Duke and then to the University of North Carolina School of Medicine at Chapel Hill, and was a pediatrician in Newton.

When *La Mer* came on, they'd risen and moved to the middle of the room, where, without touching, they turned in languid circles.

"Are you ready?" Tamika asked me.

"*Me?*"

"Am I talking to someone else?"

"I suppose not," I said.

"Then turn down the lights, please? That way if you become bored watching us, you can either take a nap or go to the window and watch the stars come out."

I turned down the lights. "The three graces are not the same as the three muses," I offered. "Did you know that? Because if..."

"Shh," Tamika said, a finger to her lips. "Be a good boy now."

They joined hands again, and continued in a circle, first one way, and then the other. Some time later—ten minutes? twenty?—the music stopped, and they stood still—immobile—their breathing deep and steady.

Then Alicia stepped toward Tamika, and rested her hands on Tamika's shoulders, while Amanda, from behind, undid Tamika's gown, and let it fall to the floor. Tamika wore no undergarments, and she was, I saw—why would I have thought otherwise?—very much a woman. Her breasts were smaller than I'd imagined, her hips wider, and her stomach surprisingly ample, with a lovely ripple of extra flesh at her waist. I sipped my champagne—my third or fourth flute by this time—and I thought: how wonderful it must be to be Tamika—to be an exceptionally tall, beautiful woman whose body, as she headed into her middle years, was just beginning to know the sweet, natural effects of time and gravity.

Amanda, still in her schoolgirl outfit, rose on her toes and kissed Tamika lightly on the mouth. She and Tamika flicked tongues for a while, after which they began to kiss with increasing passion while Alicia, on her knees, put her mouth to the base of Tamika's spine, and began kissing and licking her there. Tamika sighed, and that was when I found myself thinking not of Seana's novel, but of my father telling me about it after he'd read it the first time—about the mother-daughter-father *ménage à trois*, of how original and—his word—*delicious* he found it, and of how proud he was of Seana, and I wondered: would I ever feel free enough to tell him about what I was seeing now?

I also wondered if Nick had been invited to watch a performance like this when he'd been here, and as soon as I imagined him sitting where I was, the pleasure I'd been feeling washed out of me. I watched Alicia get down on her knees, part the folds of Tamika's sex, and lick her gently even as, still on her knees, Amanda parted Tamika's cheeks and began probing Tamika's anus with her tongue. Eyes closed, Tamika stared ahead with a look of such extraordinary contentment that for a moment I was able to put aside the bitterness I was feeling toward Nick so that I could try again to imagine what it might be like to be Tamika.

After a while I closed my eyes and drifted off into a pleasant haze, and I must have dozed off, because when I opened my eyes Amanda and Alicia were lying side by side on the floor—they were naked, their uniforms nowhere in sight—and Tamika was tending to them lovingly. I watched for a while but nothing they did aroused me, and this was surprising because when I'd watched lesbian porn films—this had started at Smith College with girlfriends there—the films had always turned me on. Nor did my presence seem to make a difference. Although they'd seemed happy enough to have me in the room, once they'd begun playing with one another, they never really noticed me again, so a bit later on, while the three of them lay on the carpeting, happy and exhausted, I set my glass down and, as quietly as I could, left the room.

The next morning, when I boarded the mini-van, Alicia and

Amanda were already there, and they acted as if we were what we were and nothing else: three American tourists staying in a luxury hotel in Kuching and looking forward to what promised to be a second fascinating day in Bako National Park. They were so friendly and pleasant, as Tamika was when she arrived a few minutes later (Did you sleep well? Have you had breakfast? Did you remember to bring bug spray? Have you been keeping up with news from the States?), that I was on the verge, several times, of asking if what had happened the night before had actually taken place.

As soon as we were in Bako, though, my mind stopped working and my senses took over. "What I trust Bako will prove to you," Tamika had announced on our way across the Sarawak River, "is that you do not have to die to enter paradise," and to demonstrate that this was so, she took us further inland to some of her favorite places: into a cave nearly a mile long that had marvelous chambers within chambers, extraordinary calcite formations, and several recently discovered wall paintings—stick figures of men, women, and birds whose meaning and date of creation were not yet known. We moved along trails that brought us to beaches of pristine white sand, and then up a mountainside to a rainforest canopy where we crossed, single file, along a catwalk suspended several hundred feet above ground, and where I felt as if I were floating through a world whose very beauty seemed an intimation of its imminent demise.

Thick mists came and went so that lakes and waterfalls, distant low-lying hills, and beaches below, were, by turns, invisible, or suddenly, magically revealed, and all the while a multitude of birds—small, large, strange—would fly by, adding splashes of bright, unexpected color to the moody greens and browns of the forests. We swam, we clambered up small ridges, and we gathered herbs, fruit, ferns, and bamboo shoots from which we prepared our midday meal. Tamika was especially delighted when, while we'd stopped for a late-afternoon snack near some swampy lowlands, a proboscis monkey suddenly appeared and moved toward us. Unlike silver-tailed monkeys or pig-tailed macaques, she said, proboscis monkeys rarely approached human beings. There were only about a hundred and fifty of them left in the world (they existed nowhere but in Borneo), and we laughed when she explained the obvious: that they received their names because of their large noses, which noses resembled nothing other than a man's private appendage. The larger the nose, Tamika said, the more attractive the male was to the females.

What seemed weird was that a woman so outrageously beautiful could seem in these moments to be the Malaysian equivalent of a Girl Scout guide. She was such a pleasant source of detailed information, and so without airs or condescension in the dispensing of the information, that by my last day in Bako I was amazed to realize I'd stopped thinking of her as a woman, or even of what might be going on with her, Amanda, and Alicia, but simply as the person who'd introduced me to a place more sublime and glorious than any I'd ever expected to see in this life.

I saw flying lizards and flying lemurs, green-crested lizards, small-clawed otters, hairy-nosed otters, and whip snakes. I hiked alongside underground rivers, explored caves whose caverns opened to plateaus of brush and scrub that were home to birds and flowers of astonishing color and beauty—owls and kingfishers, heath forests and antplants, pepper gardens and hibiscus and swamp vegetation and—our rare good luck—a single flowering rafflesia, the world's largest flower (the one we came upon was nearly three feet across and Tamika estimated it would weigh in at nearly fifteen pounds). It had red-orange, lobe-like petals that gave off an awful stench, like that of a rotting carcass, and though it had taken most of a year to transform itself from bud to flower, Tamika said, it would probably be gone by sunset the next day. And when, back in my suite at the end of each day,

I'd reflect on what I'd seen, I'd find myself thinking that were I to stay in Borneo—or in this one part of Borneo—for the rest of my life, I'd never see everything there was to see, and never grow tired of seeing again what I'd already seen.

On the evening before I flew back to Singapore, I sat outside at a waterfront café, gazing at a calm, teal-blue sea spotted here and there with fishing boats. The sunset, in striated layers of red and orange, with a stormy, turbulent purple-green bank of slow-moving clouds behind it, was, for the moment, serene. Tamika sat a few tables away, eating dinner with the Germans, and Amanda and Alicia were at a table next to them with two American men about my age they introduced as Harvard and MIT grads who were in Borneo to do post-graduate field work in archaeology. By the time they left the café, they'd paired off, Amanda holding hands with the Harvard man, Alicia with the guy from MIT, and I found myself imagining them, a few months later, getting together in Boston, strolling happily on the Common, then dining at the Harvard Faculty Club, where, perhaps, they would one day be married, and where, a year or two after this their children would be taking naps in identical bright red strollers while Amanda and Alicia and their husbands enjoyed a Sunday brunch and reminisced about their adventures in Kuching.

But the thought of never leaving Borneo—of making arrangements that would enable me to stay in this one place forever so I could come to know it as much as I loved it—put me in mind, that last evening in Kuching, of something Max had impressed upon me when I was twelve or thirteen and was first discovering girls: That you can get to know women—what they're like in all their loveliness and mystery—in two ways (and he was here quoting something from Seana's novel he said she'd borrowed from Tolstoy), either by knowing and loving many women... or by knowing and loving one woman well.

I returned to Borneo nineteen times in the next three years, and never (with the exception of visits to our production facilities) to the same place twice. Most trips were business-related, but with Nick's cooperation (we covered for each other whenever we made our getaways), I'd usually be able to tack on a day or two and visit a place I hadn't been to before. I was also able to go on a half-dozen extended trips—three- to five-day excursions (again, with Nick watching the store the way I did for him) where I explored places few Westerners had ever seen.

I climbed to the top of Mount Kinabalu—at more than thirteen thousand feet, the world's third highest island—from which, on a wickedly clear day, I saw all the way to the Philippines. I took longboats down the Kapuas, Borneo's longest river, camped in villages that had been home less than a hundred years ago to headhunters, and went on several World Wildlife Fund tours that took me into national parks (Kutai, Gunung Mulu, Tanjung Puting) and, on Nick's recommendation, to some of Borneo's coastal islands, where I snorkeled, and swam alongside giant sea turtles and hammerhead sharks.

I saw clownfish, giant sting rays, and World War Two Japanese shipwrecks shrouded in jewel-like coral. I swam close to tornado-like flurries of barracuda. I saw Sumatran rhinos and tigers, forests dense with two-hundred-foot-high flowering dipterocarp trees, and schools of migrating white sharks. I even came, eventually, to luxuriate in Borneo's heat and humidity—to love having the sweat pour from me, and to welcome friendly leeches that made their homes on the slippery slopes of my arms and shoulders. When the spirit was willing I enjoyed nights of love and companionship with women who were as skilled as they were kind. I ate spicy meals composed of plants, insects, and animals whose identities were unknown to me, and I made my way (several times without guides) to places that had until recent years been impassable and unexplored, and all the while

I was glorying in these wonders, I'd also be imagining that long before I died, everything I was seeing would be transformed utterly.

I'd stare at a peat swamp forest, a bank of orchids, or a waterfall, and I'd imagine the peat burning, the orchids being bulldozed under, the waterfall blasted away by dynamite. I imagined forests being cut down as if by giant lawnmowers, tree trunks gliding along conveyor belts as wide as highways, then propelled past huge blade-saws that sliced them into chopsticks or slats for garden furniture. And sometimes, walking through a jungle or a heath forest, the laughter and chatter of cicadas, squirrels, or thrushes permeating the air—my senses drenched in sound, smell, and color—I'd suddenly, as if on an LSD trip gone bad, be struck blind: the world would turn stark white, all sound would vanish, and the moist silence would touch my face as if made of millions of slow-falling snowflakes. *Was I even there?* My breath gone and my heart pumping away at two to three times its usual rate, I'd have to lower my head below my waist, squeeze my eyes shut a half-dozen times, and press my hands against my ears as hard as I could before the terror would leave—before I'd begin to breathe again and the whiteness that had swallowed me would dissolve and give way to what was in front of me.

When I visited our production facilities, I'd see multiples of what I'd seen on my first trip: peat swamps and montane forests burning and turning the sky black with smoke—clouds of it so vast they could, I knew, be seen from outer space as if they were floating continents. I saw remnants of Borneo's primeval rainforests ravaged by earth movers and chainsaws so that, when the machines left, it was as if the forests had never existed. I saw swarms of birds—red-crested, orange-breasted, green-billed, white-tailed, gray-feathered—careening wildly in circles as they searched for resting places—homes—now gone forever. I saw mouse deer and palm civets, Asian elephants and pygmy elephants, orangutans and packs of monkeys foraging in the garbage of company encampments, or wandering like lost, drunken souls across scorched, barren earth. And, truth be told, all the while, trip after trip, the pain and sadness I felt for what was being destroyed was at least equalled by exhilaration and joy—by the thrill that came from watching the dying of a world that would never be with us again.

But such thoughts came to me only when I was in Borneo. When I was in Singapore, I worked hard and played hard—ten- to twelve-hour days at the office, parties until dawn, and happy in my apartment, just me, on weekends while Nick was courting one of his new ladies.

I met two or three of them a year, and they all came from prosperous Chinese families, and they were all attractive, poised, well-educated, and well-mannered. They all fell in love with Nick, and once they reached a point where they believed they could not live without him, and told him so—that he was the sun, moon, and stars to them, that they hoped to marry him, to bear his children, and to live with him forever—he would dump them.

They came to me the way other young women had gone to him. But the women who'd gone to Nick, like Jin-gen, had mostly been poor women from the Chinese countryside who'd come to Hong Kong or Singapore in search of better lives for themselves and for the families they'd left behind. The women who came to me were wealthy women who'd been raised in cities like Shanghai, Hong Kong, Singapore, and Taipei, and though Nick didn't take money from them and give it to women he was helping (Tamika was right about him being no Robin Hood), he took what was decidedly more valuable.

As he'd once bragged when we were at UMass and he was plowing the twin daughters *and* the wife of a local Polish farmer, he could charm thorns from a rose when he wanted to, and once these upper-class Chinese women fell in love with him and introduced him to their families, and once their families accepted him, Nick was out of there. And after he'd taken their virtue, they were, in the eyes of their community—fathers and grandfathers especially—forever disgraced.

"Who will marry me now?" Lo-chin asked. "Tell me, please, Mister Charles—who will ever, *ever* marry me now?"

Lo-chin was the first to come to me, and with a question I'd hear again and again (she appeared at my apartment on a Saturday morning, disguised, to avoid her family's watchfulness, in a house-cleaner's uniform), but when I told Nick about her visit, he laughed.

"Hey—she took her chances the same as I did."

"But that's not so," I said. "It's not a level playing field, Nick."

"There are no level playing fields," he said.

"But can't you at least talk with her?"

"Look, Charlie," he said. "The only thing talking with me will do is to raise false hopes. Best is to let things lie, and for Lo-chin to come up with a story. So maybe she tells her mother she wasn't telling the truth about our intimacy—that she thought it would please her mother to believe that though she may have lost her cherry, she'd soon become the bride of the man who'd taken it."

"But we're talking about a young woman's *life*, Nick," I said. "I don't get it."

"But that's why I'm explaining things to you, Charlie," he said. "Because sometimes you see the world through those rose-colored, small-town glasses of yours. Because these Chinese families are more puritanical than our own born-again Christians. Because if they believe their daughter's slept with a man, they assume—and usually demand—that the man become her husband. But that's Chinese dealing with Chinese, and what Lo-chin can tell the old lady—it's worked before—is that I turned out to be just another greedy American. She can say I promised to marry her, sure, but that I said she had to give me what I wanted first, and so she fibbed about me compromising her honor to please the old lady—so the old lady would believe she'd soon be the mother of a bride—but at the last minute, see, Lo-chin had the courage to just say no."

"That's absurd."

"Probably. But you're the guy with the vivid imagination—a chip off the old block, right?—so whatever cock-and-bull story you come up with that does the job for Lo-chin will be fine by me."

As I expected, Lo-chin was horrified by the idea of deceiving her mother by claiming she'd previously deceived her, and when, a few months later, I went to Nick on behalf of another woman who'd come to me, Nick suggested that if I cared so much about these women, maybe I should marry one of them.

We were partying in Jan Martens' apartment (Jan was a young cousin of the guy I'd met on my first trip to our palm oil plantations), and Nick and I were both pretty wasted when I mentioned to him that Lin-fan, the woman he'd been with for two or three months, had visited me and declared she was going to kill herself if she lost Nick.

"Is that a threat or a promise?" Nick asked, and added that Lin-fan was full of it—that he'd been straight with her from the beginning about his intentions, or—to be more exact—his *lack* of intentions.

"You really get off on this, don't you?" I said.

Nick gestured to the party going on around us. "Get off on what—on having a good time, on spreading the wealth?"

"On being cruel," I said.

"*Cruel?!*" He jabbed me in the chest. "Don't make me laugh, buddy. Cruel in order to be kind, maybe—because I gave these women the best times of their lives. I gave them memories to cherish during the long years that lie in wait after their families marry them off to some rich Chinese dodo, and after—"

"*If!*" I said.

"*If?*"

"*If* the families can find someone to marry them now that you've gotten what you want."

"That's holier-than-thou bullshit I can live without," he said, "because the truth—and you came halfway around the world to prove it—is that money, even more than our precious palm oil, is the universal lubricant. Money buys *everything* in this life, Charlie, in case you hadn't heard, and these people have more money than God. Like I've been saying, China's the future, baby, so sign up early."

A woman who'd been nuzzling me was now stroking me along the inside of my thigh. I grabbed her hand, crushed it closed. She drew closer, whispered that she liked rough sex too, and that I could take her home whenever I wanted.

"And anyway, I'm not the marrying kind," Nick said. "I tried it once, remember? And what'd I get for it?"

"A wife and a son."

"Well, you got *that* right," he said, and roared with laughter. "You really got that right, Charlie boy."

"Goddamn it, Nick—I told you before never to call me Charlie boy," I said, and found myself taking a wild swing at him. But I was so drunk, I missed completely, lost my balance, and flopped back down onto the couch.

Then, as if he'd scripted the scene ahead of time, a woman I hadn't noticed before stood above us, said she was Yue-ming's sister and was here to thank Nick for what he'd done for Yue-ming, who'd been working as an *au pair* in Massachusetts—in Marblehead—and who'd just sent news that she was engaged to marry a nephew of the family she'd been working for.

"See what I mean?" Nick said.

"I give up," I said, and slumped down deeper into the couch.

"Yue-ming will take her husband's faith," the young woman stated. "Her new name will be Sarah—Sarah *Kaplan*, once she is married—and she wanted me to bring you the happy news."

Bowing courteously, the woman started to back away, but Nick reached out, grabbed her hand.

"And you'd like to go to her wedding, right?"

The woman nodded.

"Of course," Nick said. "So write down your info before you leave and give it to me, and I'll see that it happens."

The woman nodded, bowed again, and left.

Chuckling to himself, Nick repeated the name 'Sarah Kaplan' a few times, then draped an arm around my shoulder. "Oh you Jews, you Jews—when it comes to money, you can always smell the future, can't you?"

"Look who's talking, all these rich Chinese women you go after."

"Think about it for a second, though," he said. "If it was money I was after, I could have staked my claim back when you and I were feasting on horny Jewish sorority chicks from Brookline and Longmeadow—JAPs, not Chinese, in those days…"

"Forget it."

"That's what my old man told me to do, by the way," Nick went on. "Much as he hated Jews—envied them, you ask me— he was never too proud to take their money—told me to do the same. But I came out here instead, and I stayed. Why?" He gestured to the party going on around us. "Because life is good here, Charlie. You see that, right?"

"Yes. Sometimes…"

"You were always a fast learner."

"But you set me up," I said. "I see that too."

"You didn't need much help. I did like your spunk, though— the way you tried to haul off on me to protect the honor of a lady."

"But *why*, Nick? Why do you do it?'

"Do what?"

"Make them fall in love with you."

"Ah—a question I've asked myself many times."

"And the answer?"

He cupped his chin in his hand, furrowed his brow. Then: "That's right."

"*What's* right?"

"Yes."

"But…"

The woman who'd said I could take her home had slipped her hand inside my shirt and was pinching my nipples.

"You shouldn't disappoint the lady," Nick said, "and I'll see you Monday morning at the office."

He stood, started to wander off, then turned back. "So why do I do it?" he asked. "Okay. That's an easy one, since there's only one true answer, same as always: because I can."

Drunk as I was, it occurred to me, and not for the first time, that like a kid idolizing a star ballplayer—or my father's students idolizing him—I looked up to Nick not because I admired him and what he did, but because I wanted to be him: I wanted to be able to say and do what I wanted when I wanted to. What sheer freedom—and power—that would be! To be free, as Nick preached, of the usual burdens and responsibilities most people lived with most of the time. To do what you wanted when you wanted simply because you could…

The woman's hand was resting lightly on my stomach, her fingers moving south, and I grabbed her wrist, yanked her hand away, stood up, stumbled to the bathroom, put my finger down my throat, and puked big-time into the toilet.

After I'd flushed, and gone to the sink and washed, I looked up. In the mirror, I saw that Nick was leaning against the door, grinning.

"Vintage Hemingway," he said.

"Vintage what?"

"Hemingway," he said.

"Meaning?"

"Ask your old man—he's the expert on stuff like that. But in Papa's world-view, see, whenever someone has to face the truth—or death—and can't do it—whenever a guy sees that his life's come to shit—whenever he lies to himself and sees himself for the coward he truly is—he goes and pukes. Same crap, story after story. Trouble was that—like you, brother—Hemingway was too earnest, right?"

Pleased with his word-play, Nick grinned more broadly. "But like I said, if you don't believe me, you can ask your old man."

After a while I stopped going to Nick when his women came to me. And after a while I stopped hanging out with him after work and on weekends. He went his way and I went mine pretty much, and what this meant was that I spent what free time I had either in Borneo or figuring out how to get there.

When I was in Borneo, no matter where—in a luxury hotel, a village hut, or camping out on a beach—I was happy. My life there seemed as rich and beautiful as the trees, flowers, mountains, meadows, lakes, caves, and rivers I was discovering—and as doomed as the forests, fields, birds, and animals that were fast disappearing. In Borneo, my senses were alive in ways they'd never been before, yet at the same time I'd sometimes feel as if I weren't there at all: as if I didn't exist, and never had. High on a mountain, or in the thick of a rainforest, I'd feel so exhilarated—so comforted—that I didn't care if I lived or died, or if I ever returned home.

Slowly, slowly, even at the office, feelings generated when I was in Borneo, or alone in my apartment on weekends, began to push aside the part of me Nick had been preying on. The fact that someone else with my education and smarts could have done what I was doing—that I was both dispensable and interchangeable—this realization not only filled me with joy, but enabled me to give up any morsel of rage I might have had toward what our company was doing. I came to take pleasure from the long hours spent at the office and at our palm oil plantations precisely because it was true that if I didn't do what I was doing, someone else would. And there was this too: the more time I spent in Borneo, the smaller Nick became.

Then I got lucky. Yu-huan, a woman Nick had been seeing for a few months, came to me, not to ask me to plead with Nick, but to tell me what she was going to do if and when he broke up with her. Like the others, Yu-huan was born into a wealthy Chinese family—hers owned an import-export business in fishing gear: nets, traps, hooks, lines, motors, and various electronic gizmos. Her great-grandfather, illiterate but ingeniously shrewd in playing the Communists against the Nationalists, and in his timing—knowing which side to play when—had built up the business after the Second World War, and at ninety-three years old was still running it, still going over every detail of every contract before affixing his 'chop'—the seal that represented his name—without which 'chop' no deal could be finalized.

What was different about Yu-huan was that she didn't care if Nick married her or not. She'd fallen in love with him, yes, and had been foolish, for sure, but her foolishness, she said, had given her something more precious than love: the chance to be independent in the way men in her family were, which meant, she said (and in language that sounded like stuff I'd been hearing from women in the States for years), not being dependent upon a husband for her identity and well-being. What she *did* desire, however, was to have Nick's child, and about this she'd found within herself the ability, like her great-grandfather, to be ruthless.

'Decide what you want,' her great-grandfather had taught her, 'and take it, and in the taking beware, above all, of useless moral scruples.' Yu-huan had made inquiries, and had discovered the way Nick had treated other women from families like hers, and having this information, she said, gave her the courage to act upon her great-grandfather's teachings. So that if and when she became pregnant with Nick's son (and the child, she insisted—even mild skepticism was forbidden—would be male), and if he refused to marry her, instead of killing herself, or having an abortion (her inquiries also revealed what I didn't deny: that I'd arranged an abortion for one of Nick's ex-girlfriends), she would kill him. In this way, she reasoned, the father of her child being dead, there would be no shame in having the child, only public mourning for the man to whom, she would claim (a claim to be verified by her mother and an aunt, in both of whom she would have previously, and falsely, confided), she had been secretly betrothed.

Her plan had had its equivalent in an earlier era—it had prevailed, she said, throughout the nineteenth century—when it had been possible for a young Chinese woman to marry a dead man. The arrangement was called a 'ghost marriage,' and it enabled families to consolidate wealth and power while permitting young women to pursue their ambitions without the interference of husbands.

When she came to me the first time, she was two weeks late in her menstrual cycle, and though alarmed by her plan and by the eerily toneless way she presented it (and alarmed, too, to realize how much it appealed to me), I tried to show nothing. I heard her out, then asked why she'd chosen to confide in me.

"Because I have seen the way you look at Nick when he is not looking at you," she said, "and therefore know you will understand what I am going to do if I must, and that you will not oppose me or betray me."

"Of course not," I said.

"And because I have come to understand myself well enough to know I cannot do what I am going to do alone. Therefore, I have decided to place my trust in you."

"Yes," I said.

"Yes what?"

"Yes, you can trust me."

By the time she came to me five weeks later, she had confirmed the fact that she was pregnant and that the child would be a boy. She'd informed Nick and, as expected, he'd told her it wasn't his problem—he'd made no promises, had advised her to take precautions—and declared there was no way under the sun he was going to marry her. In fact, given her condition, it was best, he'd declared, if they never saw each other again.

"I am, therefore, going to follow through on my plan," she said, "which will embody in my newborn son a triumph of both justice and vengeance. And I am here today to invite you to be with me when I do what I must do."

She was so serene in the way she presented her decision—her gray-green eyes clear and unwavering while seeming to demand that I return her gaze with equal resolve—that I didn't know what to do except to nod assent, and to blink a few times so that we didn't get into a stare-me-down contest.

"Am I bitter?" she asked calmly. "Of course. But my bitterness, I have found, is bringing more joy than love ever has. Can you understand that?"

"I can understand why you'd want to do away with Nick," I said. "Sure. You're not the first, believe me."

"I know that," she said.

"But look," I said. "You can't just go around killing people whenever you want."

"Why not?" she said.

"Why *not*?"

"Yes. Why not? People do it all the time, in your country and in mine, though I will admit we do not often perform the act ourselves—that we have the luxury of employing other people to do it for us. Certainly the men in my family are not strangers to such matters."

For a moment, I found myself wondering what might happen to me if she came to doubt my loyalty, and I had to wonder too, as I already had, about what demons might lie below her cool affect, and whether or not I was dealing with a seriously deranged woman. The instant this thought passed through my mind, though, she put her hand on top of mine.

"I am not mad, Charles," she said. "Not at all. And I will take full responsibility for the consequences of my act, both for me and for my child. You will in no way be implicated."

She stroked my hand gently even as she repeated what she'd said before: that she took joy not only from being pregnant, but from the prospect of being a *mother without a husband*—a free woman!—and while she talked, she continued to caress my hand, glancing down at my lap now and then and smiling with amusement to let me know she'd noticed what I couldn't hide: that I was becoming aroused.

"I am strong enough to follow through on my intention," she said. "But, as I have confessed before, I am not strong enough to do so by myself. In this—my need to have a man by my side—I remain weak. But because this is who I am, I must ask you to answer one question."

"Sure," I said.

"Do you care if Nick lives or dies?"

"No," I said, and I didn't add that there were times (though this happened mostly in Borneo, rarely in Singapore) when I no longer cared whether *I* lived or died.

"Good," she said. "Then we are in agreement."

"No," I said, and when I said the word this time, I felt a strange and pleasant rush, for instead of seeing Yu-huan's smile, I saw Max looking out at me from her face. As soon as I started to smile at him, though, I felt a blazing jolt that made me double over in pain—an arrow of electricity zapping through me while I watched two wires, like snakes, uncoil inside my chest, one from each side of my rib cage, their frayed ends touching, sparking, sizzling...

"Are you all *right*?" Yu-huan was asking. "Talk to me, Charles. Please. Do you need to lie down?"

I shook my head sideways, but did not speak.

"Would you like to withdraw your answer, and think more about it?" she asked.

I shook my head sideways again, took deep breaths.

"We are not in a rush," she said. "By my arithmetic, we still have six and one half months until the time for…"

"No," I said again. "No," and I gathered the strength to stand—we were in my living room on a Sunday evening—and I walked across the room, my eyes on my shoes as they set down, one in front of the other, on the carpeting. I fixed us tall, strong drinks: vodka and tonic—eighty percent vodka, twenty percent tonic. We clinked glasses, then sat side by side without talking, and after a short while I found my voice and told her the story I'd been remembering a few moments before, from when I was nine or ten years old—about how my father had returned home one afternoon from the funeral of a colleague—a man about his age whom I'd met a few times but didn't really know—and about how, when I met my father at the front door and gave him a hug, and said something about it probably being a very sad day for him, to have gone to a funeral and seen a friend lowered into the ground, he'd shrugged.

"No loss," he'd said.

"No loss? I don't understand."

"When some people leave the world, we're better for it," he said, and he did so in a very off-hand manner, after which he smiled at me with great affection—the smile that was like Yu-huan's—put his arm around me, and walked me toward our kitchen.

"So let's talk about supper," he said. "What are you in the mood for?"

In truth, I never believed Yu-huan would or could kill Nick, though I did believe she believed she would. But she was determined to have their son, no matter the price, and somewhere along the way I'd made the decision to help her through the pregnancy and its aftermath as best I could. She took to visiting me regularly on Sunday evenings when I was in town—to report on the state of her health and the baby's, and to renew her vows concerning Nick's fate. We drank quite a lot—she declared it nonsense to think that mere alcohol could sap her son's health or strength—and once she began drinking, she became a different woman. The placid demeanor vanished, and she became animated, expansive, exuberant. She talked about her son, and the life that lay ahead for him—in her plans, the two of them would emigrate either to New York City (where she'd never been, though her English was virtually flawless from her years in British schools in Shanghai), or to France (she'd spent a year as a student at the American University in Paris), and her son would become either a brain surgeon, an architect, or an explorer and activist in Asia or Africa, like Edmund Hillary, Paul Farmer, Bono, or even, though in a secular incarnation, the Dalai Lama.

She told me stories about growing up in Shanghai, and how she'd been her great-grandfather's favorite—his first great grand-child whom he believed, because of this fact, was destined for greatness, and whom he'd endowed with a sense of ambition and self-confidence he'd previously reserved only for sons and grandsons.

"You can and will be whatever you choose," he'd said to her repeatedly from as far back as she could recall, and whenever she asked what he meant—what was it she would become?—his answer was the same: "Whatever you choose to be."

We also talked about books, for it turned out Yu-huan was a voracious reader of novels (her love of stories had started with her reading of favorite folk tales to her great-grandfather—*Madam White Snake*, *A Dream of Red Mansions*, *Pongu Creates the Universe*, and, most often, *Journey to the West*), and would, when I mentioned a favorite novel of mine she'd read, launch into an extended soliloquy about the book—its plot, characters, themes, symbols, significance, and relation to its author's life. When she talked about how *great* a book was, she became ebullient, and would roam around my apartment, gesticulating extravagantly while arguing with herself about which book was greater than which other book.

Madame Bovary was the-greatest-book-ever-written, *much* greater than *Anna Karenina*, she might proclaim one Sunday evening, and then on a subsequent Sunday apologize for having had flawed judgment, since it was clear that *Anna Karenina* was much much greater than *Madame Bovary*, though neither book, she might declare a week later, could compare with Chekhov's two greatest stories—"Ward Six" and "My Life."

Once she'd had a few drinks and got going, I could barely get a word in without her scoffing at what she called my hollow, weak-willed opinions. Now and then, though, I'd enter the conversation, quietly suggesting (and in ways I thought would have pleased Max) that what mattered most was not which book or writer was 'greater,' Chekhov or Tolstoy, Kafka or Flaubert (or others she admitted to her pantheon—Dickens, Turgenev, Gogol, Camus, Woolf), but to think instead of the particular pleasures each book, or writer, could give that were unlike the pleasures—the experience—one could get from any other novel or writer, or, for that matter, from life itself. For what I'd come to believe—this from weekends alone in my apartment—was that the *experience* of reading novels—of being immersed in worlds that had no *actual* existence—was an experience unlike any other, and was, among its other virtues, one of the last truly *private* experiences left to us in this world.

When Yu-huan was not obsessively wedded to whatever new hierarchy of books and authors she was haranguing me with, she would shake her head and agree that what I said made sense. In fact, she admitted that what I said helped explain why, since the age of fourteen—she was now twenty-four—she had taken to re-reading *Madame Bovary* and *Anna Karenina* once each year, beginning at the time of the Chinese New Year, which usually occurred in late January, and finishing in mid-April, before Vesak Day, which day commemorated the birth of Buddha, his enlightenment, and his attainment of nirvana. These two novels, she maintained, though written by men, were essential to her own private nirvana. Because the stories were set in other times and places, they had allowed her to see her life in new ways, and to understand not merely the meaning but, more important, the *texture* of a woman's life generally, and of her own small life in particular.

Although we never became physically intimate on these evenings (she let me know early on that if we did, it would ruin everything that made our friendship possible), I did begin entertaining a fantasy that made me wonder if I wasn't doing what I was doing only in order to outdo Nick in the kinds of things he'd been doing for young women who lacked Yu-huan's wherewithal. I began imagining being with Yu-huan when she had the child, and visiting her and the child at home, and then, when I saw the ways her family was rejecting her—making plans for her removal, along with her son, from Singapore—I saw myself doing what Nick would have seen as the most predictable and foolish thing I could have done: offering to save her from disgrace and poverty by marrying her and taking her back to the States as my wife.

In the scenario I conjured up, we would of course begin with a *mariage blanc* that would provide Yu-huan and her son a chance for a new life (his name, she announced one Sunday evening, would be Yun-shan, which meant cloud-mountain). But what would begin as a practical arrangement would in the course of time evolve, so that (in New York, Paris, or Kuching) we would come to care for one another as deeply as any two human beings ever had. I even saw myself, one night, after she'd given me the happy news that she was pregnant with our child, telling her how, in the Old Testament (something one of my Hebrew school teachers had taught me) it was usually written that a man and woman met, married, and then loved each other—the verbs ordered this way to emphasize what experience taught: that true love came *after* marriage—after two people had come to *know* one another, which was why the verbs, in ancient Hebrew, to know and to love were the same. I wasn't foolish enough to share my fantasy with Yu-huan, though, for I sensed that the last thing she thought she wanted was to be helped or saved by any man.

On the early evening of the day on which Nick died, however—a day on which we were planning to celebrate Singapore's mid-autumn festival together—things changed between us. The mid-autumn festival, also known as the Moon Cake or Lantern Festival, coincided with the fall harvest, and was the night on which the moon was said to be fullest and brightest. There were a host of romantic stories associated with the festival, the most famous having to do with a woman, Chang-Er, who on this day swallowed the elixir of immortality, after which she'd floated up to the moon, so that when you gazed at the moon on this night, you might catch a glimpse of her, and of her pet rabbit. The other story attached to the festival had to do with rebels who hid their secret communications in round cakes, the messages urging their fellow sufferers to rise up at a certain time and place and to overthrow their oppressors. According to legend, the uprising was successful—a foreshadowing of Singapore's liberation from colonial rule—and to commemorate the victory, people ate round moon-like cakes, cakes originally filled with red bean or lotus paste, but now filled with every kind of food, from ground beef, pork, sea food, or grasshoppers, to the sweetest jams and honeys. Lanterns were hung everywhere in the city, and they came in all shapes and sizes, from small ones that opened up accordion-style, to amazing constructions of translucent plastic in the shapes of roosters, rabbits, and—how not in this most modern of modern cities?—cartoon and movie characters: Mickey Mouse and Tweetie, Batman, Spiderman, Bugs Bunny, Scooby-Doo, Road Runner, Shrek…

Yu-huan had not seen Nick since the day he'd told her things were over between them, but as soon as she arrived at my apartment, she declared that after we went to the Chinese Gardens in Jurong to eat moon cakes and to see the famous display of lanterns there, we were going to Nick's party together.

"But why?"

"Because it is time," she said.

"Time?"

"Yes, time," she said, squeezing my arm and kissing me in a way she never had before. "And time to have a drink, I think. What do you think?"

I made us drinks, and then more drinks, and soon we were very drunk, with me teaching Yu-huan old camp songs—rounds like "Frère Jacques," "Row, Row, Row Your Boat," and "Dona Nobis Pacem"—and the two of us congratulating ourselves on what splendid singers we were while I patted Yu-huan's tummy and taught little Yun-shan the rounds so he could join in. Then, after Yu-huan fell across my lap, belly down, wiggled her butt, turned over, passed a fan across her eyes, and whispered, "I *am* Emma Bovary," I couldn't hold back any longer and, believing she was feeling the same way I was, I bent down to kiss her.

She slipped away, ran across the room, and dared me to catch her. I tried, but tripped over a stack of books and went smash on the floor, my glass and ice cubes tumbling onto the carpet while Yu-huan laughed and taunted me, saying I would never be able to catch her. I went after her again, but at my bedroom door she ducked under my arm and ran back into the living room, lay on the couch, a forearm across her eyes, her other hand raised palm forward in a gesture that said: "Come no further."

I stopped where I was, and she announced that it was forbidden by all the gods and goddesses, especially Chang-Er, for us to touch one another until the deed was done. I did not ask what deed she was referring to.

"Maybe you will have me one day," she said, "and maybe you will not have me. Who is to know, Charles? Who is to know anything in this strange, cruel, and mysterious world?"

She let her arm fall from her eyes, let her hand lie where it fell, below the bulge where Yun-shan was alive and growing, stroked herself between her legs a few times, sucked on her fingers, shuddered briefly—"And I am Madonna too," she stated—and sat up. "That is sufficient," she said.

"You like driving me nuts, don't you?" I said.

"Perhaps," she said. "Sometimes I am a bad girl."

"And you're nuts too," I said.

She closed her eyes. "Sometimes yes," she said. "But sometimes no."

She lay down again, her hands clasped on her stomach. "You may play with yourself if you wish," she said. "I won't mind, or watch if you do not wish me to."

I flopped into an easy chair, grabbed my cock, but without unzipping my fly. "Is this what you want?" I said. "Do you want to watch me bring myself off?"

"Not at all," she said. "I just want us not to become lovers today. It would destroy everything."

"Because you're pregnant?"

"No."

"Because you don't like me?"

"Don't like you?" She sat up. "But I *love* you, Charles, don't you know that? I love you like a brother, and if we do other things—things brothers and sisters sometimes do—we will complicate what is really quite simple."

"That's right," I said.

"Then we agree," she said, and she stood and walked in an amazingly straight line toward the bedroom. "I am going to take a shower now," she said, "and later on, when I am gone, you are going to make a pot of very strong coffee."

"But you do like me, yes?"

"I like you very much, and if things were different, of course I would want to be your lover, and bear your son, and even marry you. If…"

"Hey—if my aunt had balls, we would have called her my uncle, right?"

"'If my aunt had balls, we would have called her my uncle,'" she repeated. "That's very funny, Charles. In fact, you are a very funny man, I think, and quite wonderful."

"It's not my saying—about the aunt and uncle," I said. "It's something my father used to say."

"Then he was a wise man."

"Still is."

"And when did you last see him?"

"Three years ago—three years and three months, to be exact."

"And you miss him," she stated.

"Sure," I said. "I miss him, but it's okay because he has someone living with him now."

"I said that you miss *him*, not that he misses you."

"But it's true," I said, even as I felt my erection go soft. "And anyway, like I said, he has someone living with him now—a younger woman who used to be his student."

"Young women give life to older men," she said.

"Do you really *believe* that?" I said. "For a modern woman, isn't that a backward way of seeing things?"

"Not at all," she said. "As you put it in your culture—what I have come to rely on as a new and useful motto—'Whatever works.' For we certainly know what does not work, since it is all around us everywhere."

"Okay then," I said. "Sure. Whatever works."

"Do you know this woman?" she asked

"Oh yes," I said. "She's a well-known writer—Seana O'Sullivan."

"*You know Seana O'Sullivan?*" Yu-huan exclaimed.

"I've known her since I was a boy."

"Seana O'Sullivan, the author of *Triangle*?"

"The one and only."

"*Triangle* is a great book—greater than *Lolita*!" Yu-huan declared. "Greater than 'The Kiss'! Greater than the novels of Colette!"

"As good as *Madame Bovary*?" I asked.

"Do not mock me," Yu-huan said. "Do not hurt me double time."

"Double time?"

"Once to mock me, and twice to have withheld from me the knowledge that you know Seana O'Sullivan."

"But I…"

"No 'buts,' Charles."

"Okay," I said. "So you tell me: Why didn't I tell you?"

"Exactly. Why did you not tell me?"

"Because."

"Yes," Yu-huan said. "'Because' is a very proper answer." She blinked several times. "*Triangle* is banned in Singapore—you know that, of course."

"Yes."

"I acquired my copy in Hong Kong when I was there with Nick." She looked away. "In fact, I am now remembering that I had forgotten you knew her, and…"

She stopped.

"Yes?"

"That is all."

"He told you about his wife Trish—his ex-wife—and about how the three of us used to play around, right? Like in *Triangle*, only without the incest."

"Although he has done much good in the world, Nick has

never been a truly honorable man," Yu-huan stated. "That is why I am going to take a shower and go home. I will meet you later, at his party."

"You're really going there?"

"Of course. But you must rest now. Please do what I say, Charles."

"Sure," I said, and I lay down on the couch. Yu-huan covered me with a blanket, then went to the bathroom, and the next thing I knew, she was at the door, blowing me a good-bye kiss and telling me that to prove her love, she'd gone ahead and made the pot of coffee for me.

By the time I arrived at the party, Nick was totally blotto, and carrying on the way he often did when he got this way—balancing glasses on his nose, throwing peanuts and olives into the air and catching them in his mouth, making the rounds of young women and grabbing ass, then making nice to guys we did business with.

When Yu-huan arrived, dressed elegantly in a black strapless gown, and walked straight to him and extended her hand in greeting, asking if he had seen the lanterns in Jurong Park this year, he stared at her stomach for a while—gaped really—then, very politely, asked her how her family was. Yu-huan put an arm around my waist, kissed me quickly on the mouth, and excused herself, saying she was going to fetch us drinks.

"Well I'll be damned," Nick said.

"I hope so," I said.

"Congratulations, buddy," Nick said, slapping me on the back. "Though in my experience," he added, "it's never been a good idea to bird-dog a friend with his ex."

"Why not?" I said.

"Well, for starters, this one's just a little bit knocked up, and if you're the father..."

"I'm not," I said. "You are."

Nick froze for a second—he saw that others were listening—and glared at me with an anger I'd rarely seen him show. He forced a laugh. "You *are* a character, Charlie boy," he said, "so it's a good thing I'm not the jealous type, right?"

"And if you were?" I asked.

He poked me in the chest with an index finger, but lightly. "We don't really want to go there, do we?"

"No. Especially if you insist on calling me 'Charlie boy,'" I said. "I'm not drinking tonight, and you're smashed."

"So you think you could take me, huh?"

"Not interested," I said.

"Same old Charlie—all discretion, no valor. Just like the rest of your tribe, right?"

"My tribe?"

"Like lambs to the slaughter—isn't that the way it goes? I didn't agree with much my old man believed, but we did see eye to eye when it came to this."

"When it came to what, Nick? Be specific."

"Well, you *are* still a Jew, aren't you?" Nick said. "I mean, being with this little bitch doesn't change your religion, does it?"

I turned away, then swiveled back quickly, blasting an elbow hard into his gut so that he dropped his glass, doubled over, and began sucking air.

"*My* father taught me that move," I said. "He's Jewish too, and maybe you haven't heard, but Jews don't take crap anymore." I turned to Yu-huan, who was by my side, drinks in hand. "My father was once an excellent boxer," I explained.

Yu-huan handed me my drink, led me to the sliding glass doors that opened to the balcony. Nick's apartment was on the sixteenth floor, with a splendid view of the city and its harbor. Because of the festival, the harbor was lit more brightly than usual. In the distance, far to the east, noiseless puffs of fireworks were exploding in the sky. I touched Yu-huan's shoulder, and when she turned toward me, I saw that her eyes were moist.

She bowed her head, and spoke: "I will now ask your forgiveness for the way in which I behaved toward you earlier today."

"No problem," I said.

"You are a good man, Charlie Eisner," she said, "and I hope you receive your reward in this life."

"Me too."

"But for tonight, this," she said, and opened her purse to show me a switchblade. "Later I will seduce him. Despite his rage, or because of it, he will desire me. Nick remains, for all his triumphs, a very jealous man, and will want to re-possess me."

"Nick's competitive," I said. "That's for sure."

"No," Yu-huan said. "Not what you say. That is too simple. Jealousy is much more powerful."

"It's the illusion of possession," I said, and added quickly: "That's another one of my father's sayings."

"Jealousy is the illusion of possession," Yu-huan stated. "Yes. Then he is still a wise man, your father, even though you have not seen him for three years."

"Probably," I said.

Yu-huan touched the knife. "When he enters me," she said, "this will enter him."

"No," I said.

"But…"

"No buts," I said.

"Because?"

I kept my eye on Nick, who, once he'd gotten his wind back, started drinking again non-stop. Yu-huan and I ate and we drank—no alcohol, only tonic with lime—and a short while later Nick made his way back to us and began taunting me, jabbing me in the chest and asking if I was ready to step outside and settle things between us the way men should, and not with a gutless sucker punch.

I told him I was ready whenever he was. People crowded

around, some encouraging him, a few women telling him to leave me alone in exchange for pleasures more delectable than fighting could offer.

"They don't know Nick," Yu-huan said quietly.

I turned away, figuring Nick would see my move the way I wanted him to—as a spineless response to his challenge—and walked out onto the balcony. Yu-huan joined me and stood to the side. Nick started shouting now, telling everyone that the truth was that I'd always wanted him, but without a woman in the middle I didn't have the guts to go for it. "That's true, isn't it, Charlie boy?"

"Come and find out," I said.

Nick grinned madly, then pretended he was a raging bull by making horns on each side of his head with his index fingers, and scraping his feet back and forth on the floor as if preparing to charge. I played along, fluttering an imaginary cape in front of me, then holding it against my thigh like a matador daring him to come at me.

"Vintage Hemingway?" I asked.

Nick howled with laughter—he was as drunk as I'd ever seen him, and clearly unable to figure out what had gotten into me— how I could remain so calm and confident when he was getting ready to take me. He started calling me names—a lame-brained punk, a dickless wonder, a two-bit Jewish pipsqueak whose John Henry was no bigger than what was hanging between the legs of the babe he'd put in Yu-huan's oven.

"*Olé*," I said, but softly, and flapped my imaginary cape at him. "*Olé*, Nick…"

"You got it, Charlie boy," he said, and he came roaring at me. I stood where I was, and just as he was about to plow into my chest, I stepped aside and grabbed for his thigh—I was able to slip my arm under it—and then he was on his way up and over the railing.

Yu-huan had moved swiftly as soon as Nick began to charge,

stationing herself between Nick and everyone else to keep them from seeing my movements, but now, Nick's cry slicing through the air, they pushed past her and began screaming things people probably scream whenever they see somebody fall from a great height.

I looked down, hoping to see Nick's face—to see him look up at me in astonishment, as in: 'I didn't think you had it in you, Charlie boy'—but he'd already gone splat on the concrete below, face down, and instead of a look of astonishment, I imagined an expression of confusion: *Why did you do it?* he was asking, and before I could reply—and even while I was wondering if I'd done anything at all, since once I'd stepped aside, his momentum might have carried him to where he was without my assistance—he seemed to know the answer, and to hear what I might have said if we'd had the time to exchange words: *Why did I do it?* That's an easy one, Nick, since there's only one true answer, same as always: *Because I could.*

Make-A-Wish

*W*hen, my first night home from Singapore, Max had invited Seana to come on a trip with us to his old neighborhood, she'd replied by saying she preferred not to go home again if she could help it, thank you very much. Now, though, seven weeks after Max was in the grave, Seana and I were driving down to Brooklyn from Northampton, and she seemed even more eager to get there than I was.

"So let's go home again, Charlie—what would you think of *that*?" she said when, well past Hartford, we were approaching New Haven.

"Sounds like a plan," I said.

"And as long as we'll be in the old neighborhood," she said, "I've decided we should visit my mother and my sisters. I haven't seen my mother for nearly three years. My sisters say she's not quite what she used to be—that she's in the early stages of Irish Alzheimer's."

"*Irish* Alzheimer's?"

"That's where you forget everything but the grudge."

"Sounds about right," I laughed.

"And once we get there," she said, "I've decided I'll ask my sisters to invite my father. Or I'll do it myself, and surprise the bastard. My parents never divorced, but they've lived apart for most of my adult life. I told you that before, didn't I?"

"Yes."

"And who knows *what* marvelous things might happen once we're all together again," she laughed. "My father was an old song-and-dance man, you know, though I only got to see him perform once or twice, and that was when I was very young—when they were trying to revive vaudeville. But I was remembering one of his gags, about how a newspaper account of an Irish social event begins."

"So tell me, Seana," I said. "How does a newspaper account of an Irish social event begin?"

"'Among the injured were...'"

I asked if she'd called any of her sisters to let them know we'd be coming, and she said she was taking a page from my book—from the way I'd waited until we were nearby, in Maine, before calling Nick's parents. As in all wars, she said, an element of surprise could carry the day.

"Surprises are good sometimes," I said.

"Yes," she said. "In stories and in life. Like us."

"Like us."

"That was one of your father's mantras, in our writing workshop. 'Chances are,' he'd say, and he was quoting from Flannery O'Connor, 'that if what you're writing doesn't surprise you, it won't surprise anyone else either.'"

I think we both saw returning to the old neighborhood as a kind of pilgrimage, and I was about to say so—to say that it pleased me to be memorializing Max by making his last wish come true, but as soon as the thought was there, I remembered that his last wish had not been about us returning to Brooklyn, but about what he'd said when he'd phoned us at Trish's: that we shouldn't forget to be kind to one another.

Seana and I had been living together in the Northampton house for the seven weeks since Max's death, and what had surprised us was how easy—how natural—it seemed to be doing so. It surprised me too when, snuggled close to me one night before sleep, she whispered that she had a confession to make: that although she'd known a fair number of men in her time, this was a first.

"A first?"

"I've never lived with a man before," she said.

"Are you sure?" I'd said. "Because you're really good at it…"

What had also surprised was that Max had left instructions for me and for our rabbi, stating that he wanted a traditional Jewish funeral, and spelling out specifics: services for him at the synagogue, where, though he never attended services after I was Bar Mitzvahed, he had remained a dues-paying member until his death; burial in the synagogue's cemetery; observance of a full week of mourning—*shiva*—in our home, with a *minyan* of ten men and/or women, so I could say *Kaddish* for him three times a day; the wish that I observe other rituals—saying *Kaddish* for him from time to time on the Sabbath, and on major holidays such as *Rosh Hashanah* and *Yom Kippur*; that for thirty days I obey the injunction not to shave or marry; that during the week of mourning I keep all mirrors in the house covered, and not wear leather shoes; that, as an outward sign of grief, I have the rabbi cut the collar of one of my good jackets with a razor, and not merely pin on a strip of black cloth as was, generally, the contemporary practice; that I keep a memorial candle lit for him for a full week, and light a 24-hour candle for him each year on the anniversary of his death, on which day he hoped I would visit his grave, attend synagogue, and recite *Kaddish* in his memory.

As to the prohibition against engaging in festivities for a full year, he believed this was contrary to the prevailing rabbinic view, which was that it was forbidden to overdo mourning (thus, he noted, one mourned for only a single hour on the seventh day of the seven days of mourning), and he wrote that I should consider myself excused from this obligation.

The last time I'd been to his old neighborhood had been when I was teaching in New York, I said to Seana, and Max's apartment house had still been there. In fact, I'd been surprised at how little things had changed in thirty years. The houses on his block were the same ones that had been there the first time I'd come to Brooklyn with him, and though there were a few more locked gates across building entrances and alleyways, and though ethnicities had shifted—the people who lived on his block were mostly West Indian, not Jewish, Irish, and Italian the way they'd been when he was growing up—everything else had seemed pretty much the same. On Flatbush Avenue, the Dutch Reformed Church and its cemetery, where he'd hung out with his friends when they cut classes, had seemed in good shape, and a few blocks away, the building that had housed his synagogue was still there, though it had become home to a Pentecostal church. Most of the old movie theaters along Flatbush Avenue—the great picture palaces of the twenties and thirties—had survived, though none showed movies anymore, many were boarded up, and those that weren't boarded up had become vast indoor flea markets where West Indians bought and sold everything from incense, dresses, and mouse traps to canned goods, lawn chairs, and auto parts.

"But what do you think *has* changed, Charlie?" Seana asked.

"Is this a trick question?"

"Tell me what you think has changed," she said. "Please."

"Max is gone."

"What else?"

"We're going there together."

"That's part of it."

"And the part I don't get?"

"*Me*," Seana said. "What's changed is *me*. Although I may look and sound like the Seana you've known—same Jeanne d'Arc hair-do, same apostrophic chipped tooth, same haunting eyes, same brilliant chip-on-the shoulder wit—I'm essentially a new woman."

"Really?"

"You can't tell?"

"No."

"But you *are* curious, yes?"

"No."

"Come on, Charlie—be a sport," she said. "Ask me how I've changed. And it's not just our being together, or my deciding to see my family again, though they're part of it. But be my straight man and ask me how I've changed."

"Okay," I said. "So listen, Seana, I was thinking about what might have changed in the neighborhood where you and Max grew up, and it occurred to me to wonder about how maybe *you've* changed."

"Thank you," she said. "As I was saying, I've been thinking that what's changed most of all is me." She drew in a deep breath. Then: "I want children, Charlie."

"You have me," I said. "I'm a child."

"I'm *serious*. I've decided I want to have children."

"Oh."

"That's all you have to say—'Oh'—? Did you *hear* what I said? Can you understand what I'm saying?"

"But…"

"'But aren't you too old,' the man asks," she said quickly, then answered her own question: "Probably. Still, we're blessed—or cursed—you choose—with remarkable genes in my family. Caitlin—my oldest sister—had *all* her children, four of them, in her late thirties and early forties. My cousin Maggie had her first child at forty-three, her second and third at forty-four and forty-five. My mother had *me*—the family's pre-eminent 'Oops!' baby—when she was forty-two."

"But you're forty-three or forty-four, and…"

"I'm almost forty-five, thank you very much, and I'm

certainly not going to mess with all the fertility crap they put young women through these days, but I really would..."

She stopped, unable to go on. I started to reach over to take her hand, but decided, and not just for safety's sake—we were at New Haven, and were turning off the highway—to keep both hands on the steering wheel.

"Are you okay?" I asked when we came to a stop at the bottom of the exit ramp.

"I'm fine," she said. "So I guess what I've been trying to say in my lame way is that I think I made a mistake once upon a time—took a wrong turn somewhere—and that it's probably not the kind of mistake that's correctable."

"Like me with Nick?" I said.

"Something like that," she said. "Although he *did* get his wish—you see that, don't you?"

"See what?"

"That he's living nowhere now," Seana said, "which according to him—to what you wrote that he said—is the place to be these days. Then too, it's good to remember what Max used to say."

"What did Max used to say?"

"That death is not an event in life."

"That's not Max. That's Wittgenstein," I said. "Max never took credit for other people's words."

"Still—Nick, or Max, or Wittgenstein—it remains true that I do wish I'd had children—that I still might *have* children, even though I know it probably can't be."

"I believe you."

"Maybe yes, maybe no," she said. "But it doesn't matter because what I'm doing, you see, is expressing a feeling in a Seana O'Sullivan way—in triads: me, you, a child. A Catholic triad, come to think of it, because if I can't have a child, that makes the child a ghost."

"A *holy* ghost?"

"Don't get too smart with me," she said, "because I'm riled

now, and even though you may not be able to see them, flames are shooting out of both my ears at the moment. I'm expressing a *regret*, Charlie—a big, fat, fucking regret, which is something I've worked diligently to avoid—and I've chosen you as the lucky bastard with whom to share the news. Can you understand *that*?"

"I think you're angry with me because of a mistake *you* made."

"You bet. And I'm also remembering our conversation with Trish—that you feel the same way I do about having children."

"Maybe we're twins," I said.

"And have been engaging in incest?"

"An ancient tradition," I said.

She looked away. "Thanks, Charlie," she said. "And also, while we're on the subject, let me assure you I wasn't proposing that *we* have a child together."

"Could have fooled me."

"Well I was and I wasn't."

"Not to put too fine a point on it," I said, "but it's hard to have kids without having sex."

"You're probably right," she said.

"*Probably?*"

"Well," she said, "since Max died—the last week or two anyway—we *have* become like an old married couple, you and me."

"I hadn't thought of it that way," I said.

I drove into the station's parking garage, where we'd leave the car the way Max and I had done when we'd go to New York together, and take a Metro-North train into the city. I found an open space, parked, turned off the engine. Seana unfastened her seatbelt, slid sideways, leaned against my shoulder.

"But *I* have," she said. "Truth be told, my dear young friend, it's been a comfort to me, the way it was with your father—to live with a man I find attractive *and* with whom I feel safe, and part of feeling safe, despite all my words, published and unpublished, seems to lie in *not* having sex."

Bright winter sun—the light almost white—poured in through the large windows under the New Haven train station's roof, and I said something about loving times like this—times when I thought of myself as being suspended between here and there.

"It has been a gift," Seana said, "the way we've been with each other since your dad died."

"For me too."

"I didn't mean to lay my decisions on you, Charlie."

"What decisions?" I asked.

"Right," she said. Then: "I care about you deeply. You know that, don't you?"

"Yes."

"But you also know that I've never been a big fan of romantic notions of love."

"I've read your books."

"In fact, and I borrow from Auden here, I sometimes find myself believing there's no notion—no Western notion, anyway—that's been responsible for more misery—not to mention bad poetry—than the belief that a certain vague, quasi-mystical experience called 'falling in love' is something every normal man and woman is supposed to have."

"I agree about the poetry," I said.

"Don't make light of what I'm saying," she said. "Please? I'm being serious in a way I'm not used to being."

"I'm not making light of what you said—I'm just disagreeing with you. Auden notwithstanding, I guess I'm still a romantic the way Max was…"

She turned away from me, and we didn't talk for a while. I watched students come and go, with their backpacks, Yale-blue scarves, and rolling suitcases. At the end of our bench, a young couple—tall black girl, stocky white boy—were kissing playfully, nibbling on each other.

"Maybe we could adopt," I offered.

"Maybe," she said. "Not as much fun, though."

"There are lots of healthy children—orphans—in Borneo. When I considered staying on there—making it my home—I thought about adopting one of them."

"I read your story," Seana said, "and there's nothing in it about adopting children. Who would have taken care of them when you had to be away? Tamika? Jin-gen? Amanda and Alicia?"

"I said I *thought* about it. I didn't say I had a plan."

"Why adopt if you could marry and have your own?"

"Look," I said. "It was just a passing thought, and it was probably smarmy-romantic and unrealistic, like a lot of my ideas. Save-the-Children, right? But what I *did* realize—this hit home when I had to imagine what Yu-huan might have to go through—when I knew what others like her *did* go through— I realized that having kids wasn't about what I felt, or what I needed."

"Of course not."

"I mean, give me some credit for understanding that having kids is about *them* and not about me."

"Why are you telling me this, Charlie?"

"Children don't ask to come into the world."

"So?"

"So I knew women—here, not there—who, when they talked about having kids would drive me crazy with the way they'd go on and on about becoming mothers—about how much they looked forward to *the experience* of being a mother."

"You never heard me talk that way, did you?"

"No."

"Then shut up about it. I told you before, I would have made a very good mother."

"And, according to what I heard before, you think you still could be."

"Damned right."

"But come on, Seana. Talk about being romantic and unrealistic—and about driving *yourself* crazy with what probably can't be."

"Okay," she said. "I get the point. You're right, and I'm right, and we're both right." She shrugged. "So maybe, like you, what I need is a plan."

"Maybe."

"So let's make plans, you and me," she said, her eyes bright again, as if she'd just thought of something mischievous, and she began talking about how her mother and sisters might react to seeing her again. They'd be sure to ask us to stay over, and if they did, where would we sleep? She giggled at the prospect of bringing me—a handsome, young Jewish boy—home for a sleepover, and I asked if she might be under the spell of an incipient form of Irish Alzheimer's—if bringing me home wasn't just her way of acting out on old grudges.

"Ah, you really *are* smart, Charlie," she said. "Max often talked about how smart you were—'shrewd' was the word he sometimes used, 'shrewd if innocent' his operative phrase. He talked about you a lot, you know."

"I didn't."

"Whenever he sent me a letter, he'd report on what you were doing, and what he said each time you moved to a new place, or changed jobs, or had a new girlfriend, was that in his opinion you were only at the beginning of your potential."

"My potential as *what?*"

"He was proud of who you *were*, Charlie, not of what you *did*."

"And if he knew about Nick?"

"He'd be even prouder. Give him some credit for being a man whose values you come by honestly."

"Such as?"

"What you told me he said about loss and no loss."

"Still—ridiculous fact—I *am* a murderer," I said. "Max never killed anyone, as far as we know."

"According to my reading of your story, you *might* be a murderer," Seana said. "There's some essential—and intentional—ambiguity in the way you tell that part of the story."

"Is that what excites you about me—that I might have killed someone?"

She roughed up my hair. "Oh Charlie, my little rascal—my little Raskal-nikov," she said. "You really are something, aren't you, the stuff that spins around in that pretty head of yours."

"I hope so," I said. "But what's weird is that I feel almost nothing about what I did."

"*If* you did it."

"And no guilt I'm aware of. No *regrets*. I don't find myself wishing Nick were still alive."

"Who does?" Seana said. "Not his father. Not Trish certainly."

"Never Trish."

"Which reminds me," Seana said. "I took the liberty of making a copy of your story and sending it to her—a way of thanking her for our time there, and a way for the three of us to remain close to one another."

"But I never said you could—"

"It's just a story, Charlie, though it's a good one," she said. "Lots of sweet ambiguity—some of which, like whether you were or were not drunk the night of Nick's death—may remain a mystery forever."

"You noticed the disparity—between what I said and what I wrote," I said.

"I pay attention to you, Charlie," she said. "But do *you* remember what I said, about how sweet it would be if you could transpose the way you talked into a voice that could talk the same way—an equivalent—but on the page?"

"I remember."

"Well, you've done it," she said. "Beginner's luck maybe, but it gives me leave to tell you what *I* think, which is that it was your father's secret wish that you become the writer he never was. That's what his tag sale was really about. You see that, don't you?"

"No."

"He had no knowledge—no inkling—that *I'd* show up that morning, but I think he knew that setting out his wares would lure you home."

"You don't think it was *you*—him writing me with the news that *you* were living with him that did the trick?"

"No."

"What about him maybe wishing I'd come home and fall in love with you, so that after he was gone, the two of us…"

"Good try, but I think you're changing the subject."

Seana was looking past me, and I turned, watched an elderly man, his head and ankles wrapped in brightly colored scarves, wheeling a shopping cart across the waiting room floor. The man took a clear plastic bag of what looked like garbage from the cart, and stuffed it into a mail box.

"As far as I know," I said, "I never wanted to be a writer the way he did—or the way you did."

"Could have fooled me. Because you have something neither of us—me or Max—have: the ability to turn the stuff out without worrying every word and sentence to death."

"*You* worry things?"

"Stop," she said. "And think about the difference. Max lived past the proverbial three score and ten, and published one good, somewhat thin novel, and two short, serviceable literary studies. I'm forty-four—*almost* forty-five—and all I have to show for myself so far are two weird, shamelessly successful novels, but *you*—you sit down, and in ten days, with people coming and going—strangers, relatives, old friends—you knock out something Max and I would have been proud to put our names to."

"But I wasn't writing fiction," I said. "I wasn't making things up."

"Could have fooled me," she said again.

"Well maybe I did make up a few things here and there—embellish my memories—but what you believe about his secret wish—you're not saying it just to make me feel good?"

"What would make you think I'd want to make you feel good?"

The overhead PA system clicked on, a voice announcing that our train was ready for boarding. We picked up our bags, walked toward the escalator, then down and along a tunnel and up again to where the train to New York City was waiting.

A few minutes after the train left the station, Seana took a manila envelope from her overnight bag, and handed it to me.

"A gift," she said.

"From you?"

"From Max."

I opened the envelope, withdrew a manuscript. Under the title—A Missing Year—there was a hand-written note:

for my son, Charlie, from his loving father Max

"Wasn't this on the list you gave me—the title of one of the stories you asked me to choose from, my first night home?" I asked.

"Yes. So it's one story neither of us will have to write," Seana said. "It's fairly long, and I want to take a nap, so why don't you read it while I grab some Z's, and we can talk about it later."

"But if he'd already written the story, why...?"

"Shh," she said, placing a finger against my lips. "Later, please. I'm bone-tired. Also, I adore the sound and motion of trains—the rattling and rocking and clanging, plus our reflections hanging out there in the air on the other side of the window. I think I've always loved being on-my-way as much as you love being between-here-and-there, so be a good boy and give me a kiss good night, and we'll talk after you've read the story, okay? But think about this, Charlie—a thought that may surprise you, given what I said before: that if there is such a thing as love, maybe it shows itself forth in stories and in who we choose to tell them to—in the way we exchange stories of our lives with others…"

She rolled up a sweater, put it next to the window, closed her eyes. I leaned over, kissed her on the cheek.

A MISSING YEAR

Dearest Charlie,

If you are reading this, wherever you are, it will mean, of course, that I am no longer here (there?)—a shame, since when all is said and done, and here I paraphrase Orwell, I find that this world does suit me fairly well. And wherever I am, and unless we've both arrived simultaneously in some universe designed by Calvino or Borges, what I'm certain of is that there is no 'I' there. I never thought to persuade you of that—that when we're gone, we're gone and that's all there is to it, so that the only immortality, as our people (mostly) believe (Jews, but not only Jews—cf. Shakespeare's sonnets), lies in our children, in the memories others have of us (flawed and self-serving as they may be), and in whatever work we may have left behind: literary stuff, of course—poems, novels, plays, essays, stories—but *anything* made by one's mind or hands that has tangible existence: music, furniture, boats, paintings, sculpture, jewelry, clothing, houses…

Consciousness is fine—much studied and celebrated in recent times—but much overrated too, in my opinion, for even were it to survive in some way—were we, as in typical tales composed about such after-lives, to wake from death and find that, detached from any bodily being, mind and thought are, miraculously, still ongoing, I would doubtless spend whatever timeless time this 'I'—this consciousness recognizably me and no one else—had been given, lamenting the loss of senses. Taste, touch, sight, sound, smell—smell above all!—how ever, ever, ever undervalue them?

I.e., the grave's a fine and private place, as Marvell famously wrote, but none, I think, do there embrace. Other articulations of this notion, along with its innumerable *carpe diem* corollaries about preferring the sybaritic, now accelerate within, creating a rather sweet traffic jam, yet I banish them at once, even as I ask forgiveness for my literary excesses, references, and airs, yes? These vague, indulgent musings are—of course, of course—my somewhat arch way of avoiding telling you what I've decided to tell you about what I've always thought of as my 'missing' year—and also a reminder (to me) of how often in this life I've used words on paper to avoid other things. Through most of my life, that is, I've had the largely benign habit of passing whatever I experienced, in mind or flesh, through the filter (lens?) of what, other than you, my son, was the great love of my life: stories.

I tested (tasted?) all I did—my writing, teaching, wives, romances, friendships, pleasures, losses, memories, feelings— all, all, all—through stories I'd read, and people, places, and events I'd come to know in them. More: I often gave myself up as fully as I was able to the imagination of others—let myself believe I was part of the mind—the sensibility—that had conjured up these worlds so that, I suppose—vain hope!—my own imagination, like theirs, might find objects and tales equal to my desire to find them...

But to the missing year itself: My great fear, you see, was that I would kill *you*, Charlie. I *wanted* to kill you. The idea of killing you thrilled and pleased in a time distinctly bereft of thrills or pleasure. For a year—fourteen months and three days, to be exact, as I wrote earlier—I thought, every day, of killing you. The thought arrived, as you might guess, attached to my desire to do away with myself, and this desire arrived shortly before your mother left us both (nor, I note quickly, did I ever stoop, to keep her from leaving us, to blackmailing her with the threat that I would kill the two of us if she did leave us). But the desire to kill the two of us came—this dark, unwelcome guest—and it stayed for more than a year, yet could occasionally, when most robust, bring with it (paradoxically?) an exhilarating feeling of liberation.

The possibility of leaving this world, and taking you with me—of being in a place or non-place where consciousness was forever non-existent—this became balm to my pain, and the pain, let me tell you—and I hope you never know it in its dreadful particularity—was decidedly *physical*. During those fourteen months and three days I read a good deal about depression, which, I discovered, had a distinguished history, beginning at least 2500 years ago with Hippocrates, and though the reading taught me much about the melancholic disposition, about trauma and grief and their contributions to the deadly mood, and about suicidal desires and the pernicious ways they can take hold and take over, I found little about the sheer bodily pain that, as in my case, can accompany the affliction.

Though I experienced most of what have become the standard symptoms that now make major depression certifiable and reimbursable (sleep disturbances, fatigue, feelings of worthlessness, thoughts of suicide), I experienced no weight loss, or loss of sexual desire, no headaches or flu-like symptoms, no sharp internal blade-like grindings. Instead, my lows were accompanied by constant nausea (even—especially!—during love-making), along with a vise-like pressure throughout my upper body, front and back, as if I'd been saturated with something heavier than blood—inhabited by a beast that was trying to suck and squeeze breath and life from me. When it came to rising from a bed or chair, the heaviness would at times paralyze me, as if the sheer weight of my body were the palpable equivalent of my spirits.

I.e., I despaired of being able to lift either. If you've ever been drunk out of your mind, or sea-sick in the extreme, so that rather than endure any more of the lethal whooshing, you preferred to die—*nothing* seemed worth another moment of the swirling desolation—you will have a tiny intimation of what this cafard was like when it filled—drenched!—all cells of body and soul.

Aware, however, that what I was experiencing might merely (*merely?!*) be advanced coronary artery disease (from which my father passed away at 49 years old—a massive heart attack while waiting in the evening rush hour for the downtown IRT subway at the Rector Street station in lower Manhattan), I did go to my physician, who forwarded me to a cardiologist, who—hope dashed again—found nothing wrong with my heart, or the arteries that fed it and were fed by it.

Well, I told myself—much as the host of the annual sado-masochist convention is said to have announced—'The good news this year is that we seem to have lots of bad news!' For the cardiologist's evaluation meant that what I was experiencing was, in fact, what I believed it to be: the great black bile itself—melancholic depression.

So there we were, Charlie, abandoned by mother and wife, you having just passed your first birthday—the most beautiful, clever babe ever—and me relieving my newly acquired distress by imagining how sweet it would be to do away with you, and after you—my guilt now boundless!—with me (I spare you details of my how-to fantasies while assuring you that swiftness and lack of suffering for you were paramount in my considerations).

Did I consider murdering your mother? Of course, though not for long, and not at all after I received a kind offer from a former student (an advisee who went on to considerable success both as novelist and screenwriter-director), a young man from an Italian family in Springfield, Massachusetts, who, learning of my situation, told me he could have 'a man with a bent nose' (his phrase) take care of things. All I had to do was nod once and it would come to pass in a completely risk-free, cost-free manner (again, his language).

A mother abandoning a child, he said, was a mean-spirited and irresponsible act that went against both nature and biology, and it would be more than irresponsible—how I adored his repeated use of the word!—not to repair this flaw in the fabric of the world by cleansing it of its perpetrator (again, his language).

The offer was more than moderately attractive, for among the wealth of evils in human character, meanness-of-spirit and irresponsibility had always, as you know, ranked high in my private catalog. But so, alas alas, did the siren call of a beautiful woman chanting '*I love you... I love you... You're wonderful... You're wonderful...,*' which, more in my youthful years than later on, made easy prey of whatever judgment and reason I possessed. Still, no matter my former student's assurances (or my desires), I declined the offer. What I feared, you see, was error. I was, that is, afraid of being caught, for being caught—whether for having committed the deed, or having assented to it—would have resulted in your being left to the care of others, and to coping not only with the sequelae of abandonment by a mother (a dead young mother, to boot), but with the burden of having been orphaned by a convicted murderer.

There were comic possibilities here, for sure (think: the ingeniously enchanting tales of John Cheever, the wonderfully mischievous films of Pedro Almodóvar!), though at the time so constant was the animal ache in mind and body that, as with cracked or broken ribs, the mere thought of laughter was enough to lay me out for hours (hmmm: did you know that— sweet memory—you and I shared afternoon nap-time back then, you in your crib, me on my office couch?). The only way I found to escape the constant pain—as undeserving, worthless, wretched, banal, dull, hopeless, lazy, mean-spirited, stupid, vain, and homely *shlep* of a man as I'd become—was by imagining the prospect of being somewhere else, and of having you there with me.

Yet there was something else at work in the bowels of my gloom—a fear that arose from my hunger for vengeance: that should I fail to nail my courage to the sticking point in the act itself, she would come marching triumphantly back into your life, my deed confirmation of everything she wanted to believe and to have others believe. Plus, a dividend: she'd be the recipient of large quantities of cash, for she'd be seen as the long-suffering mother who'd fled an unhealthy situation—marriage to a dangerous, despicable, deranged man, the proof in the pudding of my murderous intent and botched self-annihilation.

But consequences, Charlie—let us consider consequences. As I would often remind students: if they kept two principles in mind—that character was fate, and that there were no acts without consequences—they could begin to find their way into the workings (and delights) of all tales worthy of attention. When we were home alone, and I pictured our resident would-be Humbert Humbert (me!) mocked by her, I saw, too, the consequences of my inevitable bunglings. Insurance companies do not pay out for death-by-suicide, but her likely appeal—that I was not in my right mind when, at the eleventh hour, I changed beneficiaries (assigning all to charities)—would surely have carried the day. (Actually, I realize, despite a multitude of resolutions, I never did get around to changing *anything* in my will that year, which tells you something about melancholy, and how it can cause a lasting rupture between the desire to act and the ability to act.)

Still, a question: Why did your mother leave us? You were probably hoping—how not?—that in this note you'd find answers, or at least the beginnings of answers. Why she left me—why any woman leaves a man—is rarely, on an overt level, mysterious. There are the usual suspects: She didn't love me, she didn't want to be married to me, she found me impossible, she wanted her freedom, she fell in love with somebody else, she experienced a sudden change-of-life, she was on alcohol and/or drugs, she found motherhood less than it was cracked up to be, she had a severe, debilitating post-partum chronic depression...

But why she left you—ah, to that conundrum, I plead ignorance. While it's true (and sad) that people hardly blink when men leave wives and children, I tend to agree with my Springfield student that when a mother does so, it would seem to go against nature and biology, and therefore, like a miracle—a *miracle*!—be beyond human understanding. For what defined God and God's miracles in the Hebrew Bible—from the great flood that covered the earth to the burning bush, from the ten plagues to the sun standing still in the heavens—were occurrences that, *by definition*, went against nature and the natural order, and could, thus, have been brought about only by a god who was transcendent and (also by definition) beyond our understanding.

When people asked why she left you, as ask they often did, and would suggest, thinking this would console me, that perhaps she'd suffered some kind of mental breakdown, I'd nod knowingly, as if the suggestion had merit, and say that perhaps what troubled your mother could be found in the psychiatric encyclopedia of mental disorders—the infamous *DSM*—under the letter 'A.' Under 'A?' they'd ask. Yes, I'd say: 'A'... for Absence of Character.

How else respond to such a foolish question? Still, you must wonder—we never spoke about this, did we?—about what she (this woman you never truly knew) was like, and, allied to this question, what-I-saw-in-her that led to love, marriage, and bringing you into the world.

And the answer?

Simple: We were young, she was beautiful, and she told me—insecure, neurotic, young Jewish city boy that I was—that she loved me. You've seen pictures, of course, but they don't begin to capture the seductive *wholesomeness* of her beauty: a blond-haired, blue-eyed, corn-fed Midwesterner (from Iowa: the heart of corn country)—a cheerful cheerleader with a perfect gleaming American smile and a perpetual blush in her cheeks, crossed with a full-bodied, voluptuous Scandinavian (think: Liv Ullman, Anita Ekberg)—a young, exquisitely desirable woman who, after she'd told me she loved me, said two additional things that sealed the deal: first, that she believed—she knew, she just knew!—I was going to become a truly *great* writer; and second, that I was the most wonderful lover she'd ever known.

And let me tell you, son, as I discovered too late in the game, when it came to the latter, she knew whereby she spoke. But (sigh!) even irony and distance can not keep away the return, in memory, of the excruciating feelings of hurt, shame, and helplessness that came with my discovery of her several (serial?) lovers, which news was soon followed by her leave-taking, which act itself (the better miracle, for it gave us our years together, you and me) was preceded, as I noted above, by the arrival of a constant, gnawing pain, along with sensations of a kind I'd never before known: I kept falling, falling, falling into a darkness more terrifying than the absence of the dimmest light—into a hole that was at the same time somehow a hollow *within me*, so that I felt I was disappearing into myself again and again, and without any clue as to how to stop—or name!—the falling...

To give you an inkling (ink link?) of how my baleful innocence was destroyed: we were to meet for lunch at the university's Faculty Club—a rather poor excuse for same: more like a student cafeteria, but with waitstaff—and I arrived early (to have twenty minutes or so in which to rework a lecture I was preparing on Henry James-the-Irishman), went to the men's room to wash up, heard a strange guttural sound, found the stall where the sound was coming from, opened the door, and there was your mother, skirt up around her waist, sitting astride a young man—he worked as a busboy at the club—who was himself sitting on an open toilet, his pants gathered around his ankles. 'Good morning, Professor Eisner,' he said. 'Sorry to see you here so early today.' And your mother, over her shoulder, her eyes filled with lust-fulfilled bliss, 'Oh Max, we really do have to stop meeting like this...'

I hurried home from the Faculty Club and when she joined me, and when I wept and said the obvious—bad enough that you were doing it, but you knew I would be there—*We had a date!*—she said of course she knew—that was the point, after all, for didn't this non-coincidence answer the pertinent questions? But I was a helpless, wounded beggar—distraught, destroyed, disabled. The rage, and its faithful companion, clinical depression, were to come later, though I don't think she sensed this, or ever gave such possibilities much thought. On that afternoon, however, she did for a while sit beside me, stroke my hair, lift my hands from my face, and wipe my tears away. What I think, she said before she left, is that I was trying to get your attention.

The rest—what I knew and when I knew it—is theme and variation, and my conclusion is that it turned out to be our great good fortune that once she left, she never returned. Her life, such as it became, is a void too—a mystery—though of decreasing interest. Out of sight became, literally, out of mind. Another conclusion, perhaps a trifle too generous on my part: that her intention was not to humiliate me, but more simply (mindlessly?) to please herself. The shameless narcissism—the unthinking sense of entitlement of an unusually beautiful, and, then as now (*pace* Orwell's warning about double-negatives), not unintelligent woman, seemed a not unnatural phenomenon.

There were annual birthday cards from her to you, the last when you were twelve, but the envelopes were without return addresses, and I chose not to give you the cards. Why stir up unanswerable questions, or feelings that were beyond gratification? I myself had several New Year's cards from her, with uncharacteristically bland greetings: 'with love' or 'kind regards' or 'wishing you a year of health, happiness, and adventure'—and also a letter congratulating me on the publication of *Prizefighter*, hoping it would be the first of many successes (as of this writing, there has never been a successor—her hope, then, become a curse that I embraced?), and noting that the scene in which the protagonist discovers his girlfriend has cheated on him suggested to her that I had not yet gotten over what she saw as inconsequential dalliances of a kind that occurred in most—her word—*mature* marriages. 'Grow up, Max,' she advised.

Once she left, she never inquired about you. But if she had, I might have informed her that instead of killing you, or her, or myself, I had decided to live, and that it was you, Charlie—her son—who, unwittingly, saved *all* our lives. You didn't know that, did you?

Shortly after your homecoming from Singapore, while you were sleeping off your jetlag, I shared some of this with Seana, who responded to my tales of woe with what she said was an old Irish adage: 'Ah family, family—can't live with 'em… can't kill 'em.'

Seana is a jewel, as you know—multi-faceted, sharp-edged, and with a quirky brilliance—a luminosity—that rises from deep within, and whenever and wherever you are now, it is my hope that you and she are, and will remain, friends. There's nothing that gives more comfort than to imagine this is so. As to why you might be friends, the only answer, as ever (cf. Montaigne): *because you are you, and she is she.*

So: how did you save my life (and your own)?

The quick answer: by falling, and trusting I would catch you and save you from hurt.

How it happened: I had begun drinking even before your mother left us—evenings, afternoons, mornings. On a daily basis, the numbing of senses—along with the resultant dizziness, fogged mind, and clogged sleep—got me through. I'd pour a bit of Scotch (Dewar's) into my coffee at the start of the day; while receiving students in my office, I'd fill and refill a mug with Dewar's from a flask I kept in my bottom-right desk drawer; and when I arrived home I'd treat myself to the drink I told myself I was entitled to after a long day's work. On teaching days I left you in a nursery school, three blocks away, run by two Smith College faculty wives, both of whom were members of the synagogue, and both of whom, on random occasions, without, as far as I know, their sharing confidences, I plowed royally, despite or because of the alcohol that had me working hard not to call them, in the throes, by one another's names.

But what your mother called her 'dalliances'—and what a colleague who'd been one of those favored by her generosity called her 'open-legs policy,' a policy that favored at least two other department colleagues (a 'most favored nations policy'?), along with perhaps three of my male graduate students, and two female undergraduate honors students (to her credit, she did not discriminate on the basis of age, gender, or race)—utterly destroyed me. In her presence, hoping to get some purchase on what seemed an increasingly fragile world—an apology perhaps, a vow to reform and start over, an acknowledgment of the effect of her actions on me, a suggestion that we sign up for couples counseling—I was all fumbling and trembling. The only thing I wanted was to save our marriage and family, to make her stop having lovers, and to have her love me again.

But I *do* love you, she would say. And really, Max, why the surprise? Haven't you always said that the great thing in life was to remain open to possibility (a phrase I had, to my chagrin, used frequently during our courtship, especially when in pursuit of specific physical attentions)?

Didn't I agree, given our mutual love of sensuality—of polymorphous perversity—that the prospect of making love with one person and one person only for the next half-century was absurd? Didn't I see that her act had been a gift, and would enable us, *dans le style français*, to remain together for the duration? Didn't we both adore the French movie, *L'Ordonnance*, and declare it our very favorite? (In the movie's opening scenes, a newly married couple go to their family doctor because the woman has, beginning on the day of her wedding, become severely depressed. The doctor talks with her, nods sagely, and announces the sole logical, and very French, remedy: *Elle doit prendre un amant*, after which he writes out a prescription—'*for one lover*'—which the young woman and her husband bring to the local pharmacy.) Moreover, your mother declared, what she did when she was not at home was her *private life*, and hadn't I, in at least two essays about the decline of the novel from its cultural centrality, linked this decline to the parallel (and lamentable) decline in our valuation of privacy?

Her words—the news, the facts—fell on tender ears, and on a sensibility—and ego—too blue and bruised to bear them. I was a failure—as husband, father, man—and would never recover from what everyone would surely see as well-earned punishment. Her arguments, such as they were (to her credit, she never attempted to convince me of anything), though I could acknowledge their merits, passed me by.

What did *not* pass by was the knowledge that I had turned out to be much more a man of my generation and upbringing than I had acknowledged—'distressingly conventional,' was your mother's judgment—for I had clearly (and mistakenly) believed that if vows of love and marriage were exchanged, like the bodily intimacies that were their physical manifestations, they were intended to be honored eternally. Although your mother and I (she was two years older) were born of the same generation, she had somehow escaped—evolved from?—values of fidelity I, and most people I grew up with, had pledged obedience to.

In this, she would seem not unlike our dear Seana, though there are notable differences. To my knowledge, Seana, never married, has never, therefore, had the opportunity, in such matters, to violate a contract she has been party to; nor, without children, has she had the *option* (foul word of our time—and how I abhorred your mother's use of it to rationalize indulgence) of abandoning them. Seana has also never, to my knowledge, put much stock in romantic notions of love. Nor is she, as your mother was, a devotee of women who openly celebrated their sexual appetites and exploits—e.g., Mae West, who, you may recall, makes a cameo appearance in *Prizefighter*, and who, in real life (as in my novel) would hang out at Stillman's gym on West 57th Street, watching the boxers spar, then choosing one or several to take home with her for the afternoon.

Although Seana knows I thought seriously of suicide, she does not know that I thought of doing away with you. Despite (or because of) the easy way she has always seemed to have, in and out of her fictions, about relations with men and women, she has never judged the behavior of others—their moral and ethical positions, so to speak—by her own. She has seemed, when not herself depressed, to truly believe in the priority of pleasure, and that pleasure and morality do not necessarily, as she once put it, have dibs one on the other. Pleasure—and love—seem to exist for her, I've sometimes thought, in the same way that good stories do: *because they are.* When once upon a time I asked her about such matters, she shrugged, and replied with what seemed to her an incontrovertible fact. 'You can refute Hegel,' she said, quoting Yeats, 'but not the Song of Sixpence.'

Because of a story she submitted in the third week of her first workshop, I came, early on, to understand something of her views. In the story, a young woman discovers that her boyfriend is sleeping with the young woman's best friend—a commonplace of both life and fiction, I recall her remarking in class, into which—the challenge she'd set herself—she'd hoped to breathe a bit of new life. The class had loved the story—adultery and betrayal were, of course, ancient themes with endless possible variations and permutations, I commented, while, in my best teacherly manner referring the class to Stendahl (*On Love*) and de Rougemont (*Love in the Western World*)—but I suggested that Seana's story, for all its vividness and narrative felicity, remained somewhat derivative and familiar.

When, in conference, I repeated my reservations, and added that I'd wondered about the young woman in the tale, and if—I trusted I wasn't out of line—there were some autobiographical basis for the woman's distress that had compromised her imaginative freedom, Seana had laughed in the most disarmingly open way.

'Oh, Professor Eisner,' she said, 'Not at all. I mean, I like getting laid as much as the next girl.'

Without missing a beat, I suggested she consider giving this sentiment to her heroine, and that it might lend a particularity to the tale that would do the job she'd hoped to do. In fiction, as in life, I noted in my genially ponderous way, predictability was the enemy of all that was of more than passing interest, and if she let us see that her heroine thought this way—if she provided her with a bit of her own irreverent way of seeing life—it might do wonders for the story.

But back to your fall, son, and to my wrecked and wretched condition, which was its cause. The basics: I couldn't bear knowing that what your mother gave to me, she bestowed freely (happily?) on others. In me, I discovered, jealousy easily trumped rationality, even though I knew—could proclaim—that jealousy was itself merely the illusion of possession.

But oh my, the power of that illusion in my imagination! At first, all I wanted was to win her back—for her to forgive me, for me to forgive her, for her to forgive me for my difficulty in forgiving her, et cetera et cetera. But when—to test me?—she suggested we have her favorite graduate student (not the busboy, but another) move in with us—he could, she argued, help with you, Charlie, and with chores (feedings, diapers, babysitting, lawn mowing), and help us renew what clearly, to judge from my upset, was in need of renewal. When I said no—no, never, *jamais*, *mai*, *nunca*, *nunquam*, over my dead body—*genug!*— she simply smiled, said I could have things my way, and left. I didn't see her for the next four days or nights, and these were the first evenings, and mornings, when my closest friend became Dewar's. In fact, on the fifth morning after her absence, she found me on the bathroom floor, lying in my puke while you wailed away in your crib.

'Though you're pitiable,' she said (she used the French *pénible*, a deft touch, thereby connoting both pitiable *and* pathetic, and helping the dagger of her betrayal penetrate more easily), 'I don't pity you, and I certainly don't want to listen to that little lump of flesh and diarrhea' (a reference to you, son) 'crying all day. So I'm out of here, Max.'

I managed to get to my feet and wash my face, and she smiled at me with what seemed genuine kindness: 'We gave it our best,' she said. 'I believe we really did. But it's not for me, this marriage-mommy thing, and better that we know it sooner than later, wouldn't you agree?'

I agreed, of course. 'Yes,' I said. 'Oh sure. Of course. *Bien sûr*. Whatever you say. Whatever you want...!' And then we were two, and I picked you up, set you down on the changing table, changed your diaper, and rocked you in my arms, and thought— this was, of course, nearly a dozen years before Seana arrived— were this a story, what suggestion could I make that would lend it credibility, or, better still, sympathy for its protagonist? And as soon as I asked, the answer was there—the old writer's standby, courtesy of Messrs. Twain and Faulkner: You must kill your darlings.

The fantasy, along with drink, did, as I said earlier, help get me through. What part of me believed, you see, was that the best and only way to get back at her and hurt her badly was to hurt *you* (her son, after all). But no Medea, *moi*—and give thanks to whatever gods that be, no Greek tragedy in the House of

Eisner either. At the time I didn't think through the idea of doing away with us, or believe in it—it seemed, simply, the only solution to ending the pain, which dragged with it a thunderous noise that had taken to traveling in a continual, merciless loop through the marrow of my bones.

In truth, I don't think I believed much of anything that year, which may be why it seems missing. And it has always seemed missing, obviously, because I was missing—in action, and in in-action. Although I try now and then to summon up memories—*à la recherche*, Max, I cry out silently; *à la recherche!*—I recall few details: I slept, I ate, I taught, I shaved, I pissed, I shat, and I drank; I shopped, I cooked, I put you to sleep, I took you to nursery school, I picked you up from nursery school, I took you to the doctor, I talked to you, I talked with you, I bought you clothes, I dressed you, I fed you, I changed your diapers, I toilet-trained you, I helped you learn to walk and to ride a tricycle, and I probably took some delight in your development. You were the best and brightest of them all, the nursery school ladies told me, as did a coterie of grad student babysitters (several of whom offered to stay the night, invitations I wisely, though not without ambivalence, declined): before you were fifteen months old, you could play simple games of cards (War, Go-Fish), pick out favorite CDs, sing songs on-key and hold to your part in rounds, ice-skate on double runners on Paradise Pond, and laugh at jokes. You were also enormously responsive, affectionate, and trusting, though given our circumstances, who can figure why.

A for-instance: Once, putting you to bed at night, a glass of Jim Beam in hand (seven and a half months following your mother's departure, in a decision I considered to be a mark of incipient maturity, I had switched, a month or two before, from Scotch to bourbon), you asked for a taste, and I dipped my finger in, let you lick it.

'So what's your Daddy's favorite drink?' I asked, and when

you looked puzzled, I gave you the answer: 'Why, the *next* one, of course!'

You cracked up—a bubbling belly laugh that had you clapping your hands and rolling around in your crib. Did you understand the joke? Were you just being silly? Were you reacting to the way I was laughing at my own joke? Were you laughing because you thought laughing would please me…?

Six weeks and two days after your first birthday, I received papers from a lawyer, informing me that your mother wanted nothing from me except my agreement to a divorce, and to be able to retrieve some personal possessions. In this, I suppose, her behavior was admirable. If I agreed not to contest the divorce, retained a lawyer of my own, and signed relevant papers, we could take legal and permanent leave of each other within ninety days, with no monies or properties exchanged or owed.

It was done, and the finality of documents and signatures, once processed and approved by a court, went a long way in helping to thicken the heavy, sooty fog in which I lived.

Holden Caulfield—a character I was somewhat alone at that time in not finding worthy of the loving attention he received (he seemed merely a somewhat confused *shlemiel* of a preppy to me, without, other than his sentimental love for his lost family, any significant redeeming qualities)—did come to mind whenever I thought I was ready to do the deed, for I kept thinking of what he said when he contemplated jumping from a window, and how he would have done it if not for the thought of all the strangers who would come around afterwards to gawk at his corpse.

I had similar inhibitions: not merely, What will people—strangers!—think?—but, What would *she* think?—and when the latter thought arrived, it served mainly to enhance my insecurity and immobility, sorry soul that I was, and to convince me she'd been right to ditch and humiliate me.

Still there was the blackness in which I lived, Charlie, and it was terribly real and dark, and no matter what words I or anyone put on it, let me tell you: there is nothing as awful as feeling so deeply sad that to leave the world seems not only, in prospect, a relief, but *just*! How much better life would be for everyone else were I gone! What a gift to the world my absence would be! But if I did it solo, I feared, she would get you, or, if she demurred re motherhood, the courts would get you, and such thoughts also held me back.

And there was also time—the passage of time, more exactly. At some point in the thirteenth month of my sorrows, the beast inside mind and body seemed to be tiring of me (out of boredom, I hypothesized), and I noticed, too, that I was taking occasional pleasure from simple things—eating, sleeping, holding your hand on walks, watching you eat, or sleep, or play with your toy cars and building blocks—and I began to have a distaste, not for bourbon—never, never, never—but for the foggy dizziness it induced. Then you fell.

I was, as usual, moderately sloshed, and it was your bedtime, and I had a stack of papers to grade, a few rolled and tucked snugly under my left arm, and I was very upset with you because you'd soiled yourself. Why? Why were you doing this to me? You'd been toilet-trained for six or seven weeks (precocious as ever, you had accomplished this feat a full four months before your second birthday), we'd both taken pride in the achievement, and you'd graduated from your crib to a bed—the top half of the old hi-riser that had served as *my* childhood bed in Brooklyn. Why *now*? Had I not been paying you enough attention? Were you angry with me? Were you missing your mother, or one of our babysitters (you'd taken an especial shine to a vixenish young woman named Robyn Hayes Henderson, who, by infiltrating your affections, was determined to have your father infiltrate her moist, secret places), or…

Who knew? What I do know is that when I smelled the

presence of the foul deed, and asked if you had done it, I was already too angry for anyone's good, and when you grinned with what seemed a fiendish look of feigned innocence, and said, 'I don't *know*, Daddy,' I lost it.

So I did what I did sometimes: I let loose with words as if I were battering a punching bag with them—*How many times have I told you this or that*, and *What's the matter with you, you ungrateful little schmuck*, and *When the fuck are you going to grow up*, and *I have no patience left for you, you bird-brained momzer*, and additional choice and self-pitying gabble about having to do everything, everything, everything by myself. *Give me a break, you little shit-head, you and your shit-filled pants!* I screamed. *Just give me a fucking break, you stupid lump of clumped, rotten turds!* In my fury, and without at first letting go of the student papers, I grabbed you—*snatched* you— and carried you in the crook of my right arm up the stairs and into your room, where I tried to hoist you up onto the changing table. But the flight of stairs had made the bourbon produce a major shimmer of nausea—*Hey*, I wanted to shout to the world: *Look at the noble, dead-drunk dumb daddy doing his goddamned dumb daddy thing!*—and as I lifted you with the intent of slamming you down on the table—smashing you!—you slipped out of my grasp, and for an instant, as in the memory of car crashes, all went into sickly slow motion: I saw you falling, and I saw that your head had turned upside down, and that the exposed and sharp iron corner of your bed was in perfect position to receive your skull—and yet you smiled at me with the most loving, trusting smile I had ever seen or ever expect to see again.

You showed no fear, Charlie. You seemed to believe that if I were taking care of you, no harm could come your way. However, ever forget your sublime calm—the loving trust in your eyes?

I dropped the student papers, scooped you up before you hit the bed's flanged corner ('A fumble recovered, folks!' I heard an announcer proclaim), cleaned you up, and dressed you in freshly laundered pajamas. 'Sorry, Daddy,' you said and, when you noticed the glimmering film in my eyes, you asked if I'd hurt myself.

'Not at all,' I said. 'Not at all.'

I stopped drinking the next morning. The glooms retreated, defeated by your trust in me, which was, in that moment, certainly greater than *my* trust in me. Three weeks later, I received galleys for *Prizefighter*, and you and I celebrated by driving to Maine for lunch (clam rolls became your favorite food well into your teens). I waded into revisions with gusto, and within a year I married again—Inez Palenco, a sweet, bright woman four years younger than I (a social worker at an agency in Holyoke, a competent oboist, and a master gardener), whom you may remember only through photos, for within seventeen months of our marriage (we went to Glacier National Park, we three, for a ten-day honeymoon), she was done in by that cunning variety of breast cancer that can sneak in and take over between regular check-ups.

Somehow you grew up, went to school, graduated, and set off to seek your fortune, and what I have since thought of as 'The Great Glooms' never returned with any marked force, though I feared their return, as now, every day when I woke and every night before I slept—and you turned into as fine a son as any man might be lucky enough to have.

Let me note something else that contributed to the fading away of my missing year, and I note it not to deprive you of credit for having helped me—us!—come to a better place, but to put what happened, and how it happened, into a somewhat larger context. I had, perhaps a year before the night on which you fell, come under the spell of Primo Levi, who, as man and writer, had become my hero. As you know (how proud I was when you chose several of his books, beginning with *If This Is A Man*, for book reports in high school), he wrote about his experiences in Auschwitz and journey home from Auschwitz, but also about myriad other matters: his career as a chemist, his family, other people's vocations, his friendships, his beloved city of Turin.

It has occurred to me of late—when I have, happily, been able to give freer rein to my ruminative disposition—that the slight lessening of depressive pain I began to experience may have come from reading, not about Levi's life as victim, survivor, and witness, but about his views on suicide, along with what in him is so life-affirming (to use an apt if banal phrase): his fierce ability to see the differences in other people—their particularities and idiosyncrasies—in a time when they were put to death because they were judged, as Jews, to be *no* different, one from the other.

Though, of course, they were also exterminated because they were just that: *other.* We always fear, and despise, whatever we perceive as different from who we are, and in this, he has explained, we are not that different from animals, who are much more intolerant of members of their own species than they are of those of other species. Thus, anti-Semitism, he has suggested, is simply a horrific example of a more general phenomenon.

But suicide—what about suicide? There were, I was surprised to learn from Levi, few suicides in the camps—and generally, Levi notes, fewer suicides in wartime than in times of peace. His reasoning as to why this was so appears in a self-interview that I came across a few evenings before the night on which you fell, and long before—inexplicable, profoundly disturbing mystery!—*he* fell down a stairwell in a self-willed act I trust neither of us will emulate—one that ended his life in the place he loved: the house in which he'd been born and, before and after Auschwitz, had lived.

Yet some years before this, Levi wrote that he considered suicide a distinctively human act (we had never seen evidence that animals committed suicide), and that because, in the camps, human beings, both victims and oppressors, tended more toward the level of animals—of *animality*—it was the business of the day—essentials—that ruled: what you were going to eat and if you were going to eat, how cold it would be, what you would wear against the cold, how heavy was the work and of what kind, et cetera. In short: you thought, if 'thought' is the right word, of how you were going to make it through the day and into the evening and through the night. There was, simply, no time to think about killing yourself.

So I became busy. I began exercising regularly. I began preparing, in earnest, for the book I would write about Henry James as Irishman; I began making notes for new stories and novels; I began planting a garden, and learning carpentry; I began seeking out women who would make suitable helpmates for me, and loving (step-)mothers for you. I began cooking meals regularly, breakfast and dinner, and planning vacations, and asking my department chair if I could teach new courses that would require I put myself to school in the work of authors (Cather, Wharton, Howells, Dos Passos, Beckett) with whom I had, until then, only cursory acquaintance. I took tennis lessons, joined a co-ed softball team, took a course in auto repair, and searched out (in vain for the most part) lost cousins, aunts, and uncles. I painted rooms, repaired furniture, built bookcases, created file systems, learned to do my own taxes, and to play the piano.

Not all at once, of course, and after a while—when the demon of depression seemed to have increasing difficulty finding his way back into my daily life, I began to let some of the new activities fall away. But this happened over the course of several years, and I mark what has, until this moment, been its *definitive* departure (though daily wariness remains), from the third month of my third marriage—to Janice Fullerton, whom you will recall as perhaps the most animated and lively of my wives, though herself—the aphrodisiacal cue and clue to my infatuation and our romance?—a lifelong victim of depression, which, in the glory days of falling in love, departed, only to return when a bit of the bloom, as was inevitable, began to wear off the rose of our bliss.

Janice never became suicidal—her condition was more like a ground bass, or low-grade hum—a Baroque ostinato I came to think I could actually *hear*, and some twenty-one months after our wedding, she left us, saying it was simply not *fair*—not fair!—can you *imagine*?—that it was not *fair* for anyone to have to live with someone so plagued with sadness, and with such labile changes of mood. (Why, she would write in a note a month or two later, should we have to live and ride on the nauseating sine-curve of *her* feelings?)

I tried to talk her out of leaving (I truly loved her, as, in fact, I loved *all* my wives, along with a good number of my girlfriends; my capacity for falling in love, and staying in love, being one of my more consistent capabilities), and with medications (not then as effective as they are said to be now), and some psychotherapy, she did return to her happier and more stable self for a while. Her will to be a miserable, unloved, unworthy, abandoned child, however, proved ultimately stronger than medications, therapy, or us. In the cartons of correspondence that Seana has acquired, you will, if interested, find some four to five dozen letters from Janice. She never married again, never had children, and always inquired about you, Charlie. I believe she missed you more than she missed me, the fact that you were and were not her (only) son creating complex, and somewhat anguished attachments, not to you—no guilt, Charlie, please, please!—but to parts of her earlier life that held a power over her against which all efforts, ours included—tolerant and loving though we both were—proved helpless.

But to the end of ending this meditation, let me return to what made the difference: to Primo Levi's life and to his thoughts about suicide, and thus to your life—to what I saw in your eyes, and believe I sensed of your happy prospects on the night of your fall.

I had, then as now, the highest hopes for you, Charlie, and I trust you won't confuse these hopes for expectations. Of the latter, I have none. Let me explain: When I first read *Triangle*, brilliant and wonderful as I found it, what was *most* wonderful (Mister James my guide yet again) was the mind of the writer writing it. For no matter its faults, and this goes for *Plain Jane* as well, what shone through was the presence of a unique, supremely intelligent mind—an idiosyncratic voice and shrewd sensibility informing a well(-enough) made tale.

What also came to mind when I read *Triangle*, and again when I'd finished reading *Plain Jane*, were words a friend (Mrs. Cadwalader Jones) wrote in a letter to a friend of hers after she'd come upon some early stories by Henry James. The stories were pleasing, and well enough made, she wrote. What had impressed, though, was some other quality—what Seana has, and what you have, son. What had impressed was that the stories were informed, despite their undistinguished quality *as stories*, by a remarkable and remarkably unexpected singularity of mind—a quality of mind so rare it had, taking her by surprise, moved her utterly. It is so difficult, she wrote (in a sentence with which I've always hoped—no: intended!—to end this letter)—it is so difficult to do anything well in this mysterious world.

When I finished reading my father's story, I put it back in the envelope, then gazed out the window past Seana, who was fast asleep, and watched my reflection flicker on and off among passing trees, houses, and cars while imagining that I was falling, again and again, and that Max was catching me again and again, and I wondered: had it really happened? Had he really dropped me once upon a time, and had he really thought of killing the two of us, and had a look I gave him really served to stop *his* fall? I could recall the look on his face when he had me on the changing table—or I thought I could—and when I saw him bending over and wiggling his nose against mine to make me laugh, I pictured Trish lifting Anna into her high-chair, and I wondered too: had we really inhaled Nick's ashes? And then, looking at Seana, whose mouth was open in a nearly perfect oval, but with no sound coming from it, I wondered if it were really true that she and I were together, and that we cared for each other in a way that—if I weren't afraid it would make her take flight—I would have told her could, in my opinion, be called love?

I thought, too, of how, when we made love, she would hold to me almost desperately, her nails digging into my shoulders and back, and how afterwards, without apology, her face against my chest, she would weep softly.

Seana didn't wake until the conductor announced that we were approaching the 125th Street station stop, Harlem, in New York City.

She tapped on the envelope. "So what do you think?" she asked.

"I miss him," I said.

"Meaning that for you this year of mourning will be a *missing* year?"

"If you say so."

"He was my dear friend and mentor, yes, but he was *your* father," she said.

"That's true."

"Though he surprised us by dying too soon, didn't he?"

"He surprised himself more," I said. "If, that is—and I guess I'm thinking the way he does in the letter—in his story—if, that is, he could know somehow—could *have* known—that he'd be gone sooner than he thought he'd be. He was looking forward to a longer life."

"Sixteen years of it."

"When you were going through his stuff," I asked, "did you find any pictures of him with my mother?"

"A few. I put them aside, in case you asked."

"I've seen lots of pictures of *her*," I said. "He'd show them to me when I was a kid and asked about her, but I never saw any pictures of them together. She *was* very beautiful, though not the way you are."

"How am I beautiful, Charlie?"

I shrugged. "I never think of you as pretty," I said.

"Neither do I. So...?"

"So my mother was pretty the way lots of movie stars can be pretty," I said. "You're beautiful."

"The difference?"

"I think I would have grown tired of looking at my mother after a while, but I know I'll never get tired of looking at you. The more I look at you the more mysterious you become."

"I'll take that."

"It was the same when I first met you, though I certainly couldn't have put my feelings into words back then."

The conductor announced that we were being held in the 125th Street station momentarily, but would be moving shortly. Seana took *A Missing Year* from me, put it into her overnight bag, set a different envelope on my lap.

"Another gift from your father," she said. "I'm not certain he intended you to see this, but when he presented me with his stuff—his archive, we'll call it—he said nothing about any restrictions."

THIRTEEN WAYS OF LOOKING
AT A DEAD SON
(with apologies to Wallace Stevens)

I

Among twenty sleepless hours
The only thing moving
Was the black eye of my heart.

II

I was of three moods,
Like a man
In whom there are three brains.

III

My son whirled in the autumn winds.
He was a sliver of the dark dream.

IV

A man and a woman
Are one.
A man and a woman and a child
Are none.

V

I do not know which to prefer
The beauty of drowning
Or the beauty of hanging,
The child breathing
Or just after.

VI

Icicles filled my sorry heart
And barbed-wire fencing.
The shadow of my son
Crossed, to and fro.
The dread impulse
Traced in the shadow
An indecipherable woe.

VII

O meagre men of Massachusetts,
Why do you imagine dead children?

Do you not see how the son
Walks around the corpse
Of the women about you?

VIII

I know noble sentiments
And clouded, inescapable glooms;
But I know, too,
That the son is involved
In what I know.

IX

When the son fell out of sight,
It marked the edge
Of one of many bloodless circles.

X

At the sight of my son
Lying in a green light,
Even the angels of mercy
Would cry out sharply.

XI

He crawled over Manhattan
In a stoned stupor.
Once, a fear pierced him,
In that he mistook
The shadow of his son
For himself.

XII

The train is moving.
The son, bound, must be lying on its tracks.

XIII

It was evening all afternoon.
It was snowing blood
And it was going to snow blood.
My son slept forever
On the iron bed.

In Brooklyn, when we came up from the subway and stood at the corner of Church and Nostrand Avenues, Seana said she was pleased—and relieved—to find that the Lincoln Savings Bank, where she'd had a savings account when she was a schoolgirl, was still there, across the street. As miserable as our childhoods might be, yet the objects *of* our childhood remained precious to us, didn't they? she said. And the loss of these objects, she added a moment later—places, things—people too, sometimes—no matter the years gone by, could still wound us.

An A&P and an Ebinger's Bakery were long gone, she said— they'd been there, on the other side of Nostrand Avenue, all through her childhood—and so was a corner cigar store, and a poolroom that had occupied a floor above the cigar store, where the tough guys in the neighborhood—Italians for the most part—had hung out, and where she'd sometimes hung out with them.

We walked along Church Avenue, where stores, their brightly lettered marquees advertising goods and services, were all West Indian except for a new Starbucks coffee shop, and a Rite-Aid drugstore where a theater—the Granada—had been. At Rogers Avenue, I pointed to part of an old trolley track, like a silver rib, showing through the street's pot-holed surface a few feet from the curb. My father had set most of *Prizefighter* in this part of Brooklyn, and in the book the hero had hitched rides on the backs of trolley cars, had loved to watch sparks fly from the overhead electrical wires that supplied juice to the trolleys, and to watch the motormen, at this corner, switch trolley routes by using long poles—like the kind pole-vaulters used, he'd written—to move cables from one overhead line to another.

We came to a narrow side street that ran next to the Holy Cross church—Veronica Place—and Seana told me the house in which she'd grown up and where her mother still lived, was down this street, four houses in, which was something I already knew (Max had pointed it out on one of our visits), but I didn't say so. She asked if we could walk a while longer, said she was more nervous—anxious—than she expected to be. Then she started talking, her words coming fast, about *Julius Caesar*, and how Max, who'd taught a Shakespeare seminar she'd taken, had pointed out that the main character in the play named for him dies halfway through, and that one way of understanding the play was to consider how and why, though never physically present in the play's second half, Caesar remains the play's major character, its controlling presence.

"Like my father dying halfway through *my* life?" I said. "Is that what you're trying to say?"

"It crossed my mind," Seana said.

"I'm exactly half his age—half the age he was when he died," I said. "Thirty-six to his seventy-two. Did you realize that?"

"No."

"Neither did I. Not until now."

We passed the Holy Cross schoolyard, where some black guys were playing basketball, and I remembered my father telling me about older guys he'd played with here when he was a boy, some of whom had been caught in the point-fixing scandals of the early fifties. One of them had made a cameo appearance in *Prizefighter*—a black guy kicked out of college and banned for life from professional basketball—and whenever someone asked why he wasn't playing in the big time, he'd answer: "Because I work in the Minit-Wash now, washing down cars, you know? That's how come I got such clean hands. Yeah, me, I got the cleanest hands of any fixer around...."

When we got to Bedford Avenue and stood in front of Erasmus Hall High School, where Max had gone, Seana talked again about hanging out with Italian guys when she was growing up, and told me they'd been her first lovers.

"They were football, baseball, and soccer players, most of them," she said, "and they lifted weights, and they were in great shape, and they were always in a rush. Sometimes we'd do it in the schoolyard when it was dark, me bent over and bracing myself against the wall—usually the wall where they'd chalked in the strike zone for stickball—them coming into me from behind. They took turns some nights. I was very *American* in this, Charlie—in wanting to be *well-liked*—and afterwards they'd ask if I wanted one of them to walk me home, to be with me in case any niggers—*their* word—tried to molest me, which seemed to them the very worst thing that could happen to a girl, even an Irish girl they'd just screwed."

Like the church, Erasmus appeared to have been well maintained. Built in the style of British universities, with four buildings, turrets at the corners, forming a rectangle that enclosed an inner courtyard, it looked like a medieval castle. I told her that the first time I'd come here Max had remarked on how incredible it was to find a replica of Oxford University smack in the middle of a lower middle-class Brooklyn neighborhood. He'd talked about how much he owed to his education at Erasmus: to being taught by men who, more than a handful with doctorates, had become high school teachers during the depression in order to support their families.

We headed back toward the Holy Cross church, and when I said that I knew she hadn't been back here for a while, but didn't she once own an apartment in Brooklyn, she let go of my arm.

"Yes, I own an apartment in Brooklyn," she said. "In Carroll Gardens. I also own a condo in Boston, a home in Taos, New Mexico, and a tastefully furnished flat in Paris."

"*Really?*"

"Thanks to my two books, and shrewd investments, I *am* a fairly wealthy woman," she said. "Isn't that why, even though I'm almost old enough to be your mother, you've been hot for my crotch?"

"Oh come on," I said. "I know this—going home—is hard for you, but…"

"And I don't need your two-bit sympathy or condescension," she snapped. "How the hell would *you* know what is or isn't hard for me?"

"Stop it," I said. "Just stop it, okay, or…"

"Or what? You'll throw me off a balcony?"

"If I can find one around here," I said. "Sure. Though a fire escape might do."

"Thank you, Charlie," she said. "Thanks for pushing back. Despite your story—you and Nick and whatever did or didn't happen at the party—I wasn't sure you had it in you."

"But you *are* nuts," I said. "Mean too."

"I can be," she said. "You've got that right."

"Mean to yourself first of all," I said.

"*Above* all," she said.

"Do you really have an apartment in Brooklyn?"

"I told you I did."

"And three others?"

"That's right."

"But *why*?" I asked. "Why so many different places?"

"Guess."

"So nobody can find you?"

"Maybe."

"But *I* found you." I pulled her close, and spoke the words that came to me next: "Finders keepers…?"

We were passing the Holy Cross schoolyard again, and she set her overnight bag down, then pushed me, step by step, until my back was up against the chain-link fence.

"Finders *what*?!" she said, her face close to mine. "Because if you could *find* any sense in your head, you'd keep your sentimental sentiments to yourself and realize that this woman you claim to care about, and who has, rash act, admitted she cares for you, is having a distinctly and *remarkably* hard time now. And why do you think that is, Mister Eisner?"

"Hey—slow down," I said. "I was just…"

"You were just being your usual innocent, *faux-naif*, ignorant self, but it won't wash this time, son, because it's all coming down the pike and going up the pike at the same time and nobody's directing traffic. *Everything*, buster—your father in the grave, my mother on her way there, my father too mean to die, my beloved sisters-in-waiting with their expanding litters of Catholic brats, my unwritten novels, and *my whole fucking life*, can't you see? Can't you *see*? Are you fucking blind, or a moron, or *what*?"

"I'm Charles Eisner, and I'm your friend," I said.

"My *friend*?!" she said. She grabbed me by the shoulders, shoved me against the fence. "*My friend*?! Then stop trying to cheer me up with your banal, bumbling, belittling Brooklyn banter. And tell me this—what would it take to get you to just shut up and stop asking questions and judging every goddamned thing I think and do…?"

"But I wasn't…"

She pulled me to her, then slammed me against the fence. "Can you please just shut your fucking mouth?" she said. "Or, as we used to say in these parts—where *I* grew up, young man— why don't you shut your ass and give your mouth a chance, because I don't need *words* now, can you understand that? I don't need sympathy, or empathy, or solicitude, or compassion, or condolence, or contrition, or consolation, or any other word beginning with the letter *C*, because actions speak louder than words, right?"

And saying this she slammed me against the fence again, and when she did, cheers went up from inside the schoolyard, some of the black guys yelling at her to let me have it, to bust my mouth, and chop up my balls, and wipe up the sidewalk with what was left.

She looked past me. "Maybe later," she said to them calmly, then turned back to me. "I own four homes," she said. "One-two-three-four, and, as it happens, I can not be found in any of them today, but when I can, know this: that I am writing a different novel in each of them, see, and maybe I'm a different person in each of them, and maybe I have a different lover, or set of lovers in each of them, and what's it to you? What's it to you or anyone else if I *ever* finish one of these goddamned novels or I don't? You tell me that, you goddamned Jew bastard who's still wet behind the ears—you son-of-a-bitch-motherfucking-fart-slurping-scum-bag-of-a-Kotex-sniffing-cocksucking kike…"

The black guys on the other side of the fence whooped and hollered, and when they did, I pushed at Seana with both hands, and to my surprise, she gave way—no resistance at all—and beamed her most gorgeous smile at me.

"Hey—that was pretty fucking good, don't you think?" she said. She waved to the guys in the schoolyard. "See you around, you handsome black mothers!" she called. She picked up her bag, I picked up mine, and her free arm draped around my shoulder, we started walking down the street again.

"I *am* a piece of work, right?" she said. "You have to admit it."

"I admit it. You are definitely a piece of work."

"And not dull, right?"

"And not dull," I said. "A little fucked-up maybe. And volatile. Quite volatile."

"Labile would be the more accurate term," she said.

"Labile," I said. "Good word."

"With labia like mine, how not, right?"

"There's something to that."

"Do you think I'm wasting good lines now, spouting out all this stuff—that I'm throwing away precious soliloquies?"

"No," I said. "The way I see it, you're setting your words free so they can wander happily in the ether."

"Point well taken," she said. "And there's also this: if I can *live* the stuff, why write it? Henry Miller liked to talk about that—about how you often come up with your best lines and stories when you're taking a crap, for example, and how afterwards you can never remember them or retrieve them. Like dreams or daydreams that arrive with astonishing clarity, and then are gone forever a second or two later."

"Before, when you were sleeping in the train, I dreamt that you and I fell in love with each other," I began, "and that when you woke and saw me, you didn't know if…"

"Shh," she said, and put a finger to my mouth. "Don't get me started again, okay? I do adore you, Charlie, and I adore Henry Miller too, and so did George Orwell, and so did your dad. But now it's time to visit Mom. You're in for a treat. She can be a real pistol."

"Like Eugenia?"

"At least."

When the door opened, a short, wiry white-haired woman grabbed Seana and pulled her into the house. "Oh my God, oh my dear God," the woman exclaimed. "It's you—it's really you! Oh my God oh my God oh my dear God…!"

Seana held to the woman and the two of them rocked back and forth in each other's arms for a while, after which Seana introduced me, telling me the woman was her sister Caitlin, and telling Caitlin that I was her friend Charlie Eisner.

"Then you'd be the great Max Eisner's son," Caitlin said, and kissed both my cheeks, then wiped at my cheeks with the backs of her hands and apologized for slobbering on me.

"But shh," she said. "Mum's upstairs sleeping."

Seana touched Caitlin's face, under her left eye, which seemed frozen in a half-open position.

"What happened?" Seana asked.

"Stroke," Caitlin said. "Minor, so they say."

Caitlin closed the door behind us, put a finger to her lips, and led us into a room that was small and musty, framed photos and dried flower arrangements everywhere, crocheted doilies on the back of a red-tufted couch, and on the backs and arms of two large easy chairs.

"They stented my carotid, and while I was in the hospital—better safe than sorry—I had them tie off my tubes," she said. She turned to me. "I had four children in six years, well into my forties, but tell me how *you* are, my child."

"I'm happy to be here," I said. "Seana's spoken about you often."

"We'll have none of that," she said, waving away my politeness and pointing to one of the easy chairs. I sat and she took my hands in both of hers. "You've had quite the loss, haven't you?"

"Yes," I said.

"I read about your dear father's passing in *The New York Times*. I had the honor of meeting him once, when Seana gave a reading at the main library here in Brooklyn. He was very proud of her, and so were we."

"No you weren't," Seana said.

"You'd be surprised," Caitlin said.

"Do tell," Seana said.

"No need to be snide," Caitlin said. "And I urge you not to be that way with Mum either. In fact, I'll ask you to promise to behave yourself."

"And if I don't?"

"I know you still have your own place, dear, but since you've come here before going there—" she gestured to our bags "—it would be good if you'd stay over with us."

"So I can watch Mom, and you can be off-duty?"

"There's no need for such," Caitlin said. "Mum loves you very much. We all do, even though—"

"Even though I'm the queen of sluts?" Seana said. "I used that in *Triangle*, you may recall. The mother calls her daughter 'the queen of sluts'—'the *reigning* queen of sluts.' It's one of the few autobiographical moments in my fiction traceable to my early years."

"In your book you gave the line to Mum, though it was our father who named you that," Caitlin said. "But my dear Seana— and let our friend Charles be a witness—let us agree that that's all water under the bridge and bygones be bygones, because I'm truly happy you've come home, and we *are* proud of you, and we've all said things—or *written* things—we wish we could take back, but that's why God invented forgiveness, don't you think?"

"Not in my book," she said.

"'Not in my book,'" Caitlin said. "That's very good. Very *literal*, I'd say." She spoke to me. "My sister certainly has a way with words, wouldn't *you* say, Charles?"

"Call me Charlie," I said.

"Of course, Charles," she said.

"'Not in my book,'" Seana said. "I like it. When I write my memoirs, that will be the title. What do you think?"

"I think you'll do whatever you please, same as always," Caitlin said. "Same as he did."

"He?" I asked.

"Our father," Seana said. "Patrick Michael O'Sullivan, whose name is never spoken here."

"And with reason," Caitlin said. "And how is he, you'll ask next, so I'll say at once that I wouldn't know. I haven't seen the sod in ages."

Seana took out her cell phone. "We can change that," she said. "I came prepared."

Caitlin tried to snatch the phone from Seana's hand. "*Don't you dare!*" she said.

"As I told Charlie on our way down here, I've been thinking it's time for a grand family reunion," Seana said. "And, as you just said, bygones are bygones, and water under the bridge, and forgiveness too, yes? There's always forgiveness, isn't that what you said? Isn't that what we were taught?"

"Don't do it," Caitlin said.

"Why not?" Seana said. "We're still family, and he's still our father, and good Catholics that they are, he and our mum are still married, aren't they?"

"Stop it," Caitlin said. "It will kill her."

"Till death do they part then, though perhaps, if she gets lucky, he'll go there first," Seana said. "And with her affliction—Alzheimer's—and all the years gone by, she probably won't recognize the old shitbag anyway."

"Stop it. Stop it at once. Stop provoking me. Stop being..."

"Stop being Seana?"

"May God forgive him for all he did," Caitlin said.

"Ah, but our Lord can't do that without proper confession, contrition, and penance."

"Enough, Seana. Show some respect."

"For *him*?"

"You know what I mean. Just you stop it now. Stop being so contrary, so..."

Seana put up her hand, cutting Caitlin off. "Is this Patrick Michael O'Sullivan—*the* Patrick Michael O'Sullivan?" she asked, the cell phone at her ear. "It is...? Did I wake you...? I see—no bother, you say, because you had to get up to answer the phone anyway...? Well, that's an old one, isn't it... and who is *this*, you ask...? Why this is your long-lost daughter, Seana..."

Caitlin stood. Seana stepped aside to let her pass, and Caitlin glared at her, and then, with a quick swipe, knocked the cell phone out of Seana's hands. The phone bounced once, hit a wall, and split open, its innards tumbling out.

Seana picked up a piece of the phone, placed it against her

ear, and grinned. "All gone!" she said. "So I guess that means we'll have to go fetch him. Are you with me, Charlie?"

"Sure," I said.

"If you go to get him, don't come back," Caitlin said.

Seana hesitated. "Do you *mean* that?" she asked.

Caitlin took a deep breath, exhaled, shook her head. "Of course not. But come here to me now." She spread her arms and Seana went to her. "I still love you, you know. We all do."

"*He* doesn't."

"'All' was not intended to be an *all*-inclusive term," Caitlin said. "That one never loved anyone other than himself. We know *that*. You're hardly alone there."

"True enough," Seana said. "Still…"

"And no matter your decision—to stay or to go—*I'll* be staying the night here," Caitlin said. She took Seana by the hand, and they sat on the couch, side by side. "Keira's with the children, hers and mine, God bless her. I left them at her house for a sleepover because my Hank's working night shift, and we take turns watching Mum now. We always had a talent for making do, didn't we?"

"We still do, it seems," Seana said.

"There are five of us, you know," she said to me. "I'm the oldest, and Seana's the baby, and there are three between us— Keira, Mary, and Margaret—Peggy we call her. Five sisters, each one come into the world smarter and more beautiful than the one before."

"So I've heard," I said.

Caitlin pointed to the ceiling. "And when it comes to Mum, you're in for a surprise. The Alzheimer's, or whatever you choose to call it, has made some inroads for sure. Her mind may not be what it once was, but its decline has been accompanied by some unforeseen benefits."

"The Lord works in mysterious ways," Seana said.

"Sometimes," Caitlin said. "Though not often, in my

experience. Mostly, I find Him quite transparent. He rewards good and punishes evil."

"In *this* life?" Seana said.

"In this life often, in the life-to-be eternally."

"And here on earth," Seana said, "there's the blessed Irish trinity, of course: shame, guilt, and humiliation."

"I've read your two books, you know," Caitlin said, "so little you say will shock me. And I've also read several books by your beloved Graham Greene, and what I take away from them is that straying from the fold can itself be the surest expression of faith, and that our Lord, in his abundant mercy, often pays more attention to His sinners than He does, say, to our Ladies of Sodality."

Seana covered her mouth to keep from laughing out loud.

"Have your fun," Caitlin said. "But please try not to laugh *at* us. If we mind our manners, we can get through most things. And..." She cocked her head to the side, pointed to the ceiling "...and yes, she's moving about, so I'll clean her up and bring her down, and then we can show you the surprise we prepared."

"What surprise?"

"In the event you came for a visit, which we've been counting on, we've kept it in readiness. There's not a day goes by, mind you, we don't think of you and remember you in our prayers."

Caitlin kissed me on the forehead. "And you too, dear child," she said. "We won't soon forget you and your dear father."

Caitlin and their mother were the same height, had the same short, cropped white hair, the same large hazel eyes. They stood at the entrance to the living room.

"Seana has come to visit us," Caitlin said.

Their mother spoke to Seana: "Why I once had a daughter named Seana," she said. "Did you know her?"

"I'm Seana," Seana said. "I'm your daughter."

"Well, isn't that good news," their mother said. "And you *look* quite wonderful, I must say, though you'll have to forgive my not recognizing you. My mind isn't quite what it was once upon a time."

"I'm sorry to hear that," Seana said.

"Well, these things happen, don't they, and who can know why."

"The Lord works in mysterious ways," Seana said.

"Oh that He does," their mother said. "Why just look at me, if you want proof!" She turned to me. "And who are you, young man?" She touched my cheek with her fingertips. "Why you've as beautiful and kind a face as Our Saviour Himself must have had."

I glanced at Seana, thought of saying what I imagined she was thinking: that I was a Jewish boy the way He was, and only three years older than He'd been when He died.

"I'm Charlie Eisner, a friend of Seana's," I said. "My father was Seana's teacher—her mentor."

"Meant what?" Seana's mother said. She turned to Seana and, suddenly alarmed, took a step back.

"And who are *you*, young lady, and when did *you* get here?" she asked.

"I'm Seana," Seana said again. "I'm your daughter. I'm Seana Shulamith McGee O'Sullivan."

"Ah, then you've come home at last," her mother said, after which, with great gentleness, she probed Seana's face with her fingers the way she'd probed mine. "How I missed you, and how I do love you. You were always the best and the most beautiful. You made my heart glad with happiness, didn't you?"

"Did I?"

"And with such a lovely name—except for McGee and O'Sullivan, of course." She spoke to me: "The McGees were cousins on my husband's side, and they were a sorry lot, you just ask anyone. And about O'Sullivan, who abandoned me and mine, the less said the better. But Shulamith! What a splendid name! So tell me, please, if you would—who gave you such a beautiful name, dear, for it surely wasn't me."

"I gave it to myself," Seana said. "It's Hebrew—from Solomon, for wisdom, and from 'shalom,' for peace."

"And from Salome," Caitlin said. "Let us not forget Salome."

"From Salome," Seana said.

"For *beauty*!" their mother exclaimed. "Of course. I can see that, for you *are* beautiful, with or without your veils, and isn't our life but a veil of tears, after all?"

"But that's not the same veil..." Seana began.

"I know *that*," her mother said, waving away her words. "Don't confuse me for one of those demented nursing home ladies, young woman. I was just being clever, but I'll never leave our home, do you hear? No matter what you say, you can't drive me out and set me on a slab of ice with a bag of food..."

"You'll always live here, Mum," Caitlin said. "We've made a vow—*all* your daughters have—isn't that so, Seana."

Seana said nothing.

"Oh I can be quite loveable and clever, as you've just seen, even without my memory," their mother said, and she sat down next to Seana. "And I'm glad of your visit."

"You smell like lilacs," Seana said. "The way you did when I was a girl."

"Talcum powder," her mother said. "Oh yes. Talcum powder—'an Irish shower' we call it. And would you know what young boys call an Irish priest?"

"I don't," Seana said. "What do young boys call an Irish priest?"

"A pain in the ass," her mother said. "Which is the kind of joke *he* would have made if were he still with us, and you know who I mean."

She folded her hands in her lap, and closed her eyes.

"Perhaps it's time for another nap," Caitlin said, "and afterwards we can show Seana the surprise we prepared for her."

Their mother opened her eyes, and sat up straight. "No nap while my daughter is with me," she said. "That would be rude. It's quite wonderful to have her here with us, you know, for there were times I feared I might die without ever seeing her again."

"Did you really?" Seana asked.

"I wouldn't lie to you, my child," her mother said. "Because, and no offense to your sisters, I did love you most of all. You were the child of my old age—the miracle and gift the Lord had prepared for me. You made me laugh again after he was gone, and I've read your books, the two of them, but you used your real name, though my own mother, bless her heart, said that if you're going to make a fool of yourself, you should do it out of town. So now, please, tell me all about yourself and about what you've been up to with this handsome, young man."

Seana's mother grinned broadly. Then her eyes closed again, and a moment later she was fast asleep.

"Who *is* this woman?" Seana asked Caitlin.

"It's one of the unforeseen benefits I mentioned," Caitlin said. "With her memory coming and going—going mostly— she's become all sweetness and light—the happy little girl she must have been before she married him, I've come to think, and before we all came along."

Caitlin said that after their mother woke, she would telephone their sisters, and that they were sure to come by and to bring their children—Seana's nieces and nephews—with them. Seana asked how they all were, and Caitlin talked about them and what they were up to: Keira, with three teenage girls at Sacred Heart, and two boys in middle school at Saint Francis. Built like little brick shithouses the boys were, Caitlin said, and Keira was selling real estate in Bay Ridge, and she was still married to Bill, though only God knew why, the way he played around with the college girls on his beat down by Brooklyn College.

And Mary, mostly on her own since her husband Mitchell went on permanent disability, was taking good care of *her* brood—two girls, two boys, and they were growing up just fine. A floor had collapsed under Mitchell during a fire in Red Hook, and he spent most of his days in bed watching television or at the local pub with his old firehouse buddies. And Peggy? Peggy was still vowing to leave her husband Joe—Joe a fireman too, and as much use, pardon her French, as a fart in a sausage factory for all the good he ever did, except to send out for pizza when Peggy had to work the night shift at Maimonides Hospital, where she was now chief nurse in pediatrics.

Her own husband, Hank, retired from the police force for six years and now working as a driver for a wealthy Park Avenue widow who dabbled in antiques, was probably the best of the lot, she said, and *their* four children were all out of college, three of them married and with their own children, and the baby— Fiona—engaged to a fine young man who'd been a star basketball player at St. John's. The bad news, though, was that Fiona had been diagnosed with lupus, though the doctors caught it early and believed it would prove manageable, and her young man—John—was standing by her. The wedding was set for June.

"The Lord does try us sometimes," Caitlin said, "and mostly we prove worthy of His love, and the good news is that we have one another, so we can help out when need be and—what saves the day—complain to each other on a regular basis. For isn't complaining what that man whose name will not be spoken told us it was—a great indoor sport at which the Irish excel?"

Seana smiled. "I'll look forward to complaining with you," she said.

"And what would *you* have to complain about?" Caitlin said. "You with no husband, no children, all the money in the world, men fainting at the sight of you, and this handsome, young friend doting on you."

Seana flinched visibly, but said nothing.

Their mother stirred. "Will you be calling the others now?" she asked.

"Soon," Caitlin said.

"Is it time for the surprise?"

"It's time."

"Then take my hand, please," their mother said to Seana.

Seana took her mother's hand, and we walked up the stairs, Caitlin going ahead of us. We waited at the second floor landing while Caitlin went into a room at the end of the hallway. She came out a few seconds later, motioned for us to join her.

We entered a small, narrow room. To one side was a bed and dresser, and to the other side was a two-drawer desk and a small three-shelf bookcase.

"This was once my daughter's room," their mother said.

Straight ahead, between two windows, the shades drawn, was a table, and on the table between two lit candles, there was a framed picture of a girl in a white dress—Seana's communion picture, I assumed—and next to it, propped up on display stands, copies of *Triangle* and *Plain Jane*.

Caitlin stood to one side of the table, hands clasped as if in prayer. Seana's mother touched each of the novels, then smiled at us.

"My daughter wrote these books," she said brightly. "She's quite the famous writer. Do you know her?"

"*I'm* your daughter," Seana said. "*I'm* Seana O'Sullivan."

"What excellent news!" Seana's mother said. "And how wonderful to know that you're still alive."

Caitlin put a hand on her mother's arm, but her mother pushed it away angrily, leaned on the table. "It's terrible when your memory begins to go," she said. "It's really quite terrible."

I was awake before the sun rose—I'd slept in the room that had been Keira and Mary's—and I went into Seana's room, where she was fast asleep, snoring lightly, her arms wrapped around a pillow. I lifted the shade on one of the windows, looked out at the alleyway that ran behind the house. Not far beyond the garbage cans and the litter, perhaps a five or six minute walk along Rogers Avenue, I knew, on Martense Street, was the house in which my father had grown up, and though the rooms in which he ate, slept, and studied would probably be there for a while to come, it occurred to me that the memories he had of those rooms, and of all he'd done and thought and dreamt in them, were now gone forever.

I watched a large brown and white spotted dog burrow into a pile of garbage, and come out with a piece of brown paper. One paw on the paper to hold it in place, the dog licked whatever grease or crumbs were on it, and then moved off. I thought of late fall mornings in Northampton, the leaves on the trees outside the kitchen windows mostly gone, Max at the stove, scrambling eggs for us. All through junior high and high school, despite my protests, he'd insisted on the two of us having breakfast together every morning before I left for school. When I once asked why—why was it so important, especially given that I could fix something for myself, and that he didn't have to get up (he never taught morning classes)—without looking at me, he answered by saying we were still family even when we were only two, and then asked if I wanted toast with my eggs.

I tried to let the world beyond Seana's room—the alleyway, the old wooden fence behind it, the backs of buildings behind the fence, the early morning light—have its way with me. I stared out at the stillness, wondered why I saw no cats—weren't they supposed to be scrounging around at this time of day?—and found myself wishing I could ask Max if he thought the quality of the stillness here—the quiet—was different from the quiet we'd known on mornings in Northampton.

I wasn't aware that Seana was awake and out of bed until she had her arms around me.

"Good morning, my love," she said.

"Do you live here?" I asked.

"Literally, or figuratively?"

"Either. Both."

"Mmmm," she said, nuzzling my neck.

"You must have been a happy little girl before you began collecting grudges," I said.

"Maybe," she said. "I used to love looking out this window, though. I loved it *because* there was nothing much to see. Sometimes, in the summer, there'd be a few people out on the fire escapes, cooling off. But with nothing to see—nothing new, anyway—I could daydream—I could *imagine* things."

"Such as...?"

"Read my books," she answered.

"*Again?*"

"Stop it," she said. "But listen—please?—I did something weird before I went to sleep. Come sit with me."

We sat on the side of her bed, and she told me that before she went to sleep she'd found herself standing in front of the shrine Caitlin and her mother had made to her and her books.

"I prayed, Charlie—for the first time in nearly thirty years, I prayed—and do you know what I prayed for?"

"My soul."

"Be serious. *Please?*"

"Tell me."

"I prayed for a child—I made a wish—and I had a moment when—it was like emerging from a blackout—I suddenly knew my wish was going to be granted. I just *knew*."

"But how...?"

She was squeezing my arm very hard without seeming to realize she was doing so. "I don't *know!*" she said. "But I found myself thinking of those organizations that give dying kids their dreams-come-true where they get to meet their favorite rock star or movie star or ballplayer..."

"Make-a-Wish," I said. "That's the name of the organization, and it's also the title of one of the stories Max never wrote, about someone like you coming to live with him. Maybe that's why..."

"*Damn!*" she said, and got up from the bed. "I shouldn't have told you. *Damn!* Just damn your eyes, O'Sullivan. You are such a child—such a grade-A jerk sometimes! Such a selfish, self-serving total *jerk!*"

I took her hand, tugged lightly, and she sat next to me again. "Hey—it's okay—nothing wrong with wishing for things for ourselves—even praying for them." I laughed. "Max used to tell a story about a guy in synagogue who prayed to God to send him a thousand dollars, and promised that if God did, he'd give half of it to charity... but if somehow God didn't believe him, he asked God to just send him *his* half."

"Stop humoring me and trying to make a joke out of everything," she said. "Your father did that sometimes, and it drove me nuts."

"Like father like son?"

"Just *stop it*, goddamn you! Stop trying to make things *right*," she said. "I hate it when people do that. I really do. Let me feel guilty if I want to feel guilty—let me feel embarrassed if I feel embarrassed. *Please?*"

"Sure."

She went to the table where her books were, picked up the photo of her in her communion dress. "I was pretty, wasn't I?"

"Pretty then, beautiful now," I said.

"So maybe I'm upset because I'm happy to be home again, and it surprises me to be happy here, and—don't protest or make a joke because if you do I may become violent—I'm happy to be here with you, Charlie."

At breakfast, Seana's mother didn't talk, not even to say 'good morning,' but she ate steadily—bread and jam, canned sausages, cookies, cut-up fruit—and stared ahead absently while she chewed.

Then the noise began.

Keira, Mary, and Peggy arrived with their children, and so did Caitlin's four children and *their* children. There was lots of hugging, kissing, and weeping. Caitlin pulled more food from the fridge, freezer, and pantry, and she and her sisters set out food on the kitchen table (each of the sisters had brought something), and on a glass-topped coffee table in the living room. The older children came to me one at a time and told me they were sorry my father had died, but otherwise didn't show much interest in who I was or why I was there.

Seana's mother sat on the couch, the grandchildren taking turns sitting next to her, telling her about what they were doing in school—the younger ones talked about cartoons they loved: *Scooby Doo, Bugs Bunny, Shrek, Road Runner*—and thanking her when, from her purse, she rewarded them with coins. "Be gone small change before I spend ye!" she'd say each time. Mary and Peggy had brought shopping bags with copies of Seana's novels they asked her to sign—for sale at their church bazaars, for their local libraries, for gift-giving—and they were at her with questions about her life—new books? new homes? travel plans?

They remembered my father from the time they'd met him at Seana's Brooklyn Public Library reading, and they remembered that he'd grown up a block or two away, and told me they'd enjoyed talking with him about what things had been like in the neighborhood when he was a boy. Peggy recalled him saying that the Holy Cross schoolyard had been his second home, and there were tears in her eyes when she said she knew that it was because of him that Seana had become a writer, and how she couldn't imagine what it was like to *have* a father of his quality, and then to lose him. One of Seana's nieces—Caitlin's daughter, Alexa, who was in graduate school at Teacher's College—said that she had written an essay on *Plain Jane* for her senior honors thesis at Fordham University, comparing it to *Jane Eyre*, and that she'd wowed her professor with the fact that Seana was her aunt.

They asked me about what I was doing—had I been living with my father before he died?—and I told them that I'd been living and working in Singapore, and that my best friend had died there not long before my father had passed away. Seana, smiling mischievously, told them that I'd written about my experiences in Singapore, and about my friend's death, which had occurred under mysterious circumstances, and that if she knew anything about matters literary, what I'd written was sure to be published one day soon.

Her sisters congratulated me, asked a few more questions, and then went back to comparing notes on their kids, and complaining about their husbands. They gossiped about relatives and people they'd grown up with—who was getting divorced, who'd come into money, who was dead or dying, who had moved away and to where... and I sat there drinking it all in, and wondering: Was *this*—or the *loss* of this—of extended family living near each other and sharing their ongoing lives on what was, for these sisters and their children, a daily basis—what it was all about? And where were the men, and what part of this world was theirs and bore the impress of who *they* were?

And so it went, into the early afternoon. The women kept setting out food and more food. They washed dishes, gossiped, and looked through photo albums of communions, confirmations, graduations, weddings, and family vacations. They laughed and wiped away tears and traded stories and called their children to them to show them pictures of people and events that had taken place when the children were young, or before the children were born. Seana's mother took a nap upstairs while the older children worked at their laptop computers, and the younger ones played video games on hand-held gizmos, or watched television—there were DVDs there for them: old Walt Disney movies—*Cinderella*,

Bambi, Dumbo, The Little Mermaid—and as the hours went by, I noticed that Seana was keeping to herself more and more.

When she said she was going upstairs to check on their mother, I followed.

I touched her arm. "Are you okay?" I asked.

"Of course," she said, and pulled away from me.

"But you're not," I said.

"Well aren't you the perceptive one," she said.

"Come on," I said. "What's up?"

"What's *up*? Why *we* are, Charlie—we're up here in the *up*-stairs hallway of the home in which I *grew* up, and where we are now having a joyous and spontaneous family reunion, and where there are so many memories and feelings crashing around that the Environmental Protection Agency may be called in."

"And you're *up*-set," I said.

"Oh Charlie," she said, her head against my chest. "You *are* a wonder, and I'll be fine after a few years of this. It's not complicated, after all. I forgot a few things, see? I forgot to be who I was supposed to be—a mother, a wife, secretary, a nurse, a teacher, a nun—I'm *in* the family but not *of* it, right? Same old, same old. I'm not *like* them, Charlie. It's why I…"

"So you're different—you're who you are, they're who they are, and what's wrong with that? They love you—*adore* you actually. You're their shining light, the angel who…"

She pulled away again, walked to her mother's room, peeked in, turned back to me.

"They really *are* proud of you and love you, even if they don't understand you, even if…"

"Does that go for you too?"

"No. I understand you. I *get* you."

"You really think so?" She pressed her body against me, her hands on the back of my neck. "You are my guy," she said. "Did you know that? But do leave me be for a while. It's all much more overwhelming than I expected, and, in the life I chose, I did get used to being alone most of the time."

"You can still be alone as much..."

"Shut up and kiss me," she said, and I did, and when she backed away, her eyes were suddenly blazing. She grabbed both my arms and started shaking me. "Oh my god," she said. "Oh my dear fucking God! I forgot, right? Yes! I almost forgot our plan..."

When we got to the Holy Cross schoolyard, he was there, as Seana thought he might be. He had never let her or her sisters see where he lived, and had always, from boyhood, called the Holy Cross schoolyard his home-away-from-home. He was sitting by himself, his back against the chain-link fence, watching black guys play basketball.

"What took you so long?" he said, but without smiling. "You hung up on me, so I waited for you, figuring you'd get yourself here by and by. Your wop boyfriends don't hang out here anymore, unless this young man you're with is one of them."

"This is my friend Charlie Eisner," Seana said. "He's Max Eisner's son. Max is dead—he passed away two months ago."

"Ah!" her father said. "Relieved to hear it, young man. No offense, but from the grim look on my daughter's face, I thought you might have come to tell me he died of a sudden this very day."

"This is my father, Patrick O'Sullivan," Seana said.

He took off his baseball cap, tipped it toward me. "Now when my time comes," he said, "the one room I live in being terribly small, all you'll have to do is tuck me in, turn out the lights, lock the door, put handles on the room, and carry it away."

One of the black guys came over. "This is my daughter," Seana's father said to him. "And this is her young friend, Charles Eisner."

"Your father's the man," the black guy said, and he shook each of our hands. "He's a real card."

"The joker in the pack," Seana's father said.

"You got that right," the black guy said. "This man knows more bad jokes than any man on this earth, and when I say bad, I mean *bad*. We count on him for stuff."

Seana's father stood, and to my surprise, he was nearly as tall as I was. He wore a blue pin-stripe suit, a green and white repp tie. He was clean-shaven, and what I had taken for high color in his cheeks was, I now saw, rouge.

"So Smitty," her father asked the black guy, "if you had a donkey and I had a rooster, and your donkey ate my rooster, what would you have?"

"Don't know."

"You'd have three feet of my cock up your ass."

Smitty laughed. "He gives us lines we can use with our lady friends too," he said to Seana, then whispered. "And we take care of him—look out for him—know what I mean?"

"No," Seana said. "I don't."

"Have you ever played 'County Fair' with one of your young lady friends?" Seana's father asked.

"How you do that?" Smitty asked.

"You have her sit on your face, and you guess her weight."

Smitty laughed again. "See what I mean?" he said.

"No," Seana said. Then, to her father: "It's time to go. Everyone's waiting."

"I suspected as much," her father said. Seana's father picked up his cane—black, with an ivory-white handle in the shape of a cat's head—and we started from the schoolyard, the black guys waving to us.

"Do you know what the difference is between a priest and acne?" her father asked, and when neither of us responded, he answered his own question: "Acne doesn't usually come on a boy's face until after he's twelve years old."

We walked past the church, one of us to either side of him.

"And you, Mister Eisner—given your origins, you might know the answer to this: What's the difference between a Jew and a pizza?"

I said nothing.

"When you put a pizza in the oven it doesn't scream," he said.

"Cheesy joke," I said.

"Don't," Seana said. "Don't encourage him."

"Because I'm *in-corrigible*," her father said. "Ah—and here's an ecumenical favorite: A priest walks up to the bar and orders a drink. Then a rabbi walks up to the bar and orders a drink. Then a horse walks up to the bar, and the bartender asks: 'Why the long face?'"

"I have a surprise," Seana said, when we reached her street. "I've planned a trip for you."

"Still trying to get rid of me, I see," he said. "But good of you, of course, and I accept your offer, since you must be a wealthy woman from your several best sellers." He tapped on my shoe with his cane. "Her sentences lack a certain felicity of style, and her timing is off—a matter of cadence there—and we certainly wouldn't think of talking about her work in the same breath with the work of, say, Beckett, or O'Casey, or even Edna O'Brien, though the public does seem to take to her. Still, if you ask me…"

"Nobody has," I said.

"What you might do," her father said, "is to think of me as a refugee from one of those cheerful William Kennedy novels."

"You wish," Seana said, and she opened the door.

"Not that I'm unappreciative of the effort—the sacrifice—you've made in coming here and bringing me home," he said. "As for the trip you so graciously offered, I'm game, of course, and you'll let me know the itinerary when you have it, please, so I can make plans accordingly."

We entered the house, and walked through the foyer into the

living room. Seana's sisters were there with some of the children. When they saw us, they stopped what they were doing, but none of them stood, and none of them spoke.

Seana's father tipped his cap. "Well, isn't it lovely to be here once again, and to receive your warm welcome." He looked around, in mock bewilderment. "Oh—am I in the wrong theater? This isn't 10 Downing Street?"

"Hello Dad," Caitlin said, and she came to him, kissed him on the cheek, and Keira, Mary, and Peggy did the same. Then their mother came forward, smiling brightly, but when she went to embrace him, he recoiled.

"She never gave me sons," he said, tapping on the floor with his cane to keep her away from him. "A spiteful woman in spite of her seeming charms." He took off his cap, held it to his chest, inclined his head slightly. "I am Patrick Michael O'Sullivan," he said.

"Why I once had a husband with that name!" Seana's mother pushed his cane out of the way. "He was a handsome devil, and the ladies loved him too much, you see, which was the bane of my existence, though I have to confess that I could understand why they had an eye for the brute."

"And not only an eye, my dear," he said, and then, to Seana. "Oh my—she really has lost it, hasn't she? She was the fairest of them all, you know. She was stunning in her youth—a rare, exquisite beauty." He pointed his cane at Seana. "Like you, my dear. You got the best of each of us, you know."

"Say hello to your grandchildren," Seana said, "and then I'll take you upstairs and show you the surprise."

Her sisters brought their children and grandchildren to him, one at a time, and the older children remembered him, Caitlin explained to me, since he *had* shown up through the years at ritual occasions: baptisms, communions, confirmations, graduations, weddings, funerals.

"Thank you," Seana said to me while the children were introducing themselves.

"For what?"

"For your story—what else? It inspired me."

"But what's this about a trip? You never mentioned anything…"

"Patience, Charlie," she said. "Patience."

"Sure. But now that I've met the man, I can't help but wonder: Did he ever…?"

"Never," Seana said. "He was too clever for that kind of vulgarity. If only he had, though, for it might have made overt what was covert—what was all innuendo and leering and nastiness…"

Her father was holding forth, wiggling his cane in the air. "…so when the man kept insisting that he was a moth—*'I'm a moth! I'm a moth! I'm a moth!'*—the doctor finally said, 'Now look, Timothy, you're not a moth, but if you insist on believing you are, then I really think you should see a psychiatrist,' to which Timothy replied, 'Of course—I was on my way there, but I saw the light on in *your* office.'"

There was a brief moment of silence, and then a few of the children laughed. Seana's father, sitting on the couch, his grandchildren around him and on the floor in front of him, beamed with pleasure.

"Family happiness," Seana said.

"Makes the eyes sore," Caitlin said, an arm around Seana.

"I'll say," Peggy said. "But you did get him here, and I suppose that's something. We *are* family, after all."

"'After all' is right," Seana said. "And what a rich and wondrous phrase that is! Think of what James could do with it…"

"James who?" Peggy asked.

"*Henry* James—the Irishman Henry James, about whom—after all—Charlie's father has written with grace and intelligence," Seana said.

Seana's mother sat down beside Seana's father. "My husband

had a cane like yours," she said, "and he could do a marvelous soft shoe number with it. He could have been another Fred Astaire if he hadn't been such a lazy and mean-hearted bastard."

"Gene Kelly would have been a more ethnically correct fit."

"In your dreams," Seana's mother said.

"But let me finish the story I was telling the children," he said. "And so one night, alone yet again, and in a rage, Molly left their flat and went down to Sheehan's bar, and there she found her husband, drinking with his friends the way he was wont to do, and he embraced her and kept urging her to join with them. She relented finally and took a sip and spat it out. 'By God, that's awful stuff!' she said, and he responded, 'And here you've been thinking I'm down here having a good time every night...'"

"Oh that one's so old it has hair on it," Seana's mother said.

"Well, 'hair today... gone tomorrow' is what I always say," Seana's father said.

"Now my own husband worked for the Brooklyn Union Gas Company," Seana's mother said. "He was a meter reader, which allowed him entry into many homes and many women."

"As it happens, I too worked for the Brooklyn Union Gas Company," Seana's father said.

"My husband did theater now and then—a few turns when they tried to revive vaudeville—and he liked to call himself a song-and-gas man," Seana's mother said. "His name was Patrick Michael O'Sullivan."

"My name is Patrick Michael O'Sullivan," Seana's father said.

"What a coincidence," Seana's mother said.

Keira announced that it was time for tea—milk and cookies too—and for whoever wanted some to come into the kitchen.

"Come with me," Seana said to her father. "It's time."

"Quite the autocrat you have here, son," he said to me. "Always liked to order people around, she did. If she'd been a boy, she would have been a chip off the old block, I dare say."

We walked up the stairs, and Seana led her father into her bedroom.

"This is what my sisters made for me," she said.

"Awfully tacky, wouldn't you say?"

"No," she said. "But you might."

"Is this the surprise you referred to? I thought you talked about arranging for a trip…" He picked up *Plain Jane*, then set it back on the table, face down. "Well, you have brought us all together, though to what end is unclear. Still, the Lord works in mysterious ways, they say."

"He may, but I don't," Seana said. "For I'm more like you than is good for you."

"I'm glad to hear of it," he said. "It will get you through many a thorny garden."

"I hope so," Seana said. "We'll go back downstairs now."

When we were at the top of the stairs, Seana asked her father to give her his cane, said he could use the banister for making his way downstairs. Then she called out: "Caitlin, Peggy—you should dial 911—I think there's going to be an accident!"

Her father, looking puzzled, stepped down, and when he did Seana took him by the arm.

"Here—on second thought, you might need the cane for your trip," she said, and she thrust the cane at him, but below his open hand, so that when he reached for it, and she put her free hand on his back as if to steady him, he tripped on the cane, lost his balance, and tumbled down the staircase.

Seana stood next to me. "We're even now, Charlie," she said. "But at least *I* had the good sense to keep it in the family."

Her sisters and some of their children were at the bottom of the stairs, Keira screaming, the children gaping, Caitlin on the phone.

When we turned onto my street in Northampton—it was past ten in the evening—I saw that someone was sitting on my porch, slowly rocking back and forth in a rocking chair the way Max had often done on summer evenings. We parked the car in the driveway by the side of the house, then went to the porch, and the man stood—it was Lorenzo—and without looking at Seana, and without offering his hand to either of us, he began speaking.

"I tried to reach each of you by telephone, but without success," Lorenzo said, "and so I drove down. I'm staying in town, at the Hotel Northampton, so you needn't worry about observing civilities."

The scar on his lower lip, in the dim light from the street lamp, looked like a small gray worm. I unlocked the front door, and invited him to come in.

"There is no need," he said. "My business will be brief."

We remained standing while he told us that two days earlier, Gabe had jammed all the silverware he could find into a microwave oven, turned it on, and blew up the kitchen. He had waited until Anna and Trish were away—while Trish was taking Anna to a play-date—before he did it. Trish was now in a psych ward at a hospital in Camden, for observation, and for more information it would be best that we talk with Eugenia. She was taking care of the children while Trish was gone, and Gabe, who continued to insist he intended no harm and had been working on an experiment in preparation for the next Fourth of July celebration, had been taken away by people from the local social service agency and was in a safe, secure place, and—he had been given assurances by people he knew—would not face criminal charges. Lorenzo had engaged a lawyer with whom both he and Eugenia had conferred. Having discovered the change Trish had made in her will, they had concluded it would be best if Seana and I took care of the children until Trish was well again.

"*If* she's ever well again," Seana said.

"Well that's true too, isn't it," Lorenzo said without looking at

Seana. Then he offered me his sympathy on my father's death, and left.

Early the next morning, we headed north. The highways were deserted, and we made it to Ogunquit, where we stopped in a seaside diner for breakfast, in under two hours. After breakfast, we stayed on Old Route 1 as much as we could in order to be near the ocean. Despite Max's death, Nick's death, and Seana's father's fall—Caitlin called at one in the morning to tell us that the doctors at Maimonides hospital said he'd suffered multiple fractures and various internal injuries, but that he would live—and despite what might lie in wait for us in Maine, it felt as if we were setting out on a mini-vacation—a long weekend by the sea—at a time when, the brilliant autumn colors gone, northern New England would be especially peaceful.

We were quiet on the drive, and seemed to have arrived, separately, at the decision not to talk about Seana's father, or Lorenzo, or Trish, or the possibility that we might become Gabe's and Anna's legal guardians—or about the fact that what Seana had prayed for might soon be coming true. When we talked, we talked mostly about Seana's sisters, her nieces and nephews, and her mother.

We arrived at the Falzettis' home shortly before noon. Eugenia invited us in and informed us that Lorenzo had arrived a few hours earlier, and was absenting himself because he didn't want to cause—his words—more fireworks.

"Not funny," Seana said.

Eugenia brought us coffee, and a snack—ham and cheese sandwiches, cookies, fruit—and filled us in on the current situation: Trish had been transferred to a private residential hospital outside Camden; Gabe was in a facility for developmentally challenged children—further north, near Acadia National Park; a lawyer—Trish's, not Lorenzo's—was eager to talk with us. Lorenzo had told the lawyer of their willingness to take care of Anna until the guardianship situation was resolved and, if need be, to have Gabe live with them if and when the doctors discharged him.

Eugenia assured us that, thanks to Trish's inheritance from Nick, to excellent insurance policies, and to what she and Lorenzo were prepared to contribute, there would be no problem paying for treatment and care for Trish or for Gabe, even if treatment proved long-term.

Anna, thumb in mouth, came into the room then, dragging her favorite silk-edged blue blanket behind her. Seana got out of her chair, bent down to Anna's level, and spread her arms wide. Anna gave her a hug, then came to me and gave me a hug.

"Why don't we show Uncle Charlie and Aunt Seana your room," Eugenia said, and Anna took us to the room she was staying in. Her bed was covered with stuffed animals, including the parrot we'd given her. Eugenia walked to a dresser—its top, diapers and lotions to one side, serving as Anna's changing table—and opened the drawers to show us Anna's clothing.

"It's been a help in making her feel at home that she still has her own clothes and toys," Eugenia said. "That was Gabe's doing. When he ran out of the house, he was mindful enough to take a cell phone with him, and to dial 911. Quite remarkable really. We have an excellent volunteer fire department— they were there in under four minutes—and when they arrived, Gabe was standing outside waiting for them, telling them what had happened, and where the bedrooms were. They were able to keep much of the rear section of the house, including the bedrooms, from being destroyed."

A few minutes later Lorenzo joined us in the living room. "I assume Eugenia has provided an update on essentials," he said. "Given our past history, we three, I thought it best if she be the intermediary in these matters. But I give you my word that she and I stand ready to do whatever is necessary to provide for our daughter-in-law, and for our grandchildren. I believe it was a wise move for Trish to have named you guardians—who knows how much longer we'll be available?—and I believe the children's lives will be better served by a younger couple."

He looked at me, and then, for the first time, at Seana. "Any questions?" he asked.

We had none.

"Good," he said. "Then I am going to ask you to step outside with me for a minute, young man, for some words best delivered privately."

We walked outside together, toward the end of their property, across from Wyeth's island.

"I read your story," Lorenzo said.

"My *story?*"

"I read your story," he repeated. "I found it in Trish's room when we were packing up some of her clothes, to bring to her. I know what you thought of my son—that you didn't especially like or admire him although, like many others, you were clearly drawn to him."

"Look…" I began.

"Do not interrupt," he said. "I am talking about my son, and you will hear me out."

I said nothing.

"I didn't like or admire Nick much either," he said. "I may have *liked* him less than you did. As for love, that is a word— a *notion*—I have never quite understood. Like the belief many have in God, or some Supreme Being, it is a concept beneath my powers of imagination, such as they are. But he was my son."

"Of course."

Then he grabbed me by the shoulders, and even while his voice was low and even, his eyes were on fire.

"*But he was my son!*" he said again, his grip on my arms tightening. "He was my son—blood of my blood—and I will see you crushed before I depart this world. Do you hear me?"

"I hear you."

"I have the story, which your friend sent to Trish, and I have been in touch with people in Singapore, and I am informing myself about extradition policies. Your friend's virtues as writer and woman—her recklessness and devil-may-care attitude—have done you in, you see."

"She sent the story to Trish because she *cares* for her," I said. "And anyway, the story's not all true."

"Don't talk crap to me, young man," he said. "I'm sure Nick told you that I became a self-made man because—the phrase he loved to repeat—I learned to turn shit into gold. So let me tell you the obvious: that I can do the reverse. I can turn gold—your life, sir, which includes, I have discovered, a sizeable inheritance from your father—into shit."

"Are you done?" I said.

He nodded.

"Then wipe yourself," I said, and walked away.

"Your father's smart-aleck Brooklyn lines won't help," he said, grabbing me from behind and forcing me to face him.

"I have your story," he said again, "and I will use it when and how I see fit, and if you are smart—not wise, which you will never be, but smart—you will tell no one, not even your precious Seana, for if you do, that will serve to hasten my plans, and I prefer not to be rushed. Do you hear me?"

"I hear you."

He let go of me. "You can go inside now, and I will leave you with Eugenia. I will receive reports on a regular basis, and will expect to see my grandchildren when I choose to see them. I advise you to honor my requests in a timely fashion."

The day after we returned to Northampton, it snowed heavily—an early winter storm that made the town seem especially beautiful. Seana, Anna, and I put on boots—the snow was eleven inches deep—and walked across the Smith College campus and down to Paradise Pond, which had not been plowed yet, so that there were no skaters on it. We stood outside the boathouse, and it was there that Seana proposed marriage, saying that she thought the courts would look upon us more favorably as guardians for Gabe and Anna if we were a legally married couple.

A few days later, with Max's lawyer, we negotiated a pre nuptial agreement. As with going to war, or drilling through the ocean floor, Seana said, we shouldn't undertake hazardous adventures without having viable and detailed exit strategies. She thought she might, in the next year, sell several of her apartments, have her papers and belongings packed up and shipped to Max's house—now my house, soon to be *our* house—and perhaps, on the anniversary of the day on which she had become owner of Max's archive, we could hold a tag sale of *her* literary shards, though we might put aside material a university library would find valuable in order to buy ourselves more time for writing and travel.

Two days after the snow storm, a social worker from Trish's residence called to tell us that Trish had attempted suicide by trying to hang herself with strips of cloth torn from her bed linens, but that the attempt had been unsuccessful. Later that week we drove up to Maine, left Anna with Eugenia and Lorenzo, and visited with Trish. She was heavily medicated, her speech slurred, and we spent most of our visit—less than twenty minutes—listening to her tell us again and again how sorry she was, and adding, several times, no matter our insisting that her present situation was surely temporary, that she was glad we were going to be Gabe and Anna's mommy and daddy for the rest of their lives. Before we left, she held me close. Her arms and face were slick with sweat, her body odors foul. "I really, *really* liked your story," she whispered.

We visited with Gabe, and he seemed much the same as he'd been when we'd stayed at Trish's house: bright, talkative, articulate. He liked his room, and his attendants—they were young, intelligent, well-trained—and he told us about what his days were like: the classes and tutorials, the exercise sessions and play groups, the meetings with doctors. He knew that his mother was ill and might not get well for some time, and when we said that he could come live with us in Northampton when he was discharged, he said one word, "Never," and changed the subject, asking about his model airplane collection and if it had burned in the fire. When I said it had not, he asked if, the next time we visited, we could bring model airplane kits for several World War I planes he wanted to add to his collection. Seana wrote down their names.

On a Thursday morning three weeks after our return from Maine—Caitlin and Keira driving up to Northampton and staying overnight with us so they could serve as witnesses—Seana and I were married.

In our new life together, we spent a good portion of our days caring for Anna, and were surprised, even though she was an agreeable and sweet-dispositioned child, at how much sheer time and energy it took: dealing with diapers and baths, sniffles and rashes and ear infections, naps and nightmares and eating idiosyncrasies. She was also, especially during her first three or four weeks with us, subject to tantrums, when she would become inconsolable for thirty to forty minutes, weeping and screaming and not letting us near her, and we could never figure out what had triggered a tantrum, or how and why it could disappear as quickly as it had arrived. In early February, we were able to get her into a pre-school group at the Smith College Campus Day School (where I had gone), and in this way, and by meeting other parents with children her age, and arranging for play-dates and sleepovers, we were able to have more time for writing, and for those matters we came to refer to as the detritus of illness and death: Max's lawyer, Trish's lawyer, various accountants and financial advisers, and courts in Massachusetts and Maine.

I decided not to turn *Charlie's Story* into a novel or novella, but instead, from the baker's dozen Seana had culled from his papers, to pick out one of the other stories Max had not written—*Pagello's Surgery* appealed the most—and Seana said she would do the same, and that eventually we'd make books of them all—but that she wouldn't make her initial choice until after she'd gone through the four books she was already at work on to see if any of them were worth salvaging. When I said that I didn't feel quite ready to write a novel, and would try to turn *Pagello's Surgery* into a short story first, Seana warned that it was often more difficult to write a short story than a novel—that knowing there were no limits of time and space—no page limits anyway—might give me a sense of freedom I wouldn't enjoy in the shorter form.

But it did please her that I was thinking of writing about Pagello, and if and when I did, she suggested I focus not on his love affair with George Sand, which took place in Paris when he was thirty-two, but about what she'd talked about my first night back in Northampton—about how, after his life with Sand in Paris, he'd returned to Venice, where he married, had children, practiced medicine, and died peacefully, fifty-nine years later, at the age of ninety-one. And maybe, too, we might just *have* to go to Paris and to Venice so I could do some research.

She was also, to my surprise, enthusiastic when I suggested we visit Borneo together. If and when we did, I told her I could arrange to have us fly over some palm oil plantations so we could watch the forests burning and/or blossoming.

"'*Ne détruisez pas la verdure*,'" she said.

"Sand's last words," I said.

"Yes—and I kept thinking of them when I read your descriptions of Borneo," Seana said. "Sand has always been my hero, more as a woman—a force of life—than as writer, even though, unlike me, she was an incurable romantic and believed in the divine, transfiguring power of love, in following the dictates of one's heart..."

"The way I do?"

"Probably," Seana said.

"*Probably?*"

"Probably," Seana said again. "Her energy—her passion and conviction—puts all of us to shame. She was the most prolific female author in the history of literature, yet she still had time for taking care of her children, her grandchildren, and of people who worked on her estates, as well as for numerous love affairs—with Lizst and Chopin, de Musset, Pagello, others. Such *fullness* of life, and yet her deathbed prayer, though not her last words, was for peacefulness—'*Calme, toujours plus de calme.*' So yes, Charlie—let's find a quiet place in Borneo, you and me, and maybe settle there for a while."

We began planning a trip to Borneo and, against the time when Trish might get well and take her children back, adopting a child. And we talked about buying a place of our own, perhaps near Kuching, if we could get the courts to approve our taking Anna out of the country for an extended period.

The chief psychiatrist at Gabe's institution thought Gabe might be ready for discharge within six to eight months, but he cautioned against having him live with us. His suggestion was that we find a private residential school—he could recommend several good ones—that was experienced in working with children with Asperger's syndrome. If, however, we chose to have Gabe live with us, he advised against mainstreaming him in a public school.

I began corresponding with adoption agencies in Boston, as well as in Singapore, where the main offices of several Borneo agencies were based, and it seemed that it might actually be possible to make preliminary arrangements for an adoption before we arrived, or, that failing, to make several brief trips, separately if necessary—without Anna—each of us meeting separately with agencies and children, and one of us bringing a child home when arrangements were finalized. If the adoption went well, it could, we told each other, become the first of several.

But even if we adopted children and bought a place in Borneo, or sold some or all of Seana's places, or had Trish's house in Maine restored for her and her children, we were in agreement about not selling Max's house, and on one unseasonably warm evening in mid-April, while we sat on our front porch having drinks (a vodka tonic for me, a dry martini for Seana), Anna on the floor nearby, playing with her clothespins and yogurt cups, and Seana looking especially lovely in a white linen sun-dress (since I'd mentioned that for the Chinese white, not black, was the color of death, she'd taken to wearing white virtually all the time), Seana remarked on how sad it was that Max hadn't lived to see what had resulted from his tag sale. But of course, I said, gesturing to the three of us, were he still here—and were Nick still alive—none of this would ever have happened. ∎

Also by Jay Neugeboren, available from Two Dollar Radio

1940
A NOVEL
A Trade Paperback Original; 978-0-9763895-6-9; $15 US
✶ Longlist, 2010 International IMPAC Dublin
Literary Award.

"Jay Neugeboren traverses the Hitlerian tightrope with all the skill and formal daring that have made him one of our most honored writers of literary fiction and masterful nonfiction."
—Tim Rutten, *Los Angeles Times*

SET ON THE eve of America's entry into World War Two, *1940* is built around a fascinating historical figure, Dr. Eduard Bloch, an Austrian doctor who had been physician to Adolf Hitler and his familiy when Hitler was a boy. The historical Bloch was the only Jew for whom Hitler ever personally arranged departure from Europe, and he must now, living in the Bronx, face accusations over the special treatment he received.

1940 FOCUSES ON Dr. Bloch's relationship with Elizabeth Rofman, a medical illustrator at Johns Hopkins Medical School, who has come to New York from Baltimore to visit her father, only to find that he has mysteriously disappeared. The story grows more complex when Elizabeth's son Daniel, a disturbed young adolescent, escapes from the institution in Maryland where his parents have committed him, and makes his way to New York, where he is hidden and protected by his mother... and by Dr. Bloch.

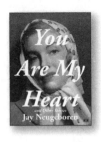

YOU ARE MY HEART AND OTHER STORIES
STORIES BY JAY NEUGEBOREN
A Trade Paperback Original; 978-0-9826848-8-7; $16 US

"[Neugeboren] might not be as famous as some of his compeers, like Philip Roth or John Updike, but it's becoming increasingly harder to argue that he's any less talented."
—Michael Schaub, *Kirkus Reviews*

FROM THE SECLUDED VILLAGES in the south of France, to the cattle crawl in the Valley of a Thousand Hills in South Africa, Neugeboren examines the great mysteries that unsettle human relationships.